"This could change all our lives for the better," Mildred said.

"If there's another world out there, an unnuked world, maybe we wouldn't want to come back."

"Mebbe *you* wouldn't want to come back," Krysty said.

"If you've got big love in your heart for Deathlands because you were born here, that's your business," Mildred told her. "From what I've seen, I'd say all the hellscape does is kick our asses."

"And what if the captain isn't telling us the whole truth?" Krysty said.

"A guy doesn't survive solo without having some neat tricks up his sleeve," J.B. said with confidence.

Ryan held up his hands. "It's about the devil we know versus the devil we don't. The familiar, bad as it is, is still familiar. We can pretty much reckon how we're gonna die. Starvation. Thirst. Gutshot. Ate by some mutie. I don't particularly care where I croak or how."

"So you're for taking this pipe-dream trip and mebbe never coming back?" Krysty said, aghast.

**Other titles in the
Deathlands saga:**

JAMES AXLER

DEATH LANDS®

Plague Lords

EMPIRE OF XIBALBA
BOOK I

A GOLD EAGLE BOOK FROM

WORLDWIDE®

TORONTO • NEW YORK • LONDON
AMSTERDAM • PARIS • SYDNEY • HAMBURG
STOCKHOLM • ATHENS • TOKYO • MILAN
MADRID • WARSAW • BUDAPEST • AUCKLAND

First edition December 2008

ISBN-13: 978-0-373-62594-9
ISBN-10:   0-373-62594-4

PLAGUE LORDS

Copyright © 2008 by Worldwide Library.

I will ransom them from the power of the grave; I will redeem them from death: O death, I will be thy plagues; O grave, I will be thy destruction.

—*The Holy Bible,*
Book of Daniel

THE DEATHLANDS SAGA

This world is their legacy, a world born in the violent nuclear spasm of 2001 that was the bitter outcome of a struggle for global dominance.

There is no real escape from this shockscape where life always hangs in the balance, vulnerable to newly demonic nature, barbarism, lawlessness.

But they are the warrior survivalists, and they endure—in the way of the lion, the hawk and the tiger, true to nature's heart despite its ruination.

Ryan Cawdor: The privileged son of an East Coast baron. Acquainted with betrayal from a tender age, he is a master of the hard realities.

Krysty Wroth: Harmony ville's own Titian-haired beauty, a woman with the strength of tempered steel. Her premonitions and Gaia powers have been fostered by her Mother Sonja.

J. B. Dix, the Armorer: Weapons master and Ryan's close ally, he, too, honed his skills traversing the Deathlands with the legendary Trader.

Doctor Theophilus Tanner: Torn from his family and a gentler life in 1896, Doc has been thrown into a future he couldn't have imagined.

Dr. Mildred Wyeth: Her father was killed by the Ku Klux Klan, but her fate is not much lighter. Restored from predark cryogenic suspension, she brings twentieth-century healing skills to a nightmare.

Jak Lauren: A true child of the wastelands, reared on adversity, loss and danger, the albino teenager is a fierce fighter and loyal friend.

Dean Cawdor: Ryan's young son by Sharona accepts the only world he knows, and yet he is the seedling bearing the promise of tomorrow.

In a world where all was lost, they are humanity's last hope....

Prologue

When a mosquito speared Okie Moore right between the eyes, he deftly squashed it against his forehead. Blood from the bug's crushed abdomen trickled in a cool bead down the side of his nose. He wiped it across his cheek with the back of his hand, smearing a fresh daub of red into the impasto of squashed bodies, legs, wings—tiny gobs of black mush trapped in the hairs of his beard. A cloud of bugs wheeled around his head; mosquitos broke formation and dive-bombed him in waves, trying to get at his earlobes, but they were protected by his greasy, shoulder-length hair.

Okie ignored the shrill, singsong whine and concentrated on the Fire Talker's rapid flow of words and exaggerated gestures. They were the evening's featured entertainment. The young 'uns squatting in the sand next to him moved a dozen steps to the right, into the shifting river of smoke that poured off the communal bonfire—the skeeter No Fly Zone.

The air this particular evening was heavy with bugs and moisture, that and the smothering heat made deep breathing difficult. Circled around the campfire were more than two hundred filthy people in brand-new, matching clothing. The men, women and older children wore baggy, gaudy Hawaiian-style shirts and shorts, still creased from the packaging, and gleaming white high-top basketball shoes. The toe boxes of the women's and kids' shoes were crammed with rags to make them fit. They looked like a band of homeless who had just looted a Wal-Mart summer clearance sale, or a gathering of Jimmy Buffett impersonators.

These Deathlanders weren't homeless, though, and they weren't defenseless. Well-oiled AKMs, semi-auto pistols, slide-action shotguns and heavy machine guns all stood close to hand, shoulder slung or holstered, or tripod swivel-mounted to spray 180 degrees of water approach with predark alloys of lead.

The price of sitting on a gold mine was eternal vigilance.

And the gold mine in question was above ground and visible for miles in all directions.

In the furious aftermath of Armageddon, the *Yoko Maru,* a container ship loaded with substandard, U.S. market-reject merchandise bound for Brazil, had been driven high and dry onto the shoal of Padre Island. The narrow slip of Padre, once two hundred miles long, had been crosscut by category 7 storms into a chain of hundreds of smaller landmasses and barely submerged sandy reefs. The little landmass that Okie and his clan shared with the *Yoko Maru* stood directly opposite the entrance to Corpus Christi Bay, which had expanded to drown the low-lying Texas port community of the same name. Tidal waves had swept away the pillars and roadway of JFK Causeway Bridge that once connected Padre to the mainland. Postnukecaust, the only access to the island was by boat.

"And then the Vikings jumped in their time dilator and

took their war to Mars," the Fire Talker announced with a dramatic, skyward sweep of his arm. A camouflage survivalist do-rag encircled the itinerant storyteller's head, layers of duct tape held together his lace-up, Nam-surplus boots. He wore a camouflage hunting vest with overstuffed pockets and no shirt underneath, and a pair of hacked-off, holed-out, olive-drab BDU pants for shorts. "They're the ones who made the stickies and scalies, the talking lungfish and the celery people," the entertainer told the audience, his voice rising in pitch and excitement. "It was part of their ancient Norse magic, what they call the Rune Stone Concatenation. And their minions launched a devastating counterattack against the Iroquois Ninja princess's cloud operatives…"

"For nuke's sake, get to the fucking point," someone from the far side of the ring growled.

Grumbles and hisses chimed from all sides. The Nuevo-Texicans, many of whom were sitting in injection-molded, white plastic lawn chairs, were getting more and more restless.

"What about the Matachìn?" someone else prompted. "That's what we want to hear about."

"I'm coming to them," the Fire Talker replied. "Patience, my friends, patience. Past is prologue. It's important you're brought up to speed on the real background of recent events…"

Okie noted the halfhearted way this stranger fanned at the swirling mass of skeeters circling his head and shoulders. He didn't squash a single one, nor did he manage to dislodge the legions feeding on his bare arms and shoulders and speckling his uncovered legs.

The Fire Talker bore vague resemblance to a picture

Okie and the others had seen before. It had been stuck inside ten thousand, thin, clear plastic cases they'd found in one of the *Yoko Maru*'s cargo containers. The predark image was of a brilliantly smiling, blockheaded guy with a dark stubbly beard and eyelashes that were way too long and lush. George Mackerel? Or was it Mackerel George? Okie couldn't recall. No one on Padre Island had had a clue what the golden disks inside the cases were for. The island's kids had torn open the cases and used the disks as flying toys. The litter of picture inserts had long since vanished, turned to pulp by torrential rain and washed out to sea. The CDs were still in evidence, stomped to golden bits and scattered through the sand.

Even from a distance, their twenty-acre, windswept island home looked like a garbage dump; downwind it smelled like one. Mounded debris—paper, plastic, wood and metal—smothered the remnants of dunes and dune grasses. All that was missing from the landfill were flocks of seagulls. With the local shortage of fresh meat, roasted gull made a nice change from fish and the other main staple, rat on a stick. Following their noses, the rats kept swimming back across the channel, but the birds weren't that stupid. Despite the complex and alluring aromas, they rarely overflew the island anymore, and those that did paid dearly for the mistake.

Thirty years before, the first families had caught a glimpse of the grounded ship from the mainland shore. Well-armed and well-provisioned, they had walked the Gulf coastline, up from below the former international border. These offspring of some of the very last Americans, saved from incineration by their Mexican expatriation, had come north to take stock of their squandered inheritance. The original Nuevo-Texicans weren't patriots. They were scroungers, looking for booty, spoils, something weakly defended to steal, and they had stumbled upon a prize so big they couldn't shift it, not in a dozen lifetimes, so they had simply moved in.

The *Yoko Maru* and its bounty had sat rusting and unmolested for seventy years because of ignorance and fear, the twinned lodestones of the reshaped planet. Vast sections of the Gulf Coast were rumored to be so nuke-poisoned as to be impassable. To just set foot there was certain death. That was myth, as the Nuevo-Texicans had soon discovered.

The people of the postnukecaust world knew even less about radiation effects than their progenitors, who didn't know very much, either, even though mortality data from Hiroshima and Nagasaki was widely available before the arsenal-emptying U.S.-Soviet exchange. Common wisdom posited a quick, horrible demise from radiation overdose when in fact, lethality depended entirely on intensity and exposure time: in the case of Hiroshima victims who weren't killed in the initial blast and who survived their burns, it had taken twenty-five or thirty years for the damage to fully manifest.

In Deathlands, the odds over a quarter century were infinitely better that something or someone was going to beat rad cancer to the punch.

One of the "somethings" in play were the muties—deadly new creatures that had crawled out of the Apocalyptic ooze to plague and slaughter the vestiges of humankind. Again in error, the survivors blamed this spreading terror on the effects of radiation. Whatever had really come to pass when civilization ended, however the cage doors to hell had been opened, the information necessary to understand it had been lost. And even if it hadn't been, the struggling humans lacked the ability and inclination to interpret it. In point of fact, the Apocalypse had tainted the invisible genetic material of every living thing: post-nukeday, there were no "norms," just degrees of mutie. That was an impossible pill for the human survivors to swallow. They had been pitched into a frightening, altered landscape where safety and survival were hardwon, and could be lost in the next instant.

For those reasons, humanity had kept its head squarely between its knees for generations.

News along the ruined Atlantic and Gulf coasts was fragmentary and transmitted by word of mouth from passing traders and wandering storytellers. These infrequent campfire soliloquies were the only entertainment on offer. The Fire Talkers swapped their tales for grub, joy juice and the gratis services of gaudy sluts. On Padre, guest speakers who failed to sufficiently amuse faced a long, almost always fatal, forced swim back to the mainland.

"Cloud operatives are pulling all the strings from their base behind the moon," the survivalist raconteur asserted.

And was immediately challenged on the facts.

"But you just said they were pawns!" a graybeard on the far side of the ring called out.

"No, I said they *might* be pawns," the Fire Talker countered, flashing his startlingly white teeth. "Obviously, there's a big difference."

"You didn't say *might*," the graybeard scoffed.

"Yes, I did."

"No, you didn't," the woman sitting beside the graybeard countered.

"What an asshole," someone catcalled.

Okie had had enough of the tap-dancing, too. Stepping forward, he thrust a grimy finger in the Fire Talker's face. "Isabel ville, Browns ville, Mata-fuckin'-moros ville," he thundered. "Tell us about something real, Mr. Mackerel George, or you're goin' skinny-dippin' with sharks."

As if a dam of tension had burst, Okie's threat brought forth braying laughter, whistles, hoots and applause.

The Padre islanders had good cause to be on edge. According to stories that had recently filtered up the Gulf shore, seafaring invaders were ransacking the villes to the south. Known as the Matachìn, they were animalistic butchers and murderers, pirate scum. If the tales were accurate, they had already raided the remnants of the biggest coastal cities of eastern Mexico, towns that had fared much better postnukeday than those in the American Southwest. According to rumor, Veracruz, Tampico and Cancun still existed, albeit much diminished in size and population. The Fire Talker claimed to have come from that direction, and to have eye-witnessed the recent pillaging; that's the only reason they had ferried him across the water, that's why they had fed and liquored him up at their own expense.

Okie and the others weren't concerned about raiders from the north. The flooded, nuked-out wasteland that was the Texas shore served as a barrier to the East Coast barons' desire for expansion. And the barons had enough trouble, anyway, defending the territory they already controlled. Armies sent off to new conquests left homelands unprotected. There were no navies worthy of the name, just a handful of intrepid traders working out of small, wind-powered boats.

The Fire Talker flashed Okie a big, pearly toothed grin and said, "The Matachìn attacked Browns ville and Matamoros ville nine days ago."

This news was met with gasps and groans.

Browns ville was just 160 miles to the south.

"They came in a fleet of tugboats, half a dozen at least," the storyteller went on. "Motored top speed right up the mouth of the Grandee."

"They were under engine power?" Okie said in disbelief.

An assault like that called for diesel in the tens of thousands of gallons. An unheard-of, even mythic quantity of fuel.

"Engine and Viking power," the Fire Talker replied. "Stacks pumping out dark brown smoke in broad daylight, horns wailing, firing cannons mounted fore and aft. Their allies, the Vikings, manipulated the virtual time continuum along the meridian lines, the power grids of Earth's magnetic core, and turned the sky black and the sea red. Just imagine the ville folks' fear. Imagine their horror when the darkness and death fell upon them.

"The Matachìn shelled the perimeter defenses with high explosive. Browns ville folk only had small arms and a few homie bombs. They couldn't make a dent in the attackers, couldn't turn them back. After cannon shells breached the berm, the pirates started lobbing explosives into the ville proper. Fires started up and spread, flames leaping high into that awful black sky. The smart folks ran north, left behind everything they had. They got out before the Matachìn landing parties hit the beach. The pirates wore special suits and helmets manufactured on Mars and given to them by the Vikings. Even bullets fired at close range can't penetrate the overlapping plates of armor. When the gates of the ville came down, then came the slaughterfest and the sacking."

Okie looked around the ring and saw doubting, distrustful, angry faces. He and his fellow Nuevo-Texicans were a hard-bitten, realist crew. Habitually cautious. Naturally suspicious. Even though they lived in a garbage dump, they could tell when something didn't smell right. Only the handful of droolies among them wore eager grins; the droolies were eating it up.

"So you're saying the Vikings are trying to take over Deathlands because of this time dohickey?" one of the men asked archly.

"No, they are servants of the Martian hordes," the storyteller said. "Vikings are just ancient barbarians who were allowed access to deep space technology, or DST, as I already explained. Do you want me to explain it again, in more detail?"

The offer was met by a booming negative chorus.

Okie joined in the boos. As a Fire Talker, Mackerel George was a flop. If he had any pertinent information, it was buried under tons of indecipherable bullshit. His story had no characters. No great battles. No romance. No titillating sex. It was just dry, boring history. So-and-so did this, then so-and-so did that. One loony idea spiraling off into the next, heading in five directions at once, and complicated by big-word double-talk and constant self-corrections. Okie had seen the handwriting on the wall the first time he mentioned the "celery people."

A smiling, oblivious Mackerel George was going over that furrowed ground again, despite the audience's complaints, connecting the existence of a race of walking vegetables to the machinations of superintelligent beings on another planet. As he spoke, skeeters landed on him and fed at will, raising overlapping circular weals on his face, arms and legs.

The islanders had had enough. Adults and children started pushing up from their plastic lawn chairs.

Only a handful sat listening with rapt attention, Okie noted. They weren't called droolies for nothing. Long, swaying strands of their saliva reflected in dancing firelight. They didn't bother to wipe it off their chins. Some of them habitually crapped their pants, as well, too stupid and slow to lower their drawers in time.

That sorry respite was all that stood between the Fire Talker and a fatal swim.

The non-droolie audience, Okie included, slipped away from the fire ring, heading for the claustrophobic comfort of their respective hovels, grumbling out loud about the waste of time and the pointless expenditure.

DANIEL DESIPIO PRESSED a palm against the gritty roof of an overturned cargo container, bracing himself, his homemade BDU shorts down around his duct-taped boot tops. The can of predark pork and beans the islanders had rewarded him with had tasted like sweetened red chalk, washed down with a half cup of harsh joy juice he was still belching, and now the pièce de résistance, an oral servicing by a toothless hag of a gaudy slut. Looking down at her bobbing gray-haired head, Daniel decided it wasn't dark enough out, not by half. He tightly closed his eyes and tried to imagine a hot young MTV star of his own era, but the calluses on her tongue and the insides of her cheeks kept intruding on and deconstructing his fantasy.

In the midst of this joyless congress, he caught himself replaying the evening's events. A familiar unfolding: helplessly watching an audience lose interest in his narrative, fielding their angry questions and challenges, watching them melt into the darkness. It was his former life all over again.

Almost.

The Big Wheel of Karma had turned, but not in the way he or Creedence Clearwater Revival had anticipated. This time, there was payback. Unimaginable payback.

Daniel didn't swat the bugs that landed ever so lightly on his face and arms. The welts raised by their bites camouflaged the tiny red whorls that dotted the surface of his skin—freezer burn from a century spent in the narrow confines of a cryotank. He let the skeeters have a good, deep taste of his tainted blood, then gently fanned them away. He didn't want the bugs to get too full. After wetting their stabbers on him, they attacked the kneeling slut. His disgruntled audience had gone back to their shacks and lean-tos with clouds of similarly infected mosquitos hovering over their heads and shoulders.

Daniel had no feelings of remorse, no pangs of conscience over what he had done to them. In fact, he gloried in it. The Big Wheel had remade him; it had given him a destiny worthy of his talent for the epic and the tragic. He was Satan's Sword, cleaving the multitudes. A transformation that gave new meaning to the twentieth–century catch phrase, "knocked 'em dead."

After a couple of minutes, Daniel decided he had had enough pièce de résistance. He put his free hand against the slut's forehead and levered himself from her suctioning grasp. She was so ugly and beat down he actually had qualms about delivering the climactic facial.

Then he thought, oh, what the hell…

Chapter One

Over Ryan Cawdor's right shoulder, five scattered, flickering, red-orange suns dawned along the horizon line to the south, sandwiched between greasy black sea and menacing black sky. Across the expanse of flat water, maybe ten miles away, a string of Gulf coast oil rigs still burned, as they had day and night for more than a century. In the distance ahead of the one-eyed warrior, the real sun—immense and an even bloodier red, squashed into an ovoid by atmospheric distortion—struggled up from deep purple night.

Ryan and his five companions ran east through the slowly lifting darkness. They drove themselves at a brutal and unforgiving pace, down the granularized ruin of an ancient, asphalt road, kerchiefs tied over their noses and mouths.

Running through the Deathlands at night and over unfamiliar ground was risky business; in this case, *not* running was far riskier. For two and a half hours they had been hard at it.

Jak Lauren was on point. Ryan could see the wild child silhouetted by the hell ball of the emerging sun, his shoulder-length mane of white hair flying, his Magnum Colt Python in his fist. In wire-rimmed spectacles and screwed-down fedora, the diminutive J. B. Dix held down the column's rear with his M-4000 12-gauge pump. Ryan's lover, the long-legged Krysty Wroth, jogged on his left with her Smith & Wesson Model 640 .38-caliber revolver in hand. Krysty's emerald eyes searched the dim verge of the roadway ahead, her red, prehensile mutie hair drawn up into tight curls of alarm. Ryan carried his SIG-Sauer P-226 with a 9 mm round chambered, safety off, index finger stiffened outside the trigger guard. His prized long-blaster, a scoped, Steyr SSG 70 sniper rifle, was strapped tightly over his shoulder and back by its sling, slap-proofed.

Behind Ryan and Krysty, in the middle of the pack, were the group's pair of time travelers.

Theophilus Algernon Tanner had been ripped from the bosom of his young family in the late 1880s, time-trawled against his will by the whitecoats of Operation Chronos. Caught in their net, he had been dragged forward to 1998, the first subject to survive the time travel experiment. If the whitecoats expected their Victorian lab rat to appreciate the Big Picture and be grateful for the sake of science and the expansion of knowledge, they were very much disappointed. They were so arrogant, so oblivious, that they never considered his outrage over the kidnapping, or his continuing grief over the loss of his loved ones. After months of captivity and near-constant poking and prodding by Operation Chronos technicians, Tanner became an intractable embarrassment. Shortly before Armageddon, to be rid of him and as punishment for his truculence, the whitecoats sent the Harvard- and Oxford-educated scholar forward in time.

It was an act of intentional cruelty that had saved his life.

Doc Tanner didn't look over two hundred years old; he looked a fit sixty and his biological age was actually mid-thirties. His teeth were still excellent. A tall scarecrow in a tattered frock coat and tall leather boots, he loped with a sheathed, ebony sword cane in one hand and his massive, Civil War-era black-powder blaster in the other.

Beside him, Dr. Mildred Wyeth kept pace, ready to cut loose, deadly accurate, with her .38-caliber Czech-made ZKR 551 target revolver, the same make and model weapon that had helped her earn a freestyle shooting silver medal in the last-ever Olympic Games. The African-American physician had been cryogenically frozen on December 28, 2000, a few weeks prior to skydark, after an adverse reaction to anesthetic during surgery. Dr. Wyeth had slept in suspended animation for more than a century before the companions freed her. Like Tanner, Mildred was still in her midthirties, biologically speaking. As she ran, the beaded plaits of her hair clicked together, keeping time with her steady footfalls.

Triple red.

Along the shoulders of both sides of the road, thorny, tangled scrub brush grew waist high. The unbroken walls of cover were made to order for a close-range cross fire and ambush.

Using the predark mat-trans system was always a gamble because so many things could go wrong, midjump and postjump. The mat-trans gateways had been designed to surreptitiously move personnel and goods between the government's deep subterranean redoubts, which were scattered across the continent. The companions had no control over their destination, except that it was someplace other than where they started. This time they had materialized in a pitch-black, east Texas redoubt, perilously close to the Houston nuke-a-thon's ground zero.

Using precious flashlight batteries for illumination, they had attempted to jump again, but the system wouldn't power up. They tried the Last Destination button with the same result. They were stuck and in the dark. The redoubt's lights wouldn't come on, either. Apparently the nuke reactor had had one last burst of power left in it. They were radblasted lucky to have materialized at all.

To conserve their batteries, they had lit torches made of paper, cardboard and rags—whatever debris they could find—and explored the deserted, underground complex, looking for a way out.

The reason why nothing worked soon became apparent. High-water marks stained the walls near the ceiling. The redoubt had been flooded at some time in the past. Dried mud, like beige talcum powder, coated walls, floors, comps, desktops, overturned chairs, and the crumbling litter of printout paper. Corrosive salts from the water had etched silicon chips and circuit boards into junk.

To keep from inhaling the potentially dangerous dust their footsteps raised, they had covered their faces with kerchiefs.

In a side room, they found a 3-D plastic topographic map of the Houston area, all the way to the Gulf coast. On the opposite wall was a row of large, glass-faced dials. J.B. and Ryan had brushed the dried mud from the faces and the engraved plastic labels beneath them. The units were radiation counters, connected to distant remote sensors. The name plates read: Central Houston, South Houston, Bunker Hill Village, Lynchburg, La Porte. The counters were nonfunctional; all but one of the needles was pinned in the red—the Barrett dial was stuck in mid-arc. Which had two possible meanings: that area had been hit by less radiation on nukeday, or the dial's mechanism had broken and its needle had fallen back from the little post at the far edge of the red.

Because the companions had no alternative, they took it to mean the former, that the Barrett direction was the only safe corridor leading away from ground zero. Every second they remained in the hotspot, they got a bigger dose of rads. Even though it was the middle of the night, they had to go, and go quickly.

There was another problem, too. Though they had water and jerky left in their packs, it wasn't enough to fuel a multiday journey. Not when they were running full-tilt. The Houston redoubt's stores, although untouched by looters, were useless to them. What wasn't ruined by the water was most likely contaminated by radiation carried in by the flooding, so there was nothing they could risk eating or drinking. Rad-tainted material was like a timebomb in the guts as well as the lungs, a constant source of poison that gradually sickened and eventually chilled.

After they found the exit to the surface and J.B. had taken a compass bearing, they headed south, cross country, until they intersected what was left of the old County Road 90. If they kept traveling east on the ruined road, they knew eventually they'd hit Louisiana, and safety. There was no way of knowing what the ambient rad levels actually were; that's why they kept the masks over their faces.

The gathering Texas dawn revealed a flat, featureless landscape, a plain of dense, twisted, black vegetation that the rising sun could not brighten or penetrate. To Ryan, the sea of brush looked like it had been burned by a terrible wildfire, but he knew it hadn't. The cruelly spiked scrub had sprung from the ashes of Armageddon, a stubborn mutation that defied the effects of toxic soil, air and water. Its fat, lobate fruits—a gaudy orange, and bigger than a man's fist—hung in heavy clusters and lay in scattered, rotting piles along the shoulder. In the motionless air they gave off a sickeningly sweet smell, like an exploded joy-juice still.

Food gathering was not an option for them. They were too close to the Houston craters; the fruit wasn't safe to eat. And they had to cover as much ground as they could before the day really heated up and the threat of death by dehydration forced them to stop and find shade until evening.

They had made the right choice for a getaway route. Dawn also revealed that County Road 90 was well traveled. Narrow, knobby tires had gouged countless, cris-scrossing ruts in the black asphalt sand. Predark motorbikes were the answer to the hellscape's ravaged highways. They used minimal fuel and could run at high speeds offroad to avoid pursuit. There was no chance of getting drive-wheels stuck in mud. Obstacles could be circumnavigated. Motorcycles were ideal for small-payload traders and bands of hit-and-git coldhearts. If someone was lucky enough to score one.

After the sun rose they holstered their sidearms; J.B. slung his scattergun. The likelihood of a surprise attack had diminished, as they could see for miles across the almost tabletop-flat landscape.

As Ryan ran, beads of perspiration trickled in a steady

stream from his hairline, following the ragged edge of the welt of scar that split his left eyebrow. He kept brushing away the sweat to keep it from seeping under the black eyepatch he wore and burning into the socket emptied by a knife slash years ago. He couldn't brush away the familiar ache in the pit of his belly or the burning dryness in his throat. Hunger and thirst were elements of daily life in the hellscape, sometimes in the background, sometimes in the foreground, but always somewhere in the mix.

With Jak in the lead, the companions climbed a slight grade for about a mile under the brightening sky, then the roadbed curved to the right and began a long, straight descent through the stands of black scrub. Looking east from the highest point, Ryan saw the horizon was pale brown, not black. The scrub dead-ended in what appeared to be a definite borderline. He remembered a north-south running river valley from the redoubt's topo map. The brown had to be that valley. There was no hint of green life ahead, just a beige flatland of bare dirt and rock.

No ambush to worry about.

No shade, either.

Mebbe the river had dried up, he thought. Not that it really mattered. If there was water flowing above or below ground in the streambed, they didn't dare even wash their faces in it. They weren't far enough from ground zero for that. Before he and the others reached Louisiana, about 150 miles distant, the odds were good that to survive they would be drinking their own warm piss.

The companions coasted downhill, running in easy strides, taking advantage of the long, gradual grade. After another mile, when they were back on the flat but still five or six miles from the riverbed, over the rasp of his own breathing, Ryan heard the sawing throb of insects. Thousands upon thousands of them. Then he hit a wall of stink. A caustic, invisible fog; not excrement, but excrement-like, on a much grander, more symphonic scale. It was the hellscape's unmistakable signature scent: ruination, the choking, searing, off-gases of biological decay.

At the front of the file, Jak drew his Colt Python and signaled for the column to slow to a walk.

The others pulled their weapons and advanced with caution. The buzzing increased in volume and intensity.

Ryan looked over Jak's slim shoulder at what lay on the road ahead. Under a haze of flying insects, half-naked bodies, at least twenty of them, were scattered from one side to the other. Some faceup, some facedown. Pale skin was blotched purple and black. The flesh looked semisoft, like it was melting from the bones; the torsos and limbs were grotesquely bloated.

Bipedal corpses.

But not norm. Definitely not norm.

"Stickies," Jak announced as he led the others into the obstacle course of decomposition and swarming insects.

For noses, this version of the race of muties known as stickies had two holes in their flat faces. Legions of hairy black flies crawled in and out of the holes, and in and out of lipless, gaping maws lined with rows of black-edged needle teeth. Emptied eyesockets were packed with masses of juddering bugs, feeding, fighting, egg-laying.

Holding her kerchief tight to her face, her eyes watering from the stench, Mildred stopped and knelt beside one of the bodies.

Ryan could see the mutie's mouth and facial bones had partially dissolved; the inward collapse created a caldera effect in the hairless flab. The creature's bare, distended belly had burst a yawning seam right up the middle.

"No way of telling what chilled them, or when," Mildred said. "Daytime temperature has got to be over a hundred degrees around here. And they've been cooking on the black sand."

"Rot quick, too," Jak said.

Even in cold weather, Ryan thought. Dead stickies disintegrated and dissolved like burning candles.

"They could have eaten the fruit and gotten poisoned," Mildred speculated as she rose from her crouch. "Or they could have died from gunshot."

"The damned bugs are eating the bodies and *they* aren't dead," Krysty said, fanning flies from her eyes.

"Neither are the wire worms," J.B. said, gesturing with the muzzle of his Smith & Wesson scattergun.

Between the lips of the gaping fissure that ran from the corpse's pubis to sternum, a bolus of the blood-washed, hair-fine parasites squirmed weakly.

"It wasn't blasters that chilled them," J.B. said, thumbing his spectacles back up the bridge of his nose. "No empty shell casings on the road. No bullet holes in the muties, either."

"Too many of the abysmal creatures to be a mere ambush party," Doc pronounced gravely. "This, my dear friends, is a steed of a different hue."

Doc had put into words what they were all thinking.

During certain times of the year, the friends had encountered an odd mating ritual. Stickies swept across the hellscape in a living wave, gathering numbers to breed. Some, like these perhaps, dropped dead of exertion along the way. The muties mated en masse, indiscriminantly, for days at a time. To be caught in the path of their sexual rampage meant horrible death. Not just from the needle teeth. Stickies had adhesive glands in their palms and their fingers were lined with tiny suckers; they killed by pulling their victims limb from limb.

"You're right, Doc," Ryan said. "They're breeders."

"Mebbe we've missed them?" Krysty said hopefully. "Mebbe they've already passed us by."

"They're in front of us, then," Mildred said. "They could be anywhere ahead."

"Mebbe so," Ryan said, shifting the sling and the weight of his Steyr SSG 70 sniper rifle from his right arm to his left, "but we've got no choice. We've got to keep following the road east. We can't bust that black brush without getting torn to shreds, and we sure as hell can't go back the way we came."

J.B. checked his weapon, cracking the combat pump gun's action just enough to see the rim of a chambered, high brass buckshot round. Snapping the slide forward, he said, "Guess we'd better get on with it, then."

Chapter Two

They were about a quarter mile from the black to brown color change when a crackle of small-arms fire erupted in the near distance ahead. At the sudden noise, the companions reacted as a well-honed unit. J.B., Doc and Mildred ducked to the left shoulder; Ryan, Krysty and Jak to the right. Crouching, weapons up, in an instant they were ready to pour withering fire down the road.

The initial burst was joined by others, which turned into a frenzy of overlapping gunshots.

But the shooting wasn't aimed at them.

"Perhaps another band of travelers has been set upon by the stickies," Doc suggested.

"Or road warriors could be resolving a dispute among themselves," Mildred countered.

"If they've got that many bullets to burn," Ryan said, "they've probably got extra food and water."

"Can't tell without a look-see," J.B. said.

"Scout ahead," Jak offered, already moving forward.

Ryan reached out a hand and stopped the albino. "No recce," he said. "There's no point. We've got nowhere to retreat. Whatever's up ahead, we've got to get past it. We need to go in full force."

As they advanced low and fast along the highway's shoulder, the melee of shooting was interrupted by two rocking booms, one after another. Too loud to be grens. Way too loud. Down the road, at the horizon line, a huge plume of off-white smoke and beige dust billowed skyward. It was hard for Ryan to imagine Deathlands' motorbike traders blowing each other up over a few knapsacks of predark spoils. High explosives were far too valuable to waste.

Ryan and the others kept moving. The firing ahead dwindled to feeble, scattered bursts. Apparently the tide of battle had turned, or the combatants had managed to destroy each other. Either way, there would be less argument over who-owned-what when the companions burst onto the scene.

Then, as suddenly as it had started, the gunfire stopped completely.

Another column of smoke slowly snaked up in front of them. This plume was oily black and much skinnier, the source hidden down in the river valley, below their line of sight.

For a moment, over the slap of his own footfalls, Ryan thought he heard the wind in his ears, high and shrill. But there was no wind; the air was dead calm. As they closed on the entrance to the highway bridge that spanned the riverbed, it sounded more like cats fighting, screaming.

The roadway ended abruptly just beyond the start of the bridge deck in a ragged lip of asphalt and concrete. The five-hundred-yard-long structure had collapsed, probably shaken apart by shock waves on nukeday. The tops of the bridge's massive support pillars stretched off in a straight line to the far side of the gorge. They were crowned by short sections of broken-off highway and guard rail. There were yawning, impassable gaps between them.

The screaming from below continued.

Unslinging the Steyr longblaster and flipping up the lens covers of its scope, Ryan crept forward, past the bike trails that had been worn into the hardpan on either side of the collapsed roadway—travelers had apparently forged an alternate route to the other end of the bridge and the resumption of the highway. Ryan peered over the verge on one knee, bringing the rifle's buttstock to his shoulder, looking over, not through, the optics.

In a fraction of a second, he took it all in.

There were two parallel, north-south running slopes in the valley below them. The first was a gradual shelf, then came the steep drop-off to the river bottom, which mostly lay out of sight because of the view angle. The edge of the drop-off was marked by overlapping blast rings with black scorch marks at their epicenters. Inside the circles, the concrete rubble had been swept clean of dust. Dead stickies and parts of same lay scattered around the joined circumferences. Beyond the litter of death, the blast rings were haloed with crimson.

The bridge deck lay in a line of massive, jumbled chunks on the ground, chunks that sprouted rusted rebar bristles. Amid the fallen blocks, about a hundred yards away, the hapless motorcycle crew had made camp for the night.

It was also where they made their last stand.

Immediately, Ryan caught frantic movement among the concrete slabs. A pair of norm survivors—the screamers—were being circled and set upon by packs of half-naked muties. Other stickies played tug of war with the corpses of fallen bikers.

And that wasn't the worst part.

"Nukin' hell!" J.B. growled over Ryan's shoulder.

Seventy-five yards away, dense black smoke poured up from a pile of offroad motorbikes. They were completely enveloped in flame. At the edges of the blaze, spindly armed muties gyrated with abandon, empty plastic jerricans of gasoline lay scattered at their feet. Stickies loved fire almost as much as they loved senseless chilling. Stickies didn't ride—machinery of any kind was beyond their limited understanding. Eight of the muties were shoving the remaining four dirt bikes toward the conflagration by the handlebars and rear cargo racks.

"Go! Go!" Ryan snarled back at the others as he thumbed the right rear of the Steyr's receiver, sliding off the safety and peering through the scope with his one good eye. He could have opened up on the muties attacking the survivors, and mebbe, just mebbe driven them off their defenseless victims before they were torn to shreds, but if he had done that, the last of the motorcycles would have surely burned.

And the motorcycles were the companions' only way out.

Ryan held the crosshairs low to compensate for the down-angled, close-range shot. He took a stationary lead on the stickie pushing the front of the first motorcycle, aiming at the head, as stickies were hard to kill otherwise. As he tightened the trigger to breakpoint, the companions were already skidding down the bike trail to his right, beelining for the pyre. His predark Austrian sniper rifle barked and bucked hard into the crook of his shoulder. With the gunshot echoing in the chasm, Ryan rode the recoil wave back onto the target. Through the optics he saw his stickie target bowled over. When it went down, it took the bike down, too, in a cloud of beige dust. Ryan worked the butter-smooth 60-degree bolt, locking down on a fresh 7.62 mm NATO round. He ignored the stickie standing frozen and empty-handed over the rear of the dropped motorcycle.

Chilling them all was secondary at this point.

Perhaps impossible.

And with any luck, unnecessary.

He swung his sights to the right, compensating for the suddenly altered course of the stickies. The daisy chain of bike-pushing muties was so focused on the bonfire, on adding more fuel to the blaze, on doing their little arm-waving, stickie fire dance, that they didn't run for cover. They just lowered their hairless heads and pressed onward. Ryan touched off a second round. The 147-grain slug hit a handlebar stickie at the base of the neck, shattering its spinal column and blowing out half its throat in a twinkling puff of pink. The nearly beheaded mutie bounced like a ragdoll off the handlebars and fork, flopping to the ground on its back. The rear pusher couldn't hold the dirt bike upright. It toppled over onto the downed stickie's legs.

From below the bridge came a chaotic rattle of single shots: Krysty and Mildred's .38s, Jak's .357 Magnum, J.B.'s 12-gauge and Doc's black-powder .44. Around the bonfire, struck by a hail of slugs, the stickie dancers jerked to a brand-new beat. As they fell to earth, the companions charged. A center-chest scattergun blast lifted and hurled the last of the dancers backward into the blaze, where it briefly thrashed, fried and died.

Suddenly sealed off from their goal by a row of blasters, the bike-pushing stickies stopped in their tracks.

As they dumped the motorcycles, the last mutie in line spun toward the campsite, toward its brother-sister creatures who were merrily disjointing dead traders and tearing off their flesh in strips. The stickie opened the black hole of its mouth and from high in its throat, shrieked like a teakettle—for help.

Already locked on target, Ryan snapped the cap. As the sniper rifle boomed, it punched hard into his temple. The NATO slug slammed the stickie sideways and down, turning off the piercing squeal like a switch. Too late. As the gunshot resounded in the valley and the mortally wounded creature dervished in the dirt, arms flapping, legs kicking, the other muties abandoned their sport and scurried to the edge of the rubble field, regrouping for an attack on new victims.

Fresh screams and bloody meat. New bones to crack, marrow to spill.

Closing fast on the dropped motorcycles, the companions spread out in a skirmish line and fired at will. J.B. shot from the hip, Mildred from her Olympic stance; both with deadly effect. Smoke and flame belched from Doc's ancient blaster, lead balls blasting through stickie chests and backs as they turned to flee.

J.B. and Doc quickly booted the corpses off the bikes while Krysty, Jak and Mildred used speedloaders to recharge their wheel guns. In front of them, fifty or more muties massed behind a slab of bridge deck. Waving their pale arms over their heads, the stickies made kissing sounds with their lipless mouths, jigging to their own silent, hardwired hip-hop, working themselves into a mindless fury.

Ryan's predark longblaster was no longer an option.

Single shots from the Steyr couldn't turn back stickies
swept up in a chill frenzy. Slinging the rifle, the one-eyed
man vaulted for the side of the road and the crude bike
trail. The downslope was close to sixty degrees, and the
path practically a straight line. He half skiied, half fell 150
feet to the bottom. He hit the ground running, yanking his
SIG-Sauer from hip leather.

At the same instant, the stickies broke from cover and
rushed the five companions, who had closed ranks to concentrate the effect of their weapons. Because Ryan knew
he couldn't reach them in time, he sprinted wide right to
flank the ten-abreast, mutie charge and give himself a
clear line of fire.

In an elegant dueling stance, left hand braced on the
silver lion's-head pommel of his unsheathed sword stick,
Doc started the fusillade with a mighty boom. A yard of
flame and gout of black-powder smoke belched from the
muzzle of the LeMat's top barrel. A fraction of a second
later the others cut loose a ragged volley.

Under the rippling smack of bullet impacts, the center
of the stickie front wave crumpled and folded. Half of the
closely following second rank crashed to earth, as well;
some from high-velocity through-and-throughs, but most
were simply tripped up, unable to avoid the sudden tangle
of legs and torsos. Which, momentarily at least, saved
their wretched lives.

The third, fourth and fifth rows of attackers split down
the middle and veered around their own fallen, like a
torrent flowing around a boulder field. The smell and taste
of the aerosolized gore, the shrill cries of pain made them
all the more frantic. As they reformed their inhuman wave,
the companions' blasters roared again.

The few muties in front who had escaped the first volley—heedless of their exposure, driven by urges too powerful to deny—high-kicked to close distance on the companions. As a result, the second round of fire was at near point-blank range, a cross-chest barrage that swept the stickies off their bare feet.

Ryan advanced on the mutie flank, holding the SIG-Sauer in a solid, two-handed grip. Because both he and his targets were moving, it wasn't the time for fine shooting. The blaster barked and bucked again and again, action cycling. Ryan punched out rapid-fire, center body shots as the tripped muties tried to scramble to their feet. The mutie bastards were so pumped up by the prospect of more chilling, that unless it was a head shot it took two slugs to put some of them down.

A round punched through a scrambler and slammed the runner behind it in the side of the head. The others dashed past like they had blinders on, even as Ryan blew their packmates to hell.

His next shot smacked a sprinting stickie high in the upper arm, and the impact spun it around ninety degrees. It then launched itself at him, banshee wild, mouth gaping, needle teeth bared, open palms leaking strands of milky adhesive. Body language notwithstanding, the stickie's black eyes were devoid of emotion, like a shark's or a doll's.

Ryan fired the SIG-Sauer into the center of the open yap. The mutie's hairless head snapped back as if it had been poleaxed, eyes skyward as a glistening strawberry mist gusted from the back of its skull. Bright arterial blood shot from the creature's nose holes as it crashed onto its back, the soles of its trembling feet black with crusted grime.

There wasn't enough time to dump the SIG's spent mag, reload, aim and fire at the stickies veering his way. He could have unslung the Steyr from his back and gotten off one or two shots before they were on him. Not enough to make a difference. Shifting the pistol to his left hand, Ryan whipped his eighteen-inch panga from its leg sheath.

He glanced to the left as the LeMat's shotgun barrel thundered. Along with a plume of caustic smoke it spewed forth the combination of broken glass and potmetal fragments that Doc called his "facelifter" load—at a range of ten feet, that's exactly what it did. It was his last shot. Doc immediately raised his edged weapon, neatly sidestepping to avoid an oncoming stickie, simultaneously rolling the wrist of his sword hand. With surgical precision and speed too quick for the eye to follow, the point of his rapier blade opened a second, grinning mouth three inches below the spike-rimmed maw the mutie had been born with. Blood sheeting down its naked chest, the hellspawn dropped to its knees in the dirt, then onto all fours.

Also out of cartridges, J.B. used the barrel of his M-4000 scattergun like a short club to bash and smash the heads of the monsters that lunged for him, beating back the horde, providing cover and time for Krysty, Mildred and Jak to reload.

From the git-go, based on the companions' rate of fire, their weapons' mag capacities, the stickie numbers and the size of the battlefield, Ryan had figured that combat would devolve to hand-to-hand. To be pulled down by this enemy was to be torn apart.

Fully aware of what was on the line, the one-eyed warrior met chill rage with chill rage. The heavy blade of his panga was made for chopping and hacking, and that's how he used it. The panga sizzled as it cleaved the air, hardly slowing when it met mutie flesh and bone. It clipped wrists into stumps, left arms dangling free from shoulder sockets, and opened godawful, diagonal torso slashes, from nipple to opposing hip. In his wake, mewling stickies scrabbled on their knees in the dust, trying to collect and stuff back the slimy gray coils of their guts.

The sight of their fellows falling in pieces under the bloody blade didn't give the stickies pause. As they threw themselves at him, Ryan's mind and body were one, measuring attack angles, kill order, the necessary rhythm of perfectly executed forehands and backhands—all in a fraction of a fraction of a second.

Stepping around another set of outstretched sucker fingers, Ryan swung the panga so hard that he sliced off the top of the stickie's head, front to back. Half a loaf of pale, cross-cut brain flopped steaming to the ground, followed by its stone-dead, former owner.

Their weapons loaded, Mildred, Krysty and Jak rejoined the fray. They split up to get clear firing lanes, then head shot the last of the surviving stickies at close range.

As quickly as he had switched it on, Ryan shut off the rampage, but the sustained burst of all-out effort left him gasping for breath. His kerchief mask's hem dripped pink from its point, pink from his pouring sweat mixed with sprays of stickie blood.

As the echoes of gunfire faded, screams from the rubble field became audible. Anguished, rasping screams.

"Start up the bikes," Ryan said, wiping the panga's blade on his pant leg before he scabbarded it. "Come with me, Doc," he called to the old man, who was recovering his sword sheath. As the two of them trotted for the remains of the travelers' campsite, Ryan dropped the SIG's spent mag into his palm and swapped it with a full one from his pocket.

Before they reached the edge of the bridge deck debris, three of the bike engines were running. Sitting astride the machines, J.B., Mildred and Krysty goosed their respective throttles to redline, making the engines whine. There was another sound, as well, much less encouraging.

Phut-phut-phut! Phut-phut-phut! Phut-phut-phut!

When Ryan looked back, he saw Jak stomping the fourth bike's starter pedal, throwing his whole weight against it, over and over again.

"This way!" Doc said.

They hurriedly followed the moans, moving past the campfire pit and the traders' abandoned, fully loaded backpacks. As they closed in on the source, the sounds became distinguishable as words.

"Sweet blessed Charity!" Doc gasped, stopping short.

"Chill me! Pleeeeease, chill me!"

The liquid, bubbling prayer came from a ruined hulk of a human being. He lay on his belly on the ground in the lee of a tipped-up slab of concrete, most of his clothes had been ripped away. "Please!"

As the trader begged, Ryan could see bloody molars and moving tongue through the huge hole torn in his right cheek. He had been scalped, as well, down to the shiny white bone. His right foot faced the wrong way, still in its duct-tape-patched boot. The other foot was missing altogether; his left arm hung semidetached, torn from its socket, hanging by a thread of golden sinew. Smeared stickie adhesive had sealed off the ruptured major blood vessels. The poor, broken bastard wasn't going to bleed out, not anytime soon.

"End it!" the man plaintively croaked, stretching out the bloody claw of his good hand. "Use your blaster!"

Doc gave Ryan a questioning look; the one-eyed man minutely shook his head. Their bullets were in short supply, and the route to safety too long and too precarious. He pointed at the steel pommel and worn leather handle of a knife sticking out of the rubble. In the heat of battle it had fallen out of the reach and sight of the mortally wounded man. The Ka-Bar's noble blade had been sharpened so many times it had been reduced to a steel sliver.

Doc used the point of his rapier to flip the knife closer to the whimpering wreck.

Without pause, without a nod of thanks, the trader grabbed the combat knife and propping the pommel on the ground, held the blade's tip below his sternum. Grunting from the effort and the pain, he rolled over hard onto the knife, driving the long steel through his heart and into his chest to the hilt. After a moment of convulsive quivering, his body lay still. The point pitched a little tent in what was left of the back of his shirt.

A faint morning breeze swept down the river valley, carrying with it an awful odor. It wasn't coming from the dead man.

"Do you smell that?" Ryan asked, pulling his sopping wet kerchief down under his chin.

Doc yanked down his mask, too. "Spoiled herring?" the Victorian said with a grimace.

Then the truth hit Ryan. Without a word, he turned and dashed for the chasm. Doc loped after him. As the one-eyed man looked down over the edge, into the riverbed, his stomach dropped to his boot soles.

Not rotten fish.

Spunk.

"Lord have mercy," Doc intoned.

The bottom third of each of the bridge's massive supports was black with stickies. Hundreds of them. They clung to the sides of the pillars, crawling, squirming over each other like bees in a hive.

Unfortunately, the dirt bike track ran right past the foot of the pillars and the puddled genetic muck before it crossed the dry riverbed to the other side.

Even more unfortunate, the smell of spilled blood from above, the screams and the gunfire and explosions had roused the writhing, hip-thrusting masses from their rut stupor. As Ryan watched, stickies disengaged and started to descend the ladder of slippery bodies to the ground.

They would follow the blood scent like a homing beacon.

"Quick!" Ryan growled, waving Doc after him as he raced back toward the campfire.

When they got there, they shouldered as many of the loaded backpacks as they could carry. As Ryan ran from the rubble field, over the sounds of the idling dirt bikes, he realized Jak's motorcycle still wouldn't start.

"Leave it!" Ryan shouted through a cupped hand. "Come on! Over here!"

The albino youth let the machine drop to the ground. Mildred passed her bike to him and climbed on the seat behind J.B. Krysty already had her motorcycle moving. When she roared up, Doc and Ryan jammed a couple of backpacks in the cargo rack, then battened them down with bungees. There was no time to check the contents.

"Gaia, what's that smell!" Krysty exclaimed as solo-riding Jak, and J.B. and Mildred joined them.

"Hundreds of stickies copulating," Doc announced.

"Down there?" Mildred said, pointing toward the drop-off and the riverbed.

"Oh, yeah," was Ryan's answer.

While he and Doc were tying down the backpacks, J.B. thumbed high brass shells into the loading port of his M-4000 as fast as he could. When the mag was plugged, he racked the action to chamber a round, stuffed a final shell in the port, then passed the scattergun back to Mildred.

"Stop for nothing," Ryan told the others as he climbed on the seat behind Krysty. "All we've got going for us is speed and surprise. That means staying on the existing path." He adjusted the Steyr strapped across his back, then unholstered his SIG. "If we try to break fresh trail and go around them, we might dump the bikes. If that happens, they'll swarm us and we're dead meat. J.B., let's go!"

The Armorer screwed down his fedora, then roared away with Mildred pressed against his back. As Krysty and passenger Ryan, and Jak and passenger Doc followed, the lead bike vanished over the verge of the chasm. A few seconds later, the 12-gauge boomed.

Mildred was doing more than riding shotgun.

Krysty slowed a little to keep from going airborne when they hit the drop-off. As soon as the front wheel pointed down, she opened the throttle wide in second gear. The slope was steep, the dished-out path worn smooth. Along with the gut-wrenching acceleration, wind howled past Ryan's ears and whipped at his clothes and his one good eye. Stickies who had been driven off the trail by J.B.'s passing and the shotgun blast watched dumbfounded by the combination of velocity and shrill engine noise.

As Krysty hurtled toward the stickie-covered pillars, Ryan leaned to the side and glimpsed Mildred standing on the dirt bike's footpegs, knees bent, left hand firmly gripping the back of J.B.'s coat collar. Holding the scattergun by the pistol grip with her right, she aimed straight ahead. Another boom rang out. The spray of close-range buckshot momentarily cleared the road of obstacles, exploding a stickie's head like a liquid-filled piñata.

Hunched over the fuel tank, Krysty shifted to third and wound the engine to redline, leaving Ryan's stomach far behind. He didn't know how fast they were going—he couldn't see the speedometer—but it felt like ninety. Firing his weapon was out of the question. He couldn't do anything but hang on.

If the muties had thrown their bodies at the bikes, they could have made them crash. Suicide in the service of chilling was certainly in their repertoire. If the strategy had occurred to them, before they could act on it, the six companions were already past the pillar bases in a screaming blur.

Dead ahead, J.B.'s brake lights flashed on, the bike shimmied as it slowed and Mildred sat down hard. Coming up on them too fast, Krysty hit her brakes, too, then downshifted an instant before they bounced into the riverbed, skidding across the loose stream gravel. To keep her from laying down the motorcycle, Ryan slammed down his left boot. Feathering the throttle and the brake, Krysty regained control and righted the bike, then she rocketed them up the much more gradual incline on the far side of the riverbed.

When Ryan glanced behind, he saw Jak powering up the slope through the dust cloud they had raised. Lanky Doc was perched on the seat behind the diminutive albino, his shoulder-length gray hair and the tails of his frock coat flapping in the breeze. With his boots propped on the footpegs, Doc's knees were level with Jak's shoulders. Ryan thought they looked like a radblasted carny act.

At the crest of the grade, there was nothing but open road ahead of the companions, stickie-free and string-straight.

Unable to contain his glee, J.B. accelerated away from the others like a madman. Holding down his treasured hat with one hand, throwing back his head, he hollered "Yee-hah!" at the top of his lungs.

Chapter Three

Under the wide brim of a straw planter's hat, Okie Moore squinted through rubber-armored minibinocs. Behind him, fixed to the rusting rail, a tattered, homemade Lone Star flag snapped in the onshore breeze. From his vantage point atop the *Yoko Maru*'s radar mast—some twelve stories above the main deck, five stories above the roof of the wheelhouse, almost four hundred feet above ground— he could see twenty nautical miles. The cheap Taiwanese optics were never quite in focus—if one eye was sharp, the other was slightly blurred—but they were good enough to spot a telltale blip along the seam between white-capped Gulf and cloudless blue sky. So far, there was nothing to see, but the combination of fuzzy images and the glare of the midday sun had given him the beginnings of a monumental headache. It felt like someone had inserted a flexible steel rod up his right nostril and then corkscrewed it through his sinus passages until the pointy tip bored into the nerves behind his eyeball.

Okie hadn't slept for twenty-four hours, not since the trader's sloop beating in from the southwest had dropped sail and coasted slowly through the sheltered anchorage on the Corpus side of the island, the black plastic, trash bag pennants on its headstay fluttering like dying crows. From the cockpit, through a megaphone, the skipper shouted a warning to the beach and the handful of moored ships. The three-man crew had seen Brownsville from a distance. It was a funeral pyre, set alight by the Matachìn.

Until that moment, only droolies had taken the Fire Talker's stories seriously.

"How long ago?" someone along the shore had shouted back.

"Four days."

"Stop!" the islanders cried. "Stop! Heave to!"

The sloop continued coasting east, the captain steering with one hand and holding the megaphone in the other.

"Are the pirates coming this way?" Okie had bellowed, running along the sand to keep up.

"Who knows?" was the reply. "Could be a day behind, or three hours behind. Or mebbe they took their spoils south. Not sticking around to find out. If you got any brains, you won't, either." The skipper tossed down the megaphone, and to his waiting crew he snarled the order "Up sail!"

The sheets filled with a resounding whipcrack and the ship accelerated away. The captain never once looked back.

The three predark vessels moored in the cove began immediate, frantic preparations to weigh anchor. Ignoring the shouts and curses of the islanders, the ships' crews had pushed half-loaded dinghies from the beach and rowed away. The only evacuation on the traders' minds was their own. As soon as the dinghies had been hoisted aboard, without even stowing cargoes belowdecks, the two battered Tartans and the Catalina winched up their hooks, raised all sails and left the Padre Islanders to meet their fate.

After the observation and blasterposts that ringed the

perimeter had been alerted, the heads of the Nuevo-Texican founding families and their lieutenants, Okie included, met in emergency session in the *Yoko Maru*'s windowless galley. They had planned to dump the Fire Talker on the mainland shore that very day. Now they didn't dare. There were unanswered questions about how he had managed to reach Padre so quickly on foot. If he was a pirate spy, and they turned him loose, he could report back on the island's fortifications and armament. Some of the headmen wanted to chill him at once, just to be safe, but when a vote of hands was taken they were in the minority. The majority decided it was better to keep him alive and close, as he might give away an impending attack, either inadvertently or under torture.

The Nuevo-Texicans had beaten back invaders on many occasions in their short, violent history, usually before the bastards even set foot on the beach. Streams of triangulated blasterfire from strategically placed blasterposts took an unholy toll on shore landings. The islanders were proud of their fighting spirit and resilience; moreover, they were supremely confident in their battle prowess. Their chip-on-the-shoulder attitude, borrowed from their nuke-fried ancestors, was "Bring it on!" Though they lived amid the unthinkable consequences of that philosophy, the irony was lost on them.

The threat of long-distance shelling by the Matachìn meant their normal defensive tactics went out the window. They couldn't count on the blasterposts surviving a high-explosive barrage from offshore. The only hardened, defensible structure on the island was the cargo ship itself. In stacked containers and vast belowdecks holds, it held virtually all of the islanders' wealth.

After a brief discussion, the headmen had decided that

if and when the enemy was sighted, they would withdraw the island's population to the freighter, and make the attackers take it, deck by deck, bulkhead by bulkhead. If the Matachìn shelled the ship to break the resistance, they'd destroy everything they came for, and waste precious ammunition in the process.

Absentmindedly scratching an angry cluster of mosquito bites on the inside of his wrist, Okie turned on the platform and gazed down on the foredeck, at lines of people carrying valuables and food into the ship, and heading back empty-handed for more. A natural incline made of compacted, wind-driven sand led from the beach to the portside gangway. Before the pirates landed, and after everyone was on board, they would blow it up, forcing the Matachìn to use grappling hooks and ladders to reach the top deck. Which would put them squarely into the kill zones of the firing ports staggered along the hull. The narrow slits hacked into the steel were just big enough for ramp and post sights and blasterbarrels.

Looking down over the crow's nest rail, feeling the rickety platform sway under him in the wind, Okie had an awful surge of vertigo. Heights normally never bothered him; they certainly never made him want to vomit. Putting it down to too little sleep and food, and too much frantic activity, he shut his eyes for a moment and concentrated on breathing deeply and evenly through his mouth.

When the whirling sensation passed, Okie once again peered through the binocs, scanning the lines of people filtering between stacked cargo containers for his two hugely pregnant wives. He didn't see either of them, or any of his six kids. Everybody who could fire a blaster was carrying one. Women and the older children wore AKs and sawed-off pump shotguns slung across their backs. There were no tear-streaked faces, no quivering lower lips. The islanders, to a person, were jut-jaw defiant.

They had all heard other Fire Talkers' stories about the Matachìn, selected, fragmented details that were, of course, calculated to entertain and raise the short hairs. There was no way of telling if any of them were true, or how much the facts had been exaggerated.

It was rumored that the pirates all carried machetes with razor-sharp cane hooks at their tips—gut rippers. It was said they used the heavy blades to chop off any hands raised against them. After cauterizing the fresh stumps with torches so their captives wouldn't bleed to death, they nailed the severed appendages in pairs to the ramparts of conquered villes, palm outward in a gesture and symbol of permanent submission.

It was rumored that they made the subjected people kneel whenever they passed, kneel with noses and foreheads pressed firmly into the dirt. It was said they wore glittering garlands of looted gold jewelry entwined in their matted dreadlocks and around their scarred boot tops. Apparently, they never washed themselves, either.

Never.

Stink was their religion. Pong was their manifesto.

According to the stories, some of the Matachìn wore bright, floral frocks over their blood-stained trousers and boots, shoulder-seam–split trophies ripped from the women they had ravaged and murdered.

According to the Fire Talkers, the Matachìn indulged in bloody and brutal ritual spectacles; they had established an extensive slave trade along the Atlantic coast of Mexico and Central America; they worked their captives to death in their agricultural fields and gaudies; and to amuse themselves during long sea voyages the pirate crews choreographed and staged slave fights to the death.

The common denominator in all the Fire Talker variations was death, unpleasant and prolonged.

Down in the ville, islanders were still gathering up everything of value, including excess stockpiles of food and fresh water. The water they couldn't move, they dumped onto the sand. The idea was to leave the pirates nothing to eat or drink. The Nuevo-Texicans were well prepared for a long siege. They had the entire storehouse of the *Yoko Maru* at their disposal. The pirates had only whatever they brought along with them. Assuming the islanders could hold the ship for the duration, sooner or later problems of resupply would drive the Matachìn back to whatever hell-hole had spawned them.

The possibility did exist that the pirates had taken their fill of spoils in Browns ville, that they weren't coming north, after all. But that wasn't something the islanders could count on. Even as the residents crisscrossed between the ville and the *Yoko Maru,* explosive charges were being laid in the narrow, winding paths between the shanties. The predark Claymore mines with their payloads of steel ball bearings wouldn't be trip-wired and armed until the enemy came into view and the last of the women and children were safely onboard the ship.

Okie raised the binocs, taking in the bow of the vessel. Surrounded by a rapt, deck-seated audience, the Fire Talker was perched on a bitt, waving his arms and talking animatedly.

Giving the droolies more to slobber about, no doubt.

The islanders' usual practice was to securely tether the

triple stupes, staking them at least three yards apart to keep them from playing hide the slime eel. When droolies mated with droolies of the opposite sex, the outcome was a foregone conclusion: more droolies. In camps elsewhere in the Deathlands, these unfortunates were not so tenderly cared for. The moment the symptoms surfaced—the slack lower jaw and vacant stare—heads were smashed in. The Nuevo-Texicans kept their little flock alive, not out of compassion or a sense of parental duty, but because the droolies were so damned amusing, even if the camp dogs failed to get the joke. Having someone around visibly more messed up than you were had another benefit, as well. It made a person feel instantly better about him or herself. "At least I'm not a droolie," was the unspoken but ever present refrain.

Okie was struck by a sudden chill that started at the base of his spine and rippled up his back and neck, and crab-crawled over the top of his scalp. Which he found very strange, given the air temperature even with the wind was in the high eighties. As the shudder passed through him, the steel rod behind his eye probed deeper into the nerve bundle. He saw bright, dancing spots of light and once again felt the urge to spew. Worse, there was a simultaneous, uncomfortable pressure building deep down in his bowels. Had to be something he ate, he thought. Underdone rat on a stick, mebbe. Closing his eyes and gripping the rail in both hands, Okie tried to will the sensations away. He still had another couple of hours before he was relieved of the watch.

"TIME DILDO-LATOR! TIME DILDO-LATOR!" The seated droolies rocked their hips, scooting their behinds on the deck in time to the gleeful chant. "Time dildo-lator! Time dildo-lator!"

Daniel Desipio sat back and basked in their adoration. They couldn't get enough of his backstories and technical explanations, although it was unclear if they understood a single word of the complex scientific and philosophical concepts that underlaid his narratives.

Still, the frenzied attention buoyed his spirits.

From the *Yoko Maru*'s bitt, Daniel surveyed the squalid little ville spread out below. Construction had started in the most weather-protected spot, in the lee of the freighter's bow. The first cluster of single-story huts used the ship's hull for their rear walls. Building materials had to be salvaged and ferried from the flooded ruins of Corpus, so subsequent structures shared both side and rear walls. Nothing in the ville was straight, not roofs, not doorways, not lanes, not side yards. Everything was made of accumulated scrap, unpainted or covered in peeling layers of paint. Over three decades the slapdash habitations had spread to the shore of the anchorage on the north side. The islanders had built monuments to themselves, expressing their personalities, desires, artistic senses with found materials, the restricted pallette of the rubbish heap. It could have been a village on the edge of a garbage dump in predark India or Brazil. Or a squatter camp in South Africa.

That said, the grounded container ship's bounty had provided every ramshackle hut with its own Taiwanese knock-off Weber kettle and fancy barbecue tools, and its own plastic lawn furniture.

The Nuevo-Texicans were damn proud of their little corner of the world.

Daniel Desipio, twentieth-century freezie, had a different perspective: a shithole by any other name.

For what had to have been the thirtieth repetition in as many hours, the Fire Talker recited the story of how the Vikings acquired the time dilator, the desperate bargain they had made with the Martian hordes, and their combined exploitation of the ancient Norse Runestone Concatenation. That terrestrial-extraterrestrial plot had been frustrated by the intervention of the Iroquois Ninja princess—proud, statuesque, with raven hair and slanted black eyes, and spots of blushing rose in the centers of her buckskin-colored cheeks—and of her singing *katana,* and her coterie of cloud operatives that moved from one human mind to another like stops on a subway line.

As he mechanically regurgitated the pulp fiction series' canon—something he could have done in his sleep— Daniel watched his audience for the initial, subtle signs of infection. A growing restlessness. A flushing of the face. A sensitivity to light. He visualized the viruses invading individual host cells, commandeering reproductive machinery, replicating until their sheer volume burst cell walls, then spewing forth in a torrent, hardwired to penetrate and infect new cells: an unstoppable, rising tide of the submicroscopic, leading to debilitation, agony and horrible death. All of which derived from the poison that lurked in his 137-year-old blood, and to which he was happily immune.

Whenever Daniel reflected on what had led him to his most peculiar fate, the answer was always the same: the blind pursuit of Art. It was what had animated and enthused him since the third grade when he started reading and collecting various pulp action series from second-hand bookstores. He had pored over the "Golden Age" titles until the yellowed, musty pages dropped from the bindings, absorbing the nuances of style and content. All Daniel Desipio had ever wanted to do was to write adventure books like those. Doggedly determined, he had eventually achieved his goal, but in the twenty years between his introduction to pulp and his first sale of a novel, the industry had changed. Series action fiction had become a franchise operation, produced by hamsterwheeling, faceless ghost writers; it was in effect a dead-end career.

Slaughter Realms, the house-owned pulp series he had slaved upon for seven years, had had several nameless authors and had run to well over 250 titles. All nagging questions of artistic control and continuity had been resolved by Armageddon, by more than a century of elapsed time, and by his unlikely survival.

Even before the nukecaust, individual books in the series had been forgotten, consigned to landfills and bonfires, and along with them Daniel's contributions to the canon. He had come up with gemlike, signature exclamations for two of the main running characters, Ragnar the Viking and Nav Licim, the wilted but defiant patriarch of the celery people. In return for his devotion to his Art, Daniel Desipio received no author credit, an hourly wage well below the established national minimum and no royalties on book sales.

The turning point for him had come on March 13, 1998, when after finishing his twenty-ninth book in the series he had asked the publisher for a hundred-dollar raise and was denied. Crushed and mortified, for the first time Daniel actually considered abandoning his lifelong dream. He considered becoming a Realtor. If he had taken that career course, he would have certainly perished along with almost everyone else in the U.S. on that January day in 2001. But in a moment of pure inspiration, fueled by the depths of his outrage and despair, Daniel had decided to do something truly radical in the name of his craft, for the sake of fresh experience, of something truly unique and exciting to write about. Without a thought to the possible consequences—not that even he could have imagined them—he had thrown himself into the meat grinder of Science.

More than a century post-nukeday, the world's values had taken a hard U-turn, and a turn for the better as far as he was concerned. The idea of bottom-rung fiction or bottom-rung consumer merchandise lost all meaning when there was nothing left for either to be compared to. Which is why the cargo of the *Yoko Maru* was worth fighting and dying for.

A self-guided sightseeing tour of the island's shanty-town had told Daniel what was stored in the container ship: white running shoes aplenty, wardrobes of summer fashion, circa 1999, and plastic lawn furniture. But also toothbrushes and toothpaste, toilet paper, linens, bathware and canned goods in profusion. Empty tins of pork and beans, peas, pearl onions, peaches, black olives and potted meat lay scorched in the camp middens, as well as cast-off plastic packaging from barbecue potato chips, honey-roasted peanuts, jerky sticks, cookies and candy bars. Daniel had seen bag charcoal, car batteries, spark plugs, fan belts, flatware, dishes, pots and pans, stuffed toys, cooking oil, and grooming and beauty products—bar soaps, lotions and lipsticks. There was also a variety of made-in-India, factory-loaded ammo: 9 mm Parabellum,

7.62 mm Russian and 12-gauge low-brass quail loads, among others. Apparently, the *Yoko Maru* held a large stockpile of predark centerfire munitions.

As he prattled away on automatic to his spellbound audience, Daniel took in the islanders' highly organized defensive preparations, the lines of people moving on and off the ship, the self-sacking of the ville. They had a good plan. Obvious, but good. From the hard looks he was getting, they suspected him of something far more nefarious than rotting the minds of droolies—as if their suspicions mattered at this point. The fight for the island was already lost; the Nuevo-Texicans just didn't know it…yet.

"Battle armor! Battle armor!" Daniel's audience hollered, shattering his reverie. "Battle armor! Battle armor!"

He held up his hands for quiet. "All right, all right," he conceded, "but this is absolutely the *last* time today…"

To the delight of his listeners, in highly numeric and acronymic detail Daniel went over the specifications of the Martian-made assault gear, down to the chemical composition of the metallic-plastic alloys, the thicknesses of individual body plates and the "theory" behind the nanotech circuitry they contained.

Chapter Four

After the companions had motored three miles up the road, Ryan signaled for a pull over and parlay. As the dust settled around them, Krysty, J.B., and Jak killed the motorcycles' engines and everyone dismounted. No longer in motion, they felt the full impact of the sweltering heat.

The first words out of Ryan's mouth were, "Check your ammo."

The one-eyed man didn't have to check his own. Every round he had left was loaded up, seven shots in the Steyr's box mag, a full 15-round clip in the SIG-Sauer. While the one-eyed warrior unslung his longblaster and stood lookout, Krysty, Mildred, J.B., and Jak started their round counts. Doc, the deep creases of his prematurely aged face rimed with dirt and sweat, retired to a wide sandstone boulder at the side of the road.

Ryan watched the time traveler take a seat on the low rock and carefully lay down his sword stick. Doc dug black-powder reloading gear from his frock coat's pockets.

More than once over the years Ryan and J.B. had tried to talk him into switching over to a weapon-chambered centerfire, but he wouldn't hear of it. Doc was one hardheaded Victorian son of a bitch. No matter what they said, he always argued that the proof was in the chilling. And that he had never had a problem doing that with the 250-year-old LeMat. Privately, J.B. assured Ryan that someday the radblasted thing was going to explode in his hand like a frag gren.

Doc prided himself on how fast he could reload his treasured if obsolete weapon. And Ryan had to admit he was plenty fast. Since the immediate danger was miles behind them, Doc gave the chambers and both barrels a quick going over with the bore brush to scour away the worst of the burned residue. He lined up the first chamber with the hammer at halfcock and the muzzle aimed skyward, then unsnapped the pistol's jointed rammer from its barrel clip. He measured the powder, poured it into the shallow chamber, and levered the rammer to seat a lead ball on top of it. After flicking away the little ring of excess lead the lip's tight fit trimmed off, he put dab of grease over the bullet to lube the barrel and keep the sparks from other chambers from causing spontaneous ignition when they fired. Rotating the cylinder a full notch, he proceeded to load the next chamber, and the next, and the next, and so on. His rate of speed was as steady as his hands. After he finished the ninth chamber he securely snapped the rammer back into its clip.

The .63-caliber shotgun chamber he loaded last, using a homemade wooden ramrod to seat the aft wadding, grapeshot and front wadding. He capped all ten chambers, lowered the hammer into one of the safety notches between nipples and slipped the massive blaster back into its hand-tooled Mexican holster.

Just under five minutes had elapsed from start to finish.

In the meantime, the other companions had taken stock of what was left of their ammo. J.B. had six high-brass rounds in his M-4000's tubular magazine. Mildred and Krysty had full cylinders in their revolvers. They had used up their speedloaders; between them they had eight loose shells. Jak had two .357 Magnum bullets left in his revolver and nothing in his pockets. Of the six, only Mildred and Krysty could swap cartridges back and forth interchangeably as they both carried .38 Specials. They evened things out with Jak, giving him a couple of bullets each. Jak could fire their .38s in his .357, but they couldn't shoot his cartridges because of the Magnum's longer case.

J.B. was the first to dig into one of the looted backpacks.

"Well, lookee here!" he exclaimed, holding up a plastic-wrapped, gold-colored brick for all to see.

Taped to the outside of the kilo of C-4 was a sealed blister pack that contained blasting caps and electronic trigger, radio detonator and two sets of lithium batteries— one to set off the cap, one for the remote detonating device. As a backup, there was also a coil of thick, white blasting cord.

Ryan and the other companions quickly dumped out the contents of the other five packs. There was no ammo. No food. No water. Just predark plastic explosive and detonators. There was enough plastique piled in the middle of the road to turn a square city block into rubble.

"Well, we know the stuff still works," Mildred said.

"Stickies found that out the hard way," Krysty said.

J.B. turned the brick over in his hand and read the text on the packaging. "Check the address," he said, showing Ryan what was written.

"What is the significance of the label?" Doc asked, staring down at a brick he had picked up.

"Back in the day," Ryan explained, "when J.B. and me were running with Trader, there was a rumor going around about a predark industrial plant in western New Mex, where the government used to turn high ex into C-4. Supposedly the finished product was stored in deep, blastproof bunkers in the desert. Looks like our dead scroungers stumbled on the motherload."

"Worth big jack," Jak said appreciatively, toeing the pile with a boot tip.

"To the right buyer," Mildred said. "The trouble is, we're a long way from the nearest baron."

Ryan nodded. Mildred was on target, as usual. HE was a useful tool in the defense of territory, and in taking territory away from someone else; it was a weapon of war. For the hellscape's smaller scale, everyday business of robbing, extortion, forced servitude and the like, it was serious overkill.

"It's still worth plenty to a middleman," Ryan countered. "We've got to find someone who has what we need, short-term. Ammo, food, water and gas for the bikes. If we can trade away a small part of the stash, we can haul the rest of it east, where it will bring the most jack. Check the fuel in the bikes."

They unscrewed the gas caps and J.B. peered inside each of the tanks.

"Fuel levels are pretty much the same," he told Ryan. "Not enough to get all of us to Louisiana, that's for sure. If we're lucky we can get mebbe another twenty miles before we start to run out. Radblasted stickies burned up all the extra gas in their victory dance."

"Then we're going to have to detour south to trade for bullets and supplies," Ryan said.

"Why south?" Mildred asked. "Beaumont is due east on this road. We've easily got enough gas to get there. Couldn't be more than ten miles."

"Beaumont is a no-go," J.B. said emphatically.

"It was hit hard on nukeday," Ryan elaborated. "Nothing there but glow-in-the-dark rubble and twisted steel. Trader always gave it a wide berth and beelined his convoys for Port Arthur ville on the Gulf shore. If the head man down there is still the same, he's a thieving pile of crap—"

"A *giant* thieving pile of crap," J.B. interjected.

"—but," Ryan continued, "it's still the closest place to swap some of the C-4 for what we need."

Jak used a hand to shield his unsettlingly red eyes from the glare as he looked up the road. "Port A ville mebbe thirty miles," he said.

If the companions had been riding solo, Ryan knew they might have made it on the little fuel they had. They wouldn't split up, though. Not a chance under these circumstances. Not of their own volition.

"How much water have we got?" Mildred asked J.B.

The Armorer produced a scarred, two-liter plastic bottle from his backpack. It was half-full of a cloudy, slightly brown-tinged liquid. There was a layer of fine sediment at the bottom. Ryan took the container; the sun beat down on his head and shoulders, the heat sang in his ears as he held it up for all to see.

"That's it?" Krysty said.

"That's it," Ryan said. Another question had to be asked, even if he already knew the answer. "We can drink it all now, or we can drink it later. What's it going to be?"

The companions were accustomed to privation, to hard,

long marches over difficult terrain. The consensus was to drink it later, when they really needed it.

The companions repacked the C-4, saddled up and rode off at a steady, fuel-conserving twenty-five miles an hour. The breeze blowing over Ryan's sweat-lubed body felt like air-conditioning.

ABOUT AN HOUR DOWN THE ROAD, J.B. lost power first. As he dropped back, his engine went dead and he and Mildred coasted to a stop. Krysty and Jak braked their bikes and turned back to join them.

"I make it we're still five or six miles from the edge of Port A ville," Ryan said as he swung off Krysty's backseat.

"Too far to push the bikes in this heat with so little water," Mildred said.

The motorcycles were valuable, all right, but they weren't worth taking the last train west for. Certainly not when they had sixty kilos of operational plastique to trade.

"Jak," Ryan said, "scout ahead and find us a good spot to hide the bikes. If we can barter some gas in Port A ville, we'll come back for them later."

Doc dismounted from the motorcycle's rear seat and the albino sped away. Jak returned a few minutes later with a typically terse report. "Gulch behind rock pile, not see from road," he said. "Quarter mile up."

They abandoned the three motorcycles in the shallow ravine, about one hundred yards from the edge of the ruined two-lane highway. It was a good location, and they could easily find it again from the sandstone outcrop.

Before they set off they shared the last of the water, which amounted to a couple of good swigs per person.

The companions left the gulch lugging one extra

backpack each, about twenty-five pounds of additional weight.

It took them almost three hours, walking at a steady pace to reach the outskirts of Port Arthur. They smelled the ville long before they saw it. The faint sea breeze carried a raw stink of sulfur. As they advanced on the southwest horizon, the skeletal, rusting ruin of the predark oil refinery came into view. Its storage tanks had ruptured long ago, spilling their precious contents into and poisoning the surrounding soil. The wide street in front of them was lined by tangled, fallen telephone and power lines and jumbled poles, and by cinder-block-rimmed foundation holes and concrete slabs sprouting stubs of plumbing and curlicues of electrical conduit. The few houses that remained standing sported caved-in roofs and buckled or bowed walls. In the aftermath of skydark, countless Category 5 storms had bored inland from the Gulf. The high-water marks were greasy brown stains on the canted, twisted eaves, stains from crude oil released from the refinery's ruptured tanks, oil floating atop the flood. As a result of the mixing effect of the water and the weather, every square foot of ground was littered with some bit of predark rubbish.

Across the panorama of decimated flatland the companions were the only things moving. Port A ville's residents had retreated like dogs into the deep shadows. Without air-conditioning, the brutal heat of the day was something best slept through.

The farther south they walked, the stronger the brimstone odor got. To a discerning nose it was as much swamp gas as petrochemical—the odor of wet rot and mold. It was coming from the direction of Port A ville's waterfront downtown, now permanently flooded thanks to the overall rise in sea level. That rise, Ryan recalled, had also swallowed up most of Pleasure Island, the 18-mile-long, man-made island on Sabine Lake. The expansion of the lake and seawater had turned one-third of the habitable land between Groves ville and Port A ville into a marshy, fetid waste. Along the former Gulf Intracoastal Waterway, which paralleled downtown, a motley fleet of traders' sail-boats would be moored to the bases of partially sub-merged, rusting loading cranes.

Two blond boys in holed-out T-shirts popped out from behind a cinder-block foundation and cut across the deserted street in front of them. Both were barefoot; one of them wore shorts, the other was bare-assed naked. They were carrying a five-gallon bucket of water between them, trying not to spill the contents as they headed for a small cinder-block structure. Metal-roofed and one-story, it looked like a power company or road mainte-nance shed. Windowless. Eight by twelve. The only door had been crudely sawn in two horizontally—the Dutch door was a way to get some air circulation. The top part of door was open. The inside looked dark and dank and blistering hot.

"Hey, how about a drink of that water?" Ryan shouted at the kids.

They stopped, turned and put down the heavy bucket. "Gimme a shotshell," the taller of the two said. He was the one wearing shorts. He was seven or eight.

A broad figure appeared above the maintenance shed's Dutch door, stepping from darkness into the light. Naked from the waist up, Mama held a rust-splotched, fold-stock AK-47 pointed skyward, her finger resting on the trigger guard. She was a big woman with stringy brown hair, huge flabby arms and massive breasts. Cradled in her other arm, a baby contentedly nursed on one of her dirt blotched, stretch-marked dugs.

"That's the price," she shouted hoarsely. "Pay it or fuck off."

Krysty muttered a curse under her breath, and her emerald eyes flashed with anger.

Appropriate anger.

The compensation being demanded was outrageous.

Ryan hated like hell to give up one of their precious few cartridges, but he had to keep the bigger picture in mind. They'd come a long way and they needed to drink now and rehydrate if they were going to be clearheaded when they got down to the business of bartering their loot. "We'll pay it," he said. "Give the boy a round, J.B."

The Armorer ejected a live shell from his scattergun. He handed it to the kid, who checked the primer and shook the shell next to his grimy ear. His eyes lit up and he smiled gaptoothed at his mama.

"Go on," she said, gesturing with the flash hider and ramp sight of the battered AK.

The companions took turns at the bucket, drinking their fill. The water was sweet, cool and fairly clean.

When they were done, Krysty said to Mama, "We paid you for the water, now what do we owe you for the air?"

At a signal from their mother, the kids kicked over the rest of the bucket on the ground. That was followed by a caustic stream of profanity and death threats from the tiny family.

"Friendly town, isn't it?" Mildred remarked as they carefully backed away and continued on.

"Make no mistake about it," Ryan said, his voice deadly cold, "this isn't your run-of-the-mill hellpit. This is the radblasted end of the line, the last outpost on the Gulf coast before the Dallas-Houston death zone. Folks don't end up in Port A ville by choice. They end up here because they were driven out of the eastern baronies on account of who they were or what they did. I'm talking about the lowest of low—diseased gaudy sluts, jolt fiends, cold-heart robbers and crazy chillers. The traders who come through here specialize in looting the interior's hotspots, and robbing the scroungers who got there first. They're used to taking the biggest risks, to chilling first and never asking questions after. Keep your eyes open and your blaster hands free. From now on, we're triple red."

After another couple of miles of deserted gridwork streets and sprawling ruination, they came to the intersection of two main roads, and in the near distance, the remains of an enormous predark shopping center. Almost all of its structures lay in piles of fractured concrete. There was no telling what had brought the buildings down: storms from the Gulf, earthquake, flood, demolition. Any or all of it was possible.

The parking lots were covered in layers of dried mud and in places trees grew up through cracks in the asphalt. Visible from a quarter mile away, four huge letters hung crooked on a concrete-block building's lone surviving wall.

"They sold 'ears'?" Jak wondered out loud.

"No," Mildred said. "No, the *S* must've fallen off. It's Sears."

Before she could elaborate, Ryan urged them on. "Let's

keep moving," he said. "We've still got some ground to cover."

Maintaining the 450-yard buffer, he led them over swampy, trash-littered, former backyards and between cinder-block foundations, filled with stagnant, black water, around to the west side of the mall. From this angle, they could see almost all of the complex's connecting interior corridors and colonnades had collapsed in on themselves. A single big-box store was still standing.

"That's BoomT's," Ryan told the others as he signaled a halt.

The entrance to the three-story building was shielded by a pair of Winnebagos sitting on their rusting wheel rims. A mob of people waited in the heat to pass single file through the gap between the RVs. Some wore heavy backpacks; some stowed their trade goods in homemade wags and dog carts. Those were the small-timers. There was a separate queue for big-time traders—a lineup of horse-drawn carts, motorcycles, pack mules and tethered-human bearers at the back bumper of the Winnebago on the right, along the building's windowless facade. Everybody stood under the watch of crude blastertowers at the corners of the roof.

As Krysty scanned the setup through minibinocs, she said, "How does the operation work?"

"Small-timers are dealt with by BoomT's sec men," Ryan said. "Before they get to go into the building, the sec men put a value on their trade goods. The customers get a chit, which they can use for any of the goods inside up to the amount of the chit. Inside there's a drop-off area for newly bartered stuff. Folks find what they're after and hand back the chit. The exit's on the south end of the building. Can't see it from here."

Krysty passed the binocs to Mildred, who had a look-see and said, "Who's the fat man coming out of the Winnie on the right? He's as big as a Sumo wrestler and it looks like he's wearing a chenille bedspread. Good God, look at that flab!" She tried to give Ryan the binocs.

The one-eyed man waved her off. He didn't need magnification to identify the man lumbering onto the tarmac. "That would be BoomT in the flesh," he told the others. "He handles the major trades and shipping deals himself."

"What are all those pinkish blotches on his arms and back?" Mildred asked as she took another look through the binocs. "He seems to have a skin condition."

"Yeah, from bullets," J.B. answered. "Those are wound scars. Definitely a hard man to chill."

"A lot of folks have tried to put BoomT in the ground," Ryan said. "He's put them all there instead. It's the flab that protects him, that and all the muscle underneath. He's one powerful son of a bitch, and he's a lot faster than he looks. Rumor has it, he can snap a grown man's neck with either hand."

"Need a dead-center hit with an RPG to take out that giant tub of guts," J.B. added.

"BoomT opened up shop about fifteen years ago," Ryan went on, "after scroungers started going into the hot zones to the north and west to look for spoils."

"By 'spoils,' I take it you are referring to undiscovered caches of predark manufactured goods?" Doc said as he accepted the binocs from Mildred.

"Correct," Ryan said.

More than a century after the Apocalypse, there was still no large-scale manufacturing in the Deathlands. The necessary machines, the understanding of engineering and assembly-line processes had all gone extinct, along with democracy, the forty-hour work week and cable TV. In actuality, nuclear Armageddon had turned back America's clock more than two hundred years, to before the Industrial Revolution. The United States of America had devolved into a feudal, agarian and hunter-gatherer society.

"Trader never trusted BoomT," J.B. said.

"He had good reason," Ryan said. "Big Boy over there is a double-dealing, backstabbing mountain of crap. And we don't have enough ammo left to defend our booty. If we take more spoils with us than we're willing to lose, chances are we'll lose everything and get ourselves chilled in the bargain."

"So, we've got to hide most of the C-4?" Mildred said. "Where?"

"I know a good place farther south," Ryan said, waving on the companions.

Circling wide around the south end of the mall, through the shimmering waves of heat they could see a pair of four-mule carts crawling for the line of moored sailboats at the water's edge. The heavily laden wags rolled on scavenged auto axles and wheels down the cracked and granularized street.

Between the mall and the distant water was a wide expanse of rolling, undeveloped land. There were stands of mature trees; some bare-limbed and dead, some living. Among the twists and turns of the landscape stood patches of irrigated fields that were bordered by little clusters of field-hand shanties.

"From the lay of it, I'd say it used to be a golf course," Mildred said.

It was a golf course no more.

It had become the breadbasket for Port A ville and vicinity.

Local folk had abandoned the city streets in favor of the open space. The soil there was unpolluted, and there were no wrecked buildings that had to be cleared before it could be cultivated. The former Babe Zaharias Memorial Golf Course was, in fact, the path of least resistance.

Ryan led the companions across the mule-cart route, past the imploded shell of the former links' clubhouse, and onto what had once been a lush and rolling green. The farm fields on either side weren't fenced. No field hands were in evidence. With the sun straight overhead, it was too hot to do grunt work. No heads appeared in the doorless doorways or glassless windows of the huts, either. If the laborers were inside, they were dozing soundly through the suffocating heat.

The companions climbed a shallow grade, then passed through a stand of tall trees. In a shallow bowl below, out of sight of the surrounding fields, was a water hazard that had once challenged golfers. The small lake's surface was choked with mats of chartreuse algae.

Ryan led them down to the shore, then handed J.B. his scoped longblaster and said, "Leave your C-4 here and head up to the ridge on the far side of the lake. Make sure no one is spying on us from that direction."

As J.B. trotted away, Krysty put two and two together and said, "We're hiding the explosives in the water?"

"It won't hurt the C-4 because it's sealed in plastic," Ryan said as he dumped the contents of his backpack onto the bank. "Everybody take out one detonator blister pack," he told the others.

The companions unshouldered their loads and did as he asked.

"Put the batteries in your detonators," Ryan said as he put batteries in his. When they were all ready, he added, "Now try the test button."

All of the remotes lit up. Green for go. They were functional.

The one-eyed man pried the two tiny power cells from the black plastic case and slipped each of them into a different pants pocket. "Okay, now remove the batteries," he said. "Hide them in your gear separate from the detonators. We don't want some drooler arming one of the remotes and pushing the 'fire' button by accident."

As Doc pocketed his depowered detonator he shook his head and said, "Batteries in, batteries out. Dear Ryan, I must admit to puzzlement. For the life of me I cannot fathom your intent."

He was not alone.

"Where are you going with this, Ryan?" Krysty said.

"I'm just buying us some getaway insurance."

With the point of his panga Ryan carefully slit the plastic on one of the bricks along a lengthwise seam. Using the components from a blister pack, he quickly rigged the two-kilo block of plastique for remote detonation. Then he pressed closed the slit he had made in the plastic wrap. Because it stuck to the explosive material, the incision was almost undetectable. He repacked the backpack with ten parcels of C-4, putting the rigged brick near the bottom.

"Now any of us can detonate the entire load if the shit hits the fan," he said.

"We better all be a long ways off when that happens,"

Mildred said. "Twelve kilos of plastique is going to raise some dust."

"But, Ryan, anybody else can set it off, too," Krysty protested. "Why did you leave the detonators and batteries in the load we're going to trade?"

"Had no choice," Ryan told her. "For all we know, BoomT is expecting this C-4 to show up. He could have contracted the dead scroungers to bring it to him from New Mex. And if he did, he could know there were supposed to be remote detonators included in the deal. If the detonators are missing when we show him the goods, you can bet the farm he'll have his sec men search us. When they find what they're looking for, it'll take the play away from us. If the detonators are in the mix, BoomT isn't going to dig deeper, and we've still got our hole card."

"So, we show up with the C-4 instead of the traders he contracted with?" Mildred said. "How's that going to go down?"

"BoomT won't care who makes the delivery or who he pays for the C-4," J.B. said. "He sure as hell isn't going to care what happened to the scroungers. That's the kind of shit-snake he is."

"But it is possible that he was expecting the arrival of all six backpacks," Doc interjected.

"In that case, he'll be happy that one actually showed up," Ryan said. "We've got a believable story. His pet scroungers were chilled by stickies. We salvaged a single load. Hell, it's almost even true."

The one-eyed warrior sat on the grass, untied his boots and kicked them off. "No sense in more than two of us getting wet," he said. "Jak, gather up a couple of backpacks of C-4 and wade out with me."

Leaving his own pack on the bank, Ryan hoisted three others and moved slowly into the warm water, careful to tear the smallest possible rip in the algae mat.

The albino kicked off his boots, grabbed up the remaining unbooby-trapped packs and waded out to midthigh. The two of them sank the packs under the water, holding them down until all the trapped air bubbles escaped. As they backtracked their path to shore, they brushed together the torn edges of the bloom.

Ryan and Jak carefully dried their feet on the grass before putting on their boots. When Ryan stood, he waved for J.B. to hurry down from the lookout.

"I am still at rather a loss here," Doc confessed. "What exactly is your larger strategy?"

"If we can get cartridges and gas in trade for the one load of C-4," Ryan told him, "we can lug the fuel and the sunken explosives back to the bikes, and ride on east to Louisiana in style. If we can't get gas, we'll have to find transport by water, or keep walking. If things go sour with BoomT, and we have enough of a head start, we can come back here and recover the rest of the C-4. If not, we can leave it where it is for now and come back later."

After J.B. rejoined them, Ryan retrieved his long-blaster, shouldered the last backpack of explosives and said, "Let's go cut ourselves a deal."

Chapter Five

They returned to the mall, retracing their circuitous route to approach it from the north, an extra but necessary precaution. If things went badly, BoomT and crew wouldn't think to look south for any spoils they had hidden. As the companions stepped onto the sunbaked parking lot, the dried mud crunched under their boots like layers of crisp pastry dough, and each step sent up a little puff of fine brown dust.

Keeping the edge of the mall's acres of mounded rubble on their left, they headed for the big-box store. As Ryan got closer, he could see that a side entrance to the mall's interior and its covered walkway were still intact and connected to the north wall of BoomT's emporium. The interior hallway and roof were supported on the opposite side by the facades of gutted storefronts. Ryan led the others wide right of the doorless opening, giving them some room to maneuver, if need be.

Just inside the shade of the corridor on the left, a bevy of rode-hard and hefty gaudy sluts reclined on tubular aluminum chaise longues. Barefoot, in carelessly belted, ratty nylon housecoats, they were showing off their wares and airing them at the same time.

There were no takers among the handful of scroungers loitering on the other side of the partially collapsed hallway.

Too hot.

Too sober.

Or mebbe the airing was incomplete.

Above the row of overtaxed chaises, a predark restaurant sign said Cantina Olé in red, three-dimensional letters. The "i" of the sign was a little cartoon cactus and the "O" was wearing a yellow sombrero.

Jak leaned close to Mildred and in a deadpan voice said, "Did H fall off?"

At first Mildred was puzzled by the question. Then she stared in amazement at the wild child. A second later she burst out laughing.

"Nuking hell!" J.B. exclaimed, turning to the others. "Did you catch that? Jak just made a joke!"

Although his mouth remained a thin line of implacable reserve, the albino's ruby-red eyes seemed to glitter merrily.

A loud scuffle and angry shouts and screams from deeper in the corridor put an abrupt end to conversation and sent hands grabbing for gun butts. From out of the darkness of the interior spilled a trio of wild-ass, go-for-broke combatants. The companions stepped clear as the herky-jerky, high-speed fist and foot fight tumbled out into the blinding sunlight of the parking lot.

It wasn't two against one; it was every man for himself.

Joltheads, Ryan thought, keeping his hand on his holstered SIG-Sauer.

The evidence for that conclusion was incontrovertible: the stringy, emaciated arms; the sagging, prematurely wrinkled skin dotted with angry sores; hair missing from the scalp in fist-size patches; the bulging, jaundiced eyes; the rotten, black-edged teeth; the clothes that looked like they'd been salvaged from a garbage dump and put through a shredder.

And the capper was the insensate violence.

The trio punched and kicked one another at extreme close range, spitting blood and fragments of teeth, tossing up tufts of ripped-out hair, raising clouds of dust when they fell through the mud crust on their backsides, jumping up again like they were on springs. Even though the battle was powered by a drug, there was no way human bodies could maintain the frenetic pace. After a couple of minutes of all-out combat, gasping for air, the fighters pulled black-powder handblasters out from under their clothing.

The moment they reached for their battered revolvers, the companions unholstered their own weapons and hastily withdrew to the cover of the hallway entrance.

Just in time.

Point-blank, the circling joltheads started jacking back single-action hammers and pulling triggers. The revolvers click, click, clicked like castanets on misfires or unloaded or uncapped chambers—a lucky thing, since the bastards weren't paying attention to background and potential inadvertent targets. Finally, thunderously, one of the weapons discharged, but an instant too late. Instead of coring the opposing drug fiend's head, it powder-blackened the left side of his face from chin to receding hairline and blew a .44-caliber chunk out of his dirty earlobe.

Three empty blasters hit the dirt and the sheathed knives came out.

When fixed blades were drawn, everyone watching from behind hard cover stepped forward to get a better view of the festivities. Even the gaudy sluts raised themselves from the horizontal. Nobody lifted a finger to intervene in the conflict. Nobody seemed to know or care what the fight was about. Given the fact that the combatants were joltheads, the chances were good they were fighting over something imaginary.

One of the male bystanders—a solidly built man with slicked-back, dark blond hair and an impressive, drooping-to-the-chest handlebar mustache—whipped out a harmonica. Tapping his foot to keep time, he provided a sprightly and rhythmic musical commentary on the mayhem.

Ryan had to admit it was a sight to behold: three wild-eyed, beat-to-shit ragbags wheeling around and around, taking turns stabbing each other in the guts, groaning and squealing with every strike, blood and spittle flying in all directions. After dozens of stabs delivered and received, the action suddenly lost its momentum. Gore-drenched arms hanging limply at their sides, one by one the fighters buckled and collapsed into the fine brown dirt.

A contest to the death had ended in a three-way draw.

The musician crescendoed with a scale-climbing flourish, and the assembled sluts and scroungers answered with lethargic applause. It was too hot to cheer.

Nobody moved to check the bodies for signs of life. Not even Mildred, who in a former life had sworn a Hippocratic oath.

Joltheads were better off dead.

As Ryan led the others past the rear of the mob of small-timer scroungers still waiting to pass through the gap between the cadaverous, 120-year-old Winnies, he could feel the gunsights up in the guard towers tracking their every step. BoomT hadn't lasted as long as he had and built his mercantile empire by luck alone. The fat man had an animal cunning and instinct for danger. He was capable of ordering an indiscriminate preemptive strike on the entire parking lot, if he sniffed out so much as the slightest threat.

The big-time queue had shortened considerably while they were gone. There was only one group of traders ahead of them, now. Five men bearing heavy backpacks awaited the judgment of the proprietor.

BoomT sat in a canopied golf cart, out of sniper sight in the lee of the southernmost Winnebago's bow. Clipped to the underside of the canopy's frame were a pair of ComBloc RPGs, their plastic pistol grips in easy reach.

If anything, the man was bigger than Ryan remembered. His five-hundred-pound, six-foot-eight-inch bulk took up the entire bench seat. Rolls upon rolls of pendulous, sweating flab hung from his chest. Close up, the gunshot scars on his torso and arms were clearly of varying calibers, waxy divots ranging from .380 Auto to 7.62 mm NATO. A mountainous wedge of shoulders and neck peaked at a head shaved to black stubble. Long wisps of beard hair trailed from his sloping cheeks. Instead of shoes or boots, he wore homemade sandals of tire tread. Boots his size were hard to come by.

To protect his eyes from the sun and to conceal the focus of his attention, BoomT wore raspberry-mirror-lensed, wraparound sunglasses.

The vast, bedspread-swaddled hipster impatiently waved his sec men forward to uncover the next batch of goods on offer. As he did so, he tossed a pale, slender rib bone onto the pile of other bones on the ground beside him. From the size of the heap it looked like he'd already eaten eight or nine of whatever the species was. He licked his fingers, one by one, and daintily wiped them on the edge of the coverlet.

The sec men shoulder-slung their fold-stock AKMs, opened the tops of the traders' overloaded packs and pulled out fistfuls of assorted predark fasteners. It was all salvaged nail by nail, screw by screw. It had to be. Screws and nails were no longer manufactured or imported. Without metal fasteners, building or repair of large structures was difficult, if not impossible. Without those once taken-for-granted items, folks were forced to live in tents, lean-tos, stone or log huts, or caves.

One of the sec men approached his boss and held out the sample for examination. With a fingertip BoomT casually flicked out a few badly rusted, bent nails and stripped-slot screws. "Looks like thirty percent is useless shit," was his verdict.

Then he addressed the traders. "If there are rocks in your packs, I'm going to use them to sink you to the bottom of the bay. Is that understood?"

The traders grimaced in response.

BoomT wrote out a chit and handed the scrap of paper to the sec man with a warning. "Don't give them this until you make sure there are no rocks."

The fat man shifted on the bench seat to take in the next trader in line. When he saw who was standing there, his mouth dropped open. He pushed his sunglasses down the bridge of his nose and squinted through slits for eyelids.

"As I live and breathe, it's One-Eye Cawdor!" he roared. Then he looked over at J.B. and added, "And fuck me triple dead if it ain't the Pipsqueak, too."

Chapter Six

"Brought your own sluts along, I see," BoomT said, sizing up Krysty and Mildred. "That was good thinking. Whores in these parts are scab-assed and wide-reamed. Still can't attract no decent help around here."

"They're fighters," Ryan informed him. "They're not sluts."

BoomT raised his hands in mock surrender. "Okay, okay, whatever you say, One-Eye." Then he winked at Mildred, theatrically adjusted his crotch beneath the bedspread and blew her a kiss.

Mildred was marksman enough to quickdraw her ZKR 551 and put a bullet through the middle of his forehead. Mebbe it would have only given him a headache. It certainly would have brought answering fire from all sides. Her expression stayed deadpan and her blaster remained in its holster.

"So, did you hear the news about Deathlands' famous Trader?" BoomT asked, his little black piggie eyes full of glee. "Word has it your old runnin' buddy croaked buttugly, sitting in a warm pile of his own dung and squawling for his mammy."

The Port A ville entrepreneur's chuckle was a series of rattling, glottal full-stops. Among the sec men, there were appreciative grins and snickers all around. BoomT's enforcement crew practically worshiped him. After all, so far he was unchillable. They were terrified of him, too, and also with good reason.

As Ryan recalled, Trader had gotten the better of BoomT in their last encounter by turning the tables and pulling a last-second double-switch. The fat man was always running a game of some kind, and it usually involved sleight of hand, like some variation on three card Monte. It wasn't healthy to try to return bogus merchandise, either. BoomT's customer service department was a firing squad.

"Guess what goes around comes around," BoomT said merrily. "You know, as righteous payback for that extry-special evil he did at Virtue Lake. All them mamas and papas, them helpless little kiddie-widdies. Chilled like gophers down a hole. You were there at Virtue Lake, right by his side, as I remember the story. Mebbe hard justice is about to bite you in your ass, too?"

Ryan made no comment.

"You got nothing to say on the subject, Mr. One-Eye?" BoomT prodded.

The fat man had that right. No way was Ryan going to let himself be diverted from the task and sucked into a lopsided, losing gunfight. It was time to pull the cat out of the bag. He unslung the backpack, took out a golden, plastic-wrapped brick and underhand-tossed it over to BoomT. "We've got ten kilos of that," he said. "What'll you give us for it?"

BoomT's piggie eyes widened, and he sniffed at the C-4 like it was a loaf of fresh-baked bread. "If this shit really goes bang," he said as he weighed the brick in his hand, "you can have whatever the fuck you want." After glancing at the attached blister pack, he chucked the parcel back to Ryan. "What I want first, though, is a demo blast with that remote detonator."

"You got it," Ryan said without missing a beat. Trying to read the fat man's face was like trying to read a seventy-pound suet pudding. Although BoomT's eyes had lit up when he recognized the explosive, that didn't prove he had been expecting it.

Ryan and his companions looked outwardly calm, even bored at the proceedings, but that was hardly how they felt. The radio signal trigger was indiscriminate. It was universal. Using it to fire a demonstration blasting cap would also set off the cap stuck in the booby-trapped brick in the bottom of the backpack, which would set off the plastique at their feet and turn them all from solid flesh and bone to glistening pink vapor faster than a person could blink.

As Ryan set to work preparing the test charge, Krysty, Mildred, Doc, J.B. and Jak hunkered down in the skinny strip of shade cast by the Winnie. So far it looked like Ryan could have removed the detonators from the load without risking anything. There was no time for coulda, shoulda, woulda. After he rigged a golf-ball-size clump of C-4 with a blasting cap and radio-controlled initiator, he carried the wad of plas-ex a safe distance to the middle of the parking lot, set it down, then walked back.

In front of BoomT he pretended to put in both of the detonator's batteries, but expertly palmed them instead.

Three card Monte.

Ryan flipped off the detonator's safety and tried the test circuit. Of course, the little green indicator light didn't go on. "Uh, it doesn't light up," he said, showing the dark indicator to BoomT. "Mebbe the bulb's burned out," he said. "I'll try the blast switch. Fire in the hole!"

The sec men, traders and companions took cover, but when he hit the switch nothing happened. He tried it several times. "I guess the nukin' thing doesn't work. Probably none of the detonators work. That's the breaks."

"Guess you're shit out of luck, then," BoomT said.

"Nah, there's still the detonator cord," Ryan countered. "That's the sure way to test the C-4, and there's plenty of extra cord and blasting caps to blow up the rest of it." He used his panga to cut off a yard length of the white braid and recrossed the parking lot. After removing the radio initiator, he crimped the blasting cap to the cord and set the safety fuse alight with a wooden match. This time he hot-footed it back to the RV.

"Better duck and cover," he told the others as he hurried around the front bumper.

An instant later came the solid whack of an explosion. Even though the plastique wad was small, its power was most impressive. Not just the ear-splitting bang, either. Flying shards of dried mud rattled the far side of the Winnie and peppered the wall of the box store, turning to puffs of dust on impact. As the echoes faded, in the middle of the parking lot a cloud of pale dirt mixed with smoke climbed into the sky.

"So, do we have a trade?" Ryan asked the entrepreneur.

"You'd be looking for what?" the fat man said.

"Ammo for our blasters, traveling rations, stuff we can carry."

"Go on inside and help yourselves," he said, scribbling out a chit and giving it to Ryan. He waved for a sec man to take charge of the backpack, warning him, "Put that someplace safe."

As BoomT slipped his raspberry shades back on, Ryan turned with the companions toward the store's entrance.

"Wait a minute now, One-Eye," the fat man said, "I want that bum detonator, too."

Ryan shrugged as if he couldn't imagine why BoomT would want the useless piece of junk. Of course he could imagine why. The fat man either didn't believe it was broken, or he thought he could fix it. Because it wasn't broken, and the problem could be easily repaired, Ryan had tried to slip the thing into his pants pocket. Called out, he had no choice but to comply. "Forgot about it," he said as he handed over the detonator.

A dozen or so men were running toward them from the direction of the gaudy and the small-time trader queue. The guy who played harmonica was leading the pack. Ryan guessed the explosion was the most thrilling thing that had happened in Port A ville in weeks. The scroungers and loungers wanted to find out what it was all about.

Ryan and the companions fell in line behind the sec man carrying the C-4. Behind them were two AK-armed escorts. Ryan still didn't know for sure, but it didn't appear that BoomT had any advance warning about the shipment of explosives. Sooner or later, however, the fat man was going to open the detonator case and find no batteries inside. Suspicious by nature, it would immediately occur to him that he'd been somehow, someway flimflammed. To confirm that, his first act would be to power up the "bum" detonator and test it for himself. The companions needed to be miles gone when that happened.

The plate glass in the box store's entry doors had been

replaced by sheets of split and delaminating plywood. Just inside the entrance, four assault-rifle-armed sec men stood guard behind a hardened blasterpost, keeping shoppers from trying to use it as an exit. Traffic flowed one way in and one way out. It was at least ten degrees cooler than outside.

The place was much as Ryan remembered it from his days with Trader. Above a wide expanse of gutted floor space, the drop ceiling had long since fallen away, exposing overhead wiring, heating ducts and drooping wads of water-stained insulation. The smell was particularly hard to forget—a combination of smoke from the torches and candelabra that lit the windowless showroom, and moldy funk. Dirt-encrusted footpaths crisscrossed the gray sheet flooring, winding through an indoor junkyard. Loot pillaged from the far corners of the hellscape was piled in heaps and in neat rows. Crudely lettered signs hung from the ceiling, indicating at a distance what kind of goods were on offer in the area beneath. Wag Stuf. Tules. Cloz. Vedgies. Meet. Hardwhere.

"Costco, post-Apocalypse," Mildred remarked as she took it all in. "There's even Muzak Monkees." Somewhere out of sight a hundred-year-old audio tape was playing at top volume. Scratchy violins made violent tempo downshifts, as if the entire string section had been plunged chin-deep in a tar pit. Predark music to shop by.

"Mildred, I do not see them," Doc said, looking around. "Where are the monkeys? They're playing the music?"

"No, Mu-zak. 'Daydream Believer.'"

She reacted to Doc's blank look with a curt, "Oh, never mind."

They followed the sec man carrying the C-4 backpack

to a screened-in enclosure on the left. BoomT kept his extra-special spoils stacked behind floor-to-ceiling hurricane fence reinforced by steel pipe. A guard sitting inside on a disintegrating couch with a machine pistol on his lap had to get up and unlock the cage.

With a sinking feeling in his gut Ryan watched the C-4 change hands. The die was cast. They couldn't very well demand to examine the pack they'd just traded and then disarm the brick in front of witnesses. Revealing the booby trap would surely get them chilled. Ditto for starting a blaster battle inside the store to recover the goods—they didn't have enough ammo for that.

After the cage clanged shut, the three-man escort left them to their shopping.

"Are we nuked, or what?" Krysty said in exasperation.

"Not nuked, yet," Ryan replied. "This is just another case of hit and git. Find what we need and make tracks."

"Munitions are over that way," J.B. said, waving the others after him as he set off.

Under the Gunz & Amo sign was a warped sheet of presswood laid across a pair of sawhorses. Lined up on the makeshift table were a selection of firearms on offer. The blasters of predark vintage all had barrels orange with rust; mostly single-shot, exposed hammer shotguns with cracked or missing butt and forestocks. Bailing wire appeared to be the repair material of choice.

Ryan scowled at the rows of newly manufactured pistols. The grips had been scrollsawed from one-inch plywood. Pairs of stainless-steel screw clamps held foot-long barrels to the stocks. The barrels were made of plumbing pipe, roughly 10-gauge in bore. There was no safety and no trigger on the single-shot, black-powder weapons. They were fired by a drawback thumb device based on a rat trap spring that drove a nail point into an exposed percussion cap.

They were much more likely to chill the shooter than the target.

J.B. commented in disgust, "The 'gunsmith' should be hanged, if he hasn't already been."

The other companions hunkered down and started going through plastic bins of loose live centerfire ammo of various standard calibers.

Jak pried a shell from his Python's cylinder, and tried to chamber one of BoomT's .357 Mag rounds. It didn't fit.

"Let me see it, Jak," J.B. said, holding out his hand. The Armorer thumbed his spectacles back up the bridge of his nose and closely examined the cartridge. "This case has been reloaded one too many times," he said. "There's a hairline crack around the rim. The reason you can't chamber it is that the triple stupe who reloaded it did such a crap job of prepping the case."

Whipping out a scarred toolkit, J.B. used pliers to unseat the bullet from the brass. He dumped the gunpowder onto his palm. "This isn't even smokeless," he said. "It's black powder. This ammo is junk, Ryan. There's no decent reloads in the lot. No point in rummaging through it. Even the rounds that'll chamber and might be safe to fire are gonna be nukeshit for knockdown power."

Not to mention the fact that they didn't have time for rummaging.

"Forget it, then," Ryan said. "We've got to move on. We can still trade for fuel and come out ahead."

They hurried away from the ammo station, weaving around rows of knives, hatchets, spears and crossbows made from salvaged leaf springs, past heaps of blankets and clothes folks had certainly died in, even if they weren't chilled for them. Three male shoppers stood buck-naked, showing off their farmer tans while they tried on previously owned sleepwear. Other shoppers sat on the floor, testing battered shoes and boots for a good fit. There were tiers of assorted plastic coolers, piles of moldy tents and sleeping bags and cardboard boxes of junk jewelry, eyeglasses and prescription drugs a century past throwaway dates. A skinny woman in a too big, antique Virginia Is For Lovers sweatshirt was uncapping and sniffing the contents of the half-rolled-up aluminum tubes of ointments and salves. On the far side of the sniffer was a folding table mounded with flatware. It was overseen by a geezer with a scraggly salt-and-pepper beard.

"Everybody needs a fork!" the red-nosed hawker informed them.

To no effect.

The companions skirted BoomT's fresh produce section, then the butcher shop. Slabs of raw meat lay in plastic tubs, unrefrigerated, on the floor. The flesh wasn't labeled as to species or cut. It looked like chicken, but it smelled more like fish. The rear of the shop was hidden behind a floral print bedsheet strung from the ceiling's exposed heating ducts. The curtain was thin, and a man, apparently the butcher, was dimly visible through it. He wasn't alone. Whatever he had penned back there was pleading for its life.

Krysty leaned close to Ryan and said, "Did you notice we picked up a shadow?"

"Yeah, I marked him." The handlebar-mustached harmonica player had been dogging them around the store, edging closer and closer as if trying to overhear their conversation.

The emporium's fuel station was a section of floor space covered by a variety of container types and sizes, all with air-tight screw tops. The only other thing they had in common was that they were translucent. That way a prospective buyer couldn't judge the quality by the color, or lack of same.

J.B. unscrewed a lid from a plastic jug, releasing a whoosh of built-up pressure. He then took a whiff of the contents.

Before J.B. could give his assessment of the product, the musician spoke up. "You don't want none of that," he said. "BoomT waters down his gas."

Ryan took in the deep tan, weather-seamed gray eyes, gnarled, scarred hands, and the densely muscled arms and shoulders. Harmonica Man wasn't nearly as old as he looked at first glance—a life of brutal work and privation had prematurely aged him. There was a light in his eyes that Ryan recognized, a young man's light. The silver mouth organ wasn't his only sidearm. A massive, stainless-steel .45 ACP revolver, a Smith & Wesson Model 625, rode in a beat-up canvas holster low on his right hip.

"Some folks say the fat man pees in it for fun," the musician added. "Whether it's stretched with water or piss, it's no more than seventy octane. Won't get you far. And it'll wreck your engines for sure."

J.B. nodded to Ryan as he screwed back the cap. "He's right. It's more crap," he said. "It's all crap."

"If you want not-crap," the musician said, "then you

need to see BoomT's private stock, the top-quality stuff he hides away for himself."

"You mean, behind the fence?" Mildred asked.

"No, that's temporary storage. He's got a treasure vault down in the basement for the best merchandise. If you go back and complain to him, there's a slight chance he might let you shop there. But since he's already got your goods, he'll probably tell you take it or leave it. You folks should really be dealing with me."

"What do you mean?" Ryan said. "The deal is done."

Before the musician could respond, Jak nudged Ryan with an elbow and pointed toward the security cage's open gate. A sec man was walking out with a brick of their C-4 in his hand.

"Oh shit," Ryan said.

Breaking into a trot, he and the others managed to cut the guy off before he reached the Winnebago exit. On closer inspection, Ryan could see the sec man had the brick that he had opened in front of BoomT and taken the test wad from.

"Say, where are you going with that?" Ryan asked him.

"Ol' BoomT found some batteries," the sec man replied. "He got that detonator's test light to go on. Come on out and watch, it should be extry good. He's gonna make himself a swimming pool."

Chapter Seven

BoomT sat in the shade of his golf cart's red-striped canopy, eating a whole, cold roast chicken barehanded like an ear of corn. Fifteen feet away, under the baking sun, a quartet of indentured servants grunted and groaned as they swung pickaxes high overhead, slamming them into the ground. They had cracked a seam in the asphalt and were burrowing into the concrete-like compacted clay beneath. The going got easier once they broke through the bottom of the layer of hardpan. They tossed aside the axes, picked up long-handled shovels and resumed work, digging a deep, narrow hole.

A half dozen of his sec men stood around their gargantuan leader with shouldered assault rifles, telescopic sights sweeping the flatland of vacant streets and exposed foundations for potential threats.

Because BoomT was unsure of the consequences when a full kilo of C-4 was detonated, he had decided to err on the side of caution. He sited his experiment as far as possible from the emporium so it wouldn't be accidently damaged, either in the initial blast or by the debris fall. That meant the swimming pool excavation was going to be much closer to the outside edge of the parking lot than he had originally envisioned.

BoomT could see a man on a bicycle pedaling madly

toward him from the direction of the big-box store, leaving behind a swirling wake of beige dust.

The entrepreneur spit a mouthful of chicken bones over his left shoulder onto the ground. Rotating the slippery carcass, he attacked the breast and thigh on the opposite side. Even One-Eye trying to cheat him by stealing the batteries couldn't dent his ebullient mood. He was humming to himself as he fed.

What was the point of having a large quantity of high explosive if you didn't use part of it to blow something up?

He had considered blowing up One-Eye, Pipsqueak and the two other male members of his crew along with the parking lot, but after weighing the risk and benefit, he thought better of it. Cawdor hadn't risen to the bait about Trader's hard and humiliating death. The fat man had watched him closely and there had been no reaction to the bad news, nor to the mocking way it had been delivered. Not so much as a finger twitch in response. BoomT couldn't deduce from that whether Cawdor thought the story was a lie or the truth, or whether he had heard the full account somewhere else and that's what had drawn him to Port A ville. Because One-Eye's weapon remained holstered, it didn't appear that he had come for vengeance and chilling, but to do some straightforward business.

By now One-Eye had already sussed out the shabby quality of the box-store merchandise. He would demand better for his trade, which meant taking him and his crew down to the private showroom, where they could be more easily overpowered and disarmed. BoomT had decided not to chill Cawdor outright; instead he was going to remove the man's remaining eye with a soup spoon and then turn him loose in the hellscape, helpless and as blind as a bat.

Pipsqueak, on the other hand, was gonna die hard. For BoomT it had been hate at first sight, years ago. Hated his stupid hat. Hated his squinting four-eyes. Hated his ankle-biting stature. Hated his weapons know-how. Hated most of all the fact that, way back when, he couldn't get Dix to turn against Trader, something that cost him plenty jack.

Of all the ways of chilling at the overweight entrepreneur's disposal, the biggest crowd pleaser was "death by backside" because it was so painful and prolonged, and at the same time so radblasted comical. BoomT simply positioned himself over a spread-eagled, helpless victim and with his full body weight, sat down. To get up again, he grabbed hold of a tow rope attached to the golf cart's back bumper and braced his heels; when a sec man drove the cart forward, it raised him to the vertical. With judicious, over-the-shoulder aim, he could break every bone and rupture every organ. Pipsqueak was going to end up a pancake, squashed like the nearsighted little bug he was.

For all BoomT cared, his sec men could use the albino and the geezer for target practice. They preferred shooting at something alive. After an interval of time working under and over him, One-Eye's tasty sluts would be consigned to Cantina Olé. Scroungers, male and female, would be lined up from here to Groves to have a go at those two. Pay a nukin' premium, too.

Committing an entire kilo of C-4 to the swimming pool experiment was a crazy extravagance, of that there was no doubt. Essentially it was blowing up a whole lot of jack, but BoomT was in the habit of indulging himself. As he sucked the chicken leg clean of meat, he knew he was worth it.

The hole was finished by the time the bicycle rider skidded to a stop in front of the golf cart.

BoomT tossed away the stripped chicken carcass, wiped his fingertips on the bedspread and set the brick on the seat beside him. He pushed his raspberry mirror shades on top of his head and opened the already torn plastic wrap.

"'Nother chicken," he said, reaching over his right shoulder with an empty hand. When the response was not immediate, he snapped his fingers impatiently.

From a Coleman cooler strapped onto the back of the cart, a sec man passed him a fresh bird.

BoomT ate with his left hand, rivulets of grease from the corners of his mouth running down his chins, and with his right he inserted the blasting cap and remote initiator into the side of the soft, golden brick.

The cart tipped alarmingly, and its springs shrieked as he slid off the seat. He waddled over to the hole and got down on his knees, dragging his baby-blue toga in the dust. Then he lowered himself onto his enormous belly. To place the charge properly, he had to reach down the hole to his armpit, straining to touch bottom. That he did while holding the roast chicken aloft in his other hand.

When he rose up from the ground, parking lot dirt had mixed with the grease on his chins and chest. Oblivious to the grime he had accumulated, BoomT pulled down his mirror shades and climbed back into the cart, taking a last bite of poultry before chucking the shredded remnant.

"Follow me," he told the sec men and the slaves through a mouthful of meat. Driving the electric cart one-handed, he cut a quick 180-degree turn and bumped off the parking lot curb onto the wide, deserted avenue. He crossed the street, maneuvering around the wide cracks and potholes, and pulled up in a driveway. A rusting, burned-out semi-tractor and trailer lay overturned across the sidewalk. BoomT drove around behind the wreck and parked the cart.

He had always wanted to own a real swimming pool. One he could jump into to cool off. One he could float around in; with all his fat, he was virtually unsinkable. He imagined himself doing business while bobbing on his back. The golf course's lake was far too shallow for that, and it was always mucked up with slimy stuff. The water level fluctuated seasonally, too. A real swimming pool required steep, deep sides.

Like a blast crater.

When the others were safely in the lee of the tipped-over semitrailer, BoomT daintily wiped the grease from his fingers onto the bedspread's fringe. Then he took out the detonator.

"Fire in your hole!" he bellowed.

His sec men stuck fingers in their ears and hunkered down. The slaves did the same, hunkering even lower.

Flipping off the device's safety, his eyes alight with glee, BoomT pressed the little red button.

Chapter Eight

Ryan made no attempt to stop the sec man from exiting the building with the C-4. The companions had already drawn the unwanted attention of the guards stationed inside the store's entrance. He told the others in a low tone, "We need to move now, and we need to quickstep. Don't run until we get outside."

"Wait a minute!" the musician called to their backs as they left him standing there.

The companions headed for the doors at the south end of the store, purposeful, determined. Their exodus drew some curious looks from other shoppers, but that couldn't be helped.

When they didn't wait as the musician had asked, he ran to catch up to them. Walking stride for stride alongside Ryan, he demanded, "Where're you going in such a radblasted hurry? You ain't taken out your trade, yet."

"We got other business, more important business."

As Ryan took in the man's confounded face, he imagined he could see the gears of his mind turning over the available facts—under different circumstances it might have been funny. A bad detonator was now a good detonator, now the pack of C-4 was under lock and key, and now the former owners of the precious commodity were hightailing it, empty-handed.

"You bastards," the harmonica player hissed at Ryan. "The detonator. It's all about the detonator, isn't it? You bastards booby-trapped the cargo."

"Unless you wanna get gut-stabbed and left behind," Ryan warned him in an even voice, "you'd better shut your yap."

The warning went unheeded. "That backpack was part of my cargo," the musician snarled. "I bought the C-4, I paid for it in advance."

"In times past, possession was considered to be nine-tenths of the law," Doc informed him as they closed on the guard post at the exit doors. "Of course the very idea of 'law' is now relegated to the realm of myth and misunder-standing. And presently none of us possess anything more valuable than our own lives. Which, I hasten to add, hang precariously in the balance."

"That shit is mine!"

"Not the time to discuss who owns what," Ryan told him. "What's done is done. We can't get into the cage to disarm the booby trap. We need to get distance from here. A far distance."

The man with the mustache shut up. From his expression he didn't like it, but he shut up.

Until that moment Ryan was unsure whether he was going to have to chill the guy on the spot, to cut his throat with one slash of the panga, and dump him on the floor to bleed out under a pile of unwashed, second- or third-hand clothing. Until that moment there was no way of telling whether the musician was going to make a ruckus and turn them in to get back his cache of explosive. In the end, he had made the smart decision. For one thing, getting the C-4 back before it blew up was a fifty-fifty proposition, at best. For another, he knew there was more of the stuff somewhere—"part of my cargo"—and he wanted it.

Ryan thought about the other folks in the store, the shoppers not the sec men. He thought about them for a full five seconds. There wasn't time to convince the innocent that they should abandon the building, and trying to do that would alert the guards and get everyone trapped inside. It would get everybody dead. The circumstance was unfortunate, but it was out of any of their control. Bottom line: you had to protect your own.

And the corollary: shit happened.

The companions and the harmonica player were forced to stop at the building's south exit. BoomT's sec men had set up a narrow, barricaded passage with tables set out for the examination of merchandise. The penalty for shoplifting was the same as the penalty for pretty much everything: death.

One of the sec men checked Ryan's chit. Noting the fact that they hadn't picked up any gear, he said, "Why are you leaving?"

"Nature calls big-time," Ryan lied. "We'll be right back."

"You got to go around to the other door if you want back in," the guard told him as he handed back the slip of paper. "Show them your chit. Move along."

Beyond the exit door, they stepped into blazing sun and stifling heat. There was no cover ahead; just the wide, mud-encrusted expanse of the mall's south parking lot. Jak took point, breaking into a jog. The others followed.

"Do you have any radblasted idea what ten kilos of C-4 can do?" the musician asked Ryan as they trotted.

"Rough idea," Ryan said.

"Then why the hell aren't we running faster?"

"We're waiting until we're a little ways from the building," Ryan replied. "Don't want to raise suspicions and get ourselves machine-gunned from behind. Okay, Jak, that's far enough. Let's pour it on."

The albino youth immediately picked up the pace, his arms pumping, long white hair flying out straight behind him.

The others strained, high-kicking, so as not to be left behind. The sun hammered against Ryan's head and shoulders. The weight of his pack and longblaster came down hard on their respective straps, rasping into his flesh on every footfall. The sound of seven pairs of tramping boots was muffled by the mud's friable crust. Those at the rear of the file fanned out a bit to avoid the dust cloud raised by the runners in front. Even so, Ryan tasted dirt in his mouth, and grit crunched between his teeth.

Nobody said a word.

They were all too busy breathing, struggling to hold position. Chins up, eyes straight ahead, this was a grim, silent race against time, a race against their luck finally running out. To Ryan it felt like a blaster muzzle was pressed hard to the back of his head, a live round chambered, and someone's finger curled around the trigger.

Any second.

Any nukin' second the wave of destruction would come, a wave so hot it would scramble the nerves of back and brain, so hot it would feel cold.

And then the black.

Forever.

The end of the parking lot and the line of trees at the edge of the golf course grew steadily closer. What was a safe distance? Who knew? Long minutes passed. Three. Four. Five. At minute four, Ryan's thighs began to ache; his legs felt like lead. Sweat peeled down the sides of his face and trickled along the middle of his back. By five, everyone was huffing and puffing, even Jak.

After six minutes of all-out sprint, they crossed the ruptured road and reached the start of the golf course.

Ryan hazarded a glance back over his shoulder, to measure the distance they'd come. He guessed it at a little more than seven hundred yards. Before he could face front again, it all went to hell.

There were two almost simultaneous detonations: a relatively small one at the edge of the parking lot on his left shot straight up in the air like a volcanic eruption; the other, an enormous one inside the box store volcanoed and went sideways in all directions. The horizontally spreading blast ring lifted the parking lot mud twenty feet in the air. In a blinding flare of light, the store's concrete-block walls vanished; and the Winnies disintegrated in the same microsecond. Before Ryan could bat his eye, the larger explosion swallowed up the smaller.

The shock and sound wave struck him in the same instant. He was unprepared for their power; in truth, there was no way to prepare for it. The explosion made the ground fly up and smash him in the face. One moment he was running, the next he was on his stomach, seeing stars and tasting his own coppery blood. He wasn't alone, everybody was thrown violently to the earth.

As the sound boomed past them, Ryan scrambled to his feet. He heard someone gasping for air.

"Nukin' hell," J.B. wheezed as he got up. "I think I cracked a rib."

Where the predark mall had been, a vast column of roiling dust and smoke uncoiled into the blue sky.

"There's nothing left of it," Krysty said in awe. "It's all gone."

Not quite true.

Huge chunks of debris from the store began falling through the smoke, clusters of still-joined concrete blocks crashing onto the parking lot. The lighter debris flew even farther from ground zero, as if it had been fired from a catapult. Pieces of asphalt, metal and rock sizzled down around them, bouncing on the grass.

"We need to move farther away!" Ryan said. "Go, Jak! Go!"

They ran deeper into the golf course, out from under the debris fall. J.B. dropped behind at once, cradling his rib cage on the left side. He couldn't keep up because he couldn't take a full breath. To run any distance required air. Lots of air. Ryan knew it had to have hurt like holy hell. J.B. was not a groaner by nature, but he groaned with each footfall. Seeing how badly his old friend was banged up, Ryan quickly relieved him of his pack and hung back to jog alongside him.

Jak led them up a familiar rise, through the grove of trees and down the slope to the shore of the chartreuse-matted water hazard.

At the edge of the lake, they all sat, exhausted.

First thing, Mildred had a look at J.B.'s ribs.

"I heard something go snap when I hit the ground," he told her, holding open his shirt. "It's hard to breathe deep…"

"You might have cracked one," she said. "Or maybe it's just a deep bruise. Either way all I can do is wrap you up to immobilize it." She pulled a bandage roll from her medical kit and started binding his chest in tight, overlapping turns.

As she was working, the musician lifted his head from between his knees and addressed the one-eyed man. "Where's the rest of my C-4?" he said.

"Mebbe you'd better explain how you figure it's yours before we get into whether there's any more of it," Ryan told him.

"You want an explanation? Sure, I'll give you the whole story. I heard about a predark C-4 storage site from a scrounger who'd just come back from the New Mex hot zone. He didn't know what the fuck he'd stumbled onto. The triple stupe couldn't read a lick. He thought the packaged kilos might be worth something, though. He came to me with the information and a sample of the stuff because he didn't trust BoomT to give him an honest deal. I hired a full bike crew to go back to New Mex with him. Took a big risk and staked them gas, food and ammo to go get me a load of plastique. That's why I'm here with my ship. I skipper a forty-foot sloop, working the coast route up into the Lantic. I've been waiting to make the exchange for the explosive, and then to personally deliver it to my buyers."

"East Coast barons?" Mildred said.

"Nah," the musician said. "I'm not sailing east with it, I'm sailing west. You ever hear of Padre Island?"

"Rumors," Krysty said. "Pot of gold at the end of the rainbow. Grounded freighter, fully loaded, on the southwest edge of the Houston radpit."

"To be more precise, my dear, what we've heard is rumors of rumors," Doc corrected the tall redhead. "We've never actually made the acquaintance of anyone who claimed to have visited that particular garden spot, only people who claimed to know people who claimed they knew people, and so on, and so on. Smoke and mirrors, not to put too fine a point on it."

"We don't put much stock in things we haven't seen for ourselves," Ryan told the man with the mustache.

"Well, I've been there regular, mebbe twenty times total," the musician countered, "and I'm telling you it's as real as you and me. The islanders have brand-new predark goods coming out their ears. They're ready to trade plenty for something this extra special. Once they've got it, they'll cut it up into little chunks and sell it for ten times my price. But hey, that's business."

"So if these people are paying you," Ryan said, "you can pay us."

"I'll give you just what I was going to give the cold-hearts I hired. I paid them half up front. Promised to pay them half on delivery. I'll give you the delivery part of what I agreed to."

Over the man's shoulder, submerged not thirty feet away, was the disputed stash.

"That isn't good enough," Ryan said. "We want half of whatever the islanders are going to pay you."

"Are you kidding? You want me to make you partners?"

Ryan's expression said he wasn't kidding, and that was exactly what he wanted.

"Without us, you've got nothing," Krysty said. "And you're out all your upfront costs. With us you've got fifty kilos of C-4 to trade."

"So there *is* more of it," the musician said, a wide smile lifting the corners of his drooping lip shrubbery.

"We need you, and you need us," Mildred told him. "That's what partnerships are made of."

After a moment of consideration, the companions had their answer. "All right," the musician said, "I'll admit you've got me."

"We need ammo for our blasters," Ryan told him. "Nines, .38s, .357s, 9 mm and 12-gauge."

"Not a problem. I've got a good selection of new—not reloaded—cartridges stowed away on my ship. It's islanders' ammo, from their stockpile. The bikers were going to take it as part of their pay. You can help yourselves."

"And you're taking us with you to Padre," Krysty declared.

"Of course. We ship together until the deal is finished. Afterward we go separate ways. Now, where's *our* C-4?"

By way of an answer, Ryan started unlacing his boots. Jak did the same. Then the two of them waded out into the lake to retrieve the sunken treasure.

As they dropped five dripping packs onto the shore, the musician muttered, "Well, fuck me sideways and call me Sally…"

"What *do* people call you?" Mildred asked.

"I answer to Tom, among other things," he replied.

Then the man turned to Ryan, who was drying his feet prior to putting on his boots. "Before we head out, I've got to ask you something else," he said. "No matter what you tell me, it won't change anything that we've agreed on. After all, a deal's a deal. I just want to know. Did you chill those bikers to get the booty?"

Before Ryan could reply, J.B. chimed in.

"We ain't coldheart robbers," the Armorer hissed through clenched teeth.

"And I'm supposed to know that from looking at you?" Tom countered, amused at the idea.

"The bikers were already chilled when we found them," Mildred explained. "Stickies swarmed them."

Tom frowned and shook his head. "Son of a bitch, that's a triple nasty way to go."

"We need to get a move on," Ryan said. "Some of BoomT's sec men could have survived the explosion. When they look around they're not going to be real happy with the way things turned out."

"My ship's moored over thataway," Tom said, pointing due south, toward what a century ago had been the Gulf Intracoastal Waterway, and what now was a narrow slip of a makeshift harbor.

There were five extra twenty-five-pound packs to lug. J.B. couldn't carry anything but his M-4000, and he had stiffened up so much he needed Mildred's help just to get to his feet. When she reached for her load of C-4, their new business partner brushed away her hand. "Don't worry, I'll take it," Tom said. "You see to your friend there."

The pack of plastique felt cool against Ryan's back as its moisture soaked through his coat and shirt. They climbed out of the water hazard's bowl and set off down the slope, onto the flatland, past the cultivated fields. Ryan took the rear guard, behind Mildred and J.B.

There was no longer any need to run. They walked at a brisk steady pace. Ryan kept looking over his shoulder to make sure they weren't being followed.

The sound of the explosion had awakened the field hands from their midday snoozes. Ryan saw them standing outside their shanties, one hundred or more yards away, hands on hips or shielding their eyes from the sun, looking in the direction of the mall and the rising pillar of smoke.

Beyond the south end of the golf course, the companions stepped back onto the gridwork of ruined and deserted city streets.

Almost at once, a group of armed men appeared around a corner, running toward them from the direction of the Gulf.

"Easy now," Ryan cautioned the others as hands moved for weapons. "They don't know what's happened. And we're not going to tell them. Keep walking nice and slow, like we're in no particular hurry."

That wasn't the case for the strangers. Ryan measured the opposition as they rapidly closed ground. A half dozen sec men carried Soviet-made assault rifles on shoulder slings and five crusty sailors had the butts of their sidearms hooked over their waistbands. There was shock on all their faces. They didn't go for their blasters. They didn't see the companions as a threat.

A sec man stepped up and addressed Tom, whom he obviously knew. "What the fuck?" the deeply tanned, bald-headed guy exclaimed, pointing behind them at the massive smoke cloud. The wrinkles in his forehead extended past the middle of his scalp.

"Damned if I know," Harmonica Man replied. "We'd just left the emporium, heading for my ship when there was a giant explosion at our backs. Fuck-awful blast. Never seen the like. Don't know what the hell BoomT had squirreled away, but I'm telling you it all went up in a single go. We were three-quarters of a mile away and it still nearly chilled us."

"What about other survivors?" the sec man asked, dread creeping into his voice. "Wounded?"

"We didn't see anybody," Tom said. "Fires were burning red-hot and there was too much smoke. Don't see how anyone could have lived through it, though."

"We've got to find out for sure," the sec man said. "Some of our crew might have made it. They might be hurt. Come back with us and help recce."

"There's no point," Tom said, shaking his head. "There's nothing up there but ashes. It'll take three days for them to cool down enough so you can start sifting through them. I'm not sticking around for that. I'm leaving Port A ville on this tide, and you've seen the last of me."

"Well, fuck you, then," the bald sec man said, angrily waving his crew onward.

"I wish you luck," Harmonica Man said to his back.

The companions watched the would-be rescuers hurry off. The sec men and sailors didn't cut through golf course, but took the street route, which was faster.

"Well, that makes things a whole lot easier," Tom said when they were out of earshot. "Those were BoomT's harbor guards. They could have made things dicey. Now there's nothing to stop us from sailing off into the sunset."

Standing water started at the railroad tracks, which divided Port A ville roughly in two, lengthwise. They sloshed through ankle-deep black brine; there was no way around it. The rise in sea level had inundated Big Hill Reservoir and the associated holding ponds. Sabine Lake had become a new invagination of the Gulf of Mexico. At closer range, the oil refinery was even more of a decrepit shambles, cracking towers canted at odd angles, gangways ending in space, and it was surrounded by an iridescent marsh of spilled oil. The reek of sulfur was like a snapkick in the solar plexus. Ahead of them, beyond the swamped and decaying downtown, Ryan could see huge, engine-powered ships—rusting hulks of tugs and tankers—listing on their sides in the shallows. Violent storms had driven them up onto the city streets and left them wedged there.

"Best you all follow me from here on," Tom said. "I know the route the mule carts take." He led them through knee-high water to the concrete ramp where the carts were off-loaded and loaded. The top of the ramp was connected to a system of crude floating docks. Big blocks of oil-stained, closed cell plastic foam and sealed, empty fifty-five-gallon drums supporting scrap lumber planks lay side by side. The pathway floated alongside the drowned buildings, past the ruined ships, and then cut a straight line across the deep predark channel to the sailboats tied up at the bases of the cargo cranes.

The dock moved under their weight, bobbing, undulating like the body of a giant mutie snake. At the tail end of the line, the motion was the most extreme. Ryan had to concentrate on every step and anticipate the rolling rise and fall.

As they negotiated the final, unprotected stretch of the walkway, a bullet whined past Ryan's head and slapped into the water in front of him on the right. The wake of the near-miss longblaster round brushed the side of his neck and a chill ran down his spine to the soles of his feet.

Seconds later came the bark of a rifle shot.

Chapter Nine

When BoomT pushed the little red firing switch, he was expecting a loud and satisfying result.

He wasn't expecting cataclysm.

He wasn't expecting to black out from the explosion's pressure wave.

The entrepreneur came to after a split second of oblivion, his head reeling. He couldn't tell there had been two explosions—they had come too close together and his ears had been instantly overloaded. Now it felt like wads of cotton had been rammed into them. Or like he was thirty feet under water. Momentarily the world was as silent as the grave.

Then his senses began to return, one by one.

He tasted blood on his lips; it was leaking out of his nostrils in a steady trickle. Because he had taken cover behind the overturned semitrailer, he couldn't immediately see what had happened to his world. Even so, he realized that the blast was exponentially bigger than he had planned. It had not only ripped the steel sheathing from the top side of the trailer, leaving bare the skeleton of the frame, it had lifted and scooted the massive rig six feet across the sidewalk, which in turn pushed the golf cart with him on it.

The sec men hunkered around him looked stunned, too. They were bleeding from their noses and ears.

Though his mind was clearing, he couldn't seem to make his limbs obey him. Before he could get the cart in gear a choking pall of dust and smoke swept over the trailer. There was a lot more of both than he had anticipated.

Only when still-joined sections of his emporium's concrete-filled exterior wall began to rain down around them through the haze, screaming to earth like unexploded 250 pound bombs, did BoomT realize the extent to which something had gone wrong.

Those bombs crashed onto the ancient pavement, shattering it and themselves in sprays of shrapnel and showers of sparks. The impacts actually shook the ground.

Whether seeing an opportunity in the confusion and smoke to escape their bondage, or simply fleeing in panic, his four slaves chose that moment to put wings on their heels. They sprinted away from the semi-trailer and the parking lot, arms covering their heads as hunks of building continued to fall.

Imagine june bugs caught between concrete and the head of a ball-peen hammer.

In midstride, the indentured servants were driven face-first into the ground by man-made meteors. The weight, speed and mass of the projectiles blew out the sides of their rib cages, pulverized their skulls and sent aerosolized guts, brains and marrow flying in all directions.

In the next instant, a chunk of concrete block wall slammed into the trailer, crashing completely through it.

BoomT managed to get the golf cart in gear and moving. Cranking over the steering tiller, he bid the suddenly worthless cover adieu. Accelerator pedal floored, head lowered, he sped off, following the sidewalk south. His sec men ran after him.

Until he circled out of the choking dust plume, he had no idea what had happened, what he had in fact done. As he took in his former domain, he couldn't recognize it.

It took a moment for the truth to sink in.

Sure enough, there was a crater big enough for a swimming pool.

That vacant hole, still belching smoke, was his entire net worth.

Everything BoomT had worked and fought for his whole life—his magnificent edifice to post-Apocalyptic commerce, its stock of previously owned merchandise, the contents of his treasure room, his devoted sec crew, his gaudy, his assemblage of willing if less than appetizing whores—was obliterated. In its place was more fire and more smoke than he had ever seen. Towering flames danced behind the shifting wall of dust. The vast, roiling smoke column had risen a thousand feet in the air and was still climbing.

Worst of all, the direct connection between the excavation of the swimming pool and his total ruination was impossible to ignore. BoomT had been hornswoggled into pushing the button that brought his empire to an end.

He'd been rogered in a way that Deathlands' legends were made of.

Legends that never died.

That he knew just got bigger and bigger, over time.

"Look over there! Radblazes, somebody made it out alive!" one of the sec men shouted, gesturing toward the end of the south parking lot as he passed BoomT a pair of full-size binoculars.

The entrepreneur peered through the optics. Better than a mile away, a handful of people stood on the edge of the golf course, staring back at the destruction. Even at that distance, BoomT could make out what looked like a black eye patch on one of them; the red-haired slut and the sawed-off little turd in the fedora were much easier to see. There was no mistaking who it was.

Or who had engineered his demise.

"One-Eye," he growled. Even as he spoke, Ryan and his crew turned tail and ran to get out from under the falling debris.

It was too late for BoomT's sec men to bracket them with blasterfire.

And besides, the sec men had their own concerns about being struck by objects dropping out of the sky. The relatively lighter stuff had been thrown higher by the blast. It took a lot longer to reach apogee and reverse course. And all of a sudden it was raining down around them. Some of the junk was the size and weight of cast-iron pipe fittings; some of it was three feet long, pointy and sharp.

Before the entrepreneur could order a retreat, one of his crew was struck from above, and the force of the blow dropped the sec man instantly to his knees. The end of a length of rebar angled up from his left collarbone and the steel rod's tip poked out through the middle of his right buttock. His innards were skewered crossways. Blood gushed from the dying man's mouth as he tried to speak.

BoomT stomped the accelerator, cutting the tiller arm over hard, swerving away from the gurgling horror. With debris bouncing off the ground on either side of him, he made a beeline for a perpendicular street and rumbled up onto the sidewalk. When he was out of range, he stopped the cart and let his men catch up.

He knew where One-Eye was heading. In that direction

there was only one place to go. Cawdor and crew were making for the ships tied up at the crane. A getaway by sea. BoomT realized he could still cut them off and keep them from escaping. If they didn't die in the ensuing gun battle, if they were taken prisoner, he would have his revenge, and it would be mythic.

It would have to be to make up for his loss of face.

What Trader had done to him so many years ago had been bad, so bad that the story of his hosing still circulated, still tainted his reputation, but this was a defeat of an entirely different order of magnitude. This was a total wipe-out. An extermination.

But why?

BoomT racked his brain for an answer that made sense. There was no material gain for Cawdor that he could see. One-Eye hadn't plundered the treasure room. If he'd tried, the guards posted there would have responded with bullets and a major firefight would have ensued. The fat man had come away holding the shitty end of the stick in his final deal with Trader, so there was no reason for One-Eye to risk his life and the lives of his crew to get payback. If there was payback due, it was BoomT's to collect.

His mention of Trader's death had been a test. He had held back critical details of the story, to try to find out what Cawdor knew. For years BoomT had been spreading rumors about being in the room with Trader in his last helpless moments, sometimes implying that he had hastened the legend's departure with his own two butt cheeks. The tales were complete fabrications, of course; they were intended to restore his lost status and prestige. The fat man hated to be bested, and since Trader had disappeared without a trace, there was no one to question him on the facts.

Unfortunately there was no one to refute them, either. Which was something that hadn't occurred to him until now.

It occurred to BoomT that he had been punished for the crime of running off his mouth.

And the punishment meted out was inconceivable.

Why were Cawdor and Pipsqueak hauling ass for the moored ships? That one was easy to answer—in case BoomT had somehow miraculously escaped.

His sec men joined him, coughing, sweat streaking the soot that covered their faces. The whites of their eyes were scoured pink from dust and ash. BoomT was down to five soldiers. Cawdor had six. An even match, except in firepower. His sec crew was armed with automatic weapons and extra mags.

"The scum who did this to us are headed for the water," he told his troops. "No way are they getting away with this. We're going to stop them from sailing out of here, no matter what it takes. Follow me."

With a whir of the cart's electric motor, BoomT accelerated away and his sec men fell in line behind. He kept his speed down, fearing his escort would either fall too far back to be of any use or faint dead away from exertion in the sweltering heat. His own massive, sweat-lubed buttocks were sliding around on the vinyl bench seat. Even though he was driving parallel to the golf course, he couldn't see the opposition. That was a good thing. If he couldn't see Cawdor, chances were Cawdor couldn't see him.

BoomT already had a plan in place to stop an attempted escape by sea; a plan he had devised after the Trader deal gone bad. Because of the sunken tankers at the upper end of the Port A ville moorage, the only way in—from the south—was also the only way out for deep-keel vessels. That meant exit and entry could be blocked off in a matter of minutes, keeping robbers and cheats from reaching the open Gulf, and stopping would-be robbers from invading the moorage.

He was two-thirds of the way past the golf course when he saw a column of sec men running his way. He sped up to meet them.

The troopers were visibly relieved to find their boss still not-chilled.

BoomT was less sanguine about seeing their faces. His first question was addressed to the bald guy in charge of harbor security. "Why did you desert your posts?"

"To help with the rescue," the sec man said. "We thought you'd need help to get out the wounded."

"We're all that's left," BoomT informed him. "There's no one else to rescue. Everybody was blown to bits. The emporium is gone, too. Hell, the whole damn mall is gone."

The sec men were struck mute by the news.

"Did you see a man with an eye patch?" BoomT demanded. "A stumpy little shit was with him, and a tall slut with red hair."

"Yeah, we passed them on the way up," the head sec man said. "Six strangers. And Captain Tom was with them."

"They were the ones who did it, you droolies," the fat man said. "They destroyed everything we had, and you let them go."

Blood drained from the sec men's faces.

They were thinking firing squad. And this time they were going to be the shootees instead of the shooters.

The sailors looked plenty worried, too. They backed away from the sec men, hands in plain sight and nowhere near their waistband-tucked blasters. Their body language said, This has nothing to do with us. Not our responsibility. It said volunteering for the rescue team was looking more and more like a mistake.

"We've got them outnumbered," BoomT said, the collective pronoun taking summary execution off the table. "We can still stop them from escaping." He turned to the sailors. "You guys are coming along, too." Before they could protest, he added, "If you don't help us win this fight, I'll sail your boats out into the Gulf and scuttle 'em."

With a wave of his hand, BoomT engaged the pursuit. The sixteen men followed behind him at a trot. Minutes later, when he first caught sight of their quarry, he hit the brakes and stopped the column. One-Eye and his crew were about five hundred yards ahead, just crossing the railroad tracks, starting to slog through the black water toward downtown. Picking up the binocs, the fat man counted seven, not six opponents. Captain Tom was indeed among them. In point of fact, the traitorous trader was heading the nukin' parade. And not apparently at gunpoint. BoomT watched him lead Cawdor and Pipsqueak and the others up the ramp and onto the floating dock. When they disappeared between the half-submerged buildings, it was time to act.

"We've got to close on them before they get under way," BoomT said. He pointed to his four quickest and strongest surviving lackeys. "You, you, you and you," he said, "beat feet down to the skiff loaded with the harbor net, and string it across the entrance. Don't engage the bastards. Don't return fire. Just lay the barrier net and then find positions on the crane side to defend it. If we can seal them in, we've got them. We can take our own sweet time with the chilling."

The quartet shoulder-slung their AKs and ran toward the water in the direction of the harbor mouth.

"The rest of you come with me," BoomT said, then he flattened the accelerator pedal against the firewall.

When the heavily loaded golf cart bumped over the railroad tracks and splashed into the brackish water, BoomT once again hit the brakes. The vehicle had tiny wheels. If he went any farther the water level would rise to reach the motor and batteries, and short everything out. Cinching up his bedspread toga, the fat man unclipped an RPG from the canopy frame. It was the killshot. The ship sinker. It looked like a child's toy in his huge hands.

BoomT slid off the seat into the warm, shallow water. He sloshed toward downtown at top speed, and his sec men and the sailors trailed in his foaming wake.

Grunting from the effort, the fat man waded knee-deep between redbrick buildings, then mounted the concrete ramp to the floating dock. "We're going to lower the odds," he told his men. He picked the two best shots from among the survivors. They only had iron sights on their AKs, but 30-round clips gave them plenty of wiggle room. "Get up on the rooftops," he ordered the pair. "Hold your fire until they're on the open stretch of dock. Then they've got nowhere to go except in the water. Take out as many as you can, pin down the rest. We'll do the mop-up."

The snipers ran ahead down the dock, alongside the drowned buildings. Just before they vanished from sight, they slipped through broken-out, lower-story windows.

BoomT sent the rest of the men ahead. It irked him but he had no choice. If he went first, he'd slow down the advance. Not only would five hundred pounds of running weight overstress the dock's salvaged planking, it would create a rocking motion so violent it would make standing difficult and aimed fire impossible.

When his crew was forty yards distant, BoomT set out after them, taking care where and how heavily he stepped, steadying himself with a hand against the buildings' sides. Even so, the dock lurched sickeningly under him.

A string of single shots barked from the rooftop of the building to his left.

The fat man hurried, his arms extended like a tightrope walker, to catch up to his main force, which had already reached the start of the unprotected section of dock. The undulation became so extreme that to keep from falling in the water, he dropped to his hands and knees and madly crawled the last ten yards.

The dock's violent motion continued, as did the sniper fire.

To the right, he could see four men in a small skiff, two rowing for all they were worth, two frantically pushing a folded, weighted net over the stern. They were halfway across the harbor mouth.

Two hundred yards away, One-Eye was scrambling aboard a moored sailing ship. The vessel lay broadside to BoomT, across the open stretch of water, a sitting target.

The fat man shouldered the RPG, but because of the dock's movement he couldn't keep the ship in his sights. He had to hold fire. He couldn't waste the shot.

"Go get 'em!" he shouted at the huddled sec men and sailors, waving them onward, toward the unprotected section of dock. "Don't let 'em cast off!"

Chapter Ten

Ryan broke into an all-out sprint as single-fire rifle shots rained down on the exposed dock. Bullets zinged over his head, splintering the thirty-foot stretch of planking that separated him from Jak. The companions knew better than to bunch up while crossing open space. Hitting an individual, moving target was much more difficult than lobbing rounds into a pack of bull's-eyes. The up and down, wavelike movement of the dock both helped and hurt the companions' cause: it messed up the snipers' stationary leads, but the tricky footing meant it took longer to reach hard cover.

The one-eyed man counted at least two AKs steadily popping off behind him. He couldn't stop, turn, locate the targets and return fire with the Steyr to put up cover for his battlemates. Headlong forward motion was all that was keeping them from being hit.

And even that wasn't enough.

Directly in front of him, Jak's C-4 backpack took a solid whack, jerking sideways on its backstraps. The slug drilled through and left to right into the water, missing the albino's rib cage by a fraction of an inch. The impact caught him in midstride and knocked him off balance, driving him to a knee. Unhurt, unfazed, the albino teen bounced back up at once and ran on.

One hundred feet away, the far end of the dock was tied to the partially sunken base of the Big Arthur crane. Ryan saw Tom lead Krysty, Mildred, J.B. and Doc onto the crane deck then to the right, behind the cover of the moored sailboats. Five ships blocked the sniper fire.

Ryan and Jak raced to close ranks, bullets dogging their heels. As they jumped onto the crane and ran behind the stern of the first ship, a flurry of slugs slapped its fiberglass superstructure, plowing into the hull and ricocheting off the steel masts. All along the moorage the live-aboard crews of the trader vessels were shouting and cursing as they dived for cover.

The snipers were tracking and zeroing in on the companions' movement between the ships. A tall, stringbean of a sailor stood at the precisely wrong moment. A shot intended for Ryan hit him squarely in the shoulder, twisting him, and he went over the port rail backward, screaming as he fell into the gap between the ship and the crane's base. He entered the water headfirst.

Captain Tom bellowed through a cupped hand along the line of ships, "Keep the fuck down!" He had stopped beside an off-white sloop with an oil- and chem-stained hull and battered steel masts.

As Ryan and Jak ran low and fast toward him, Tom hurried Krysty, Mildred, Doc and J.B. aboard the amidships' gangway, guiding them down into the cockpit and out of sight belowdecks.

Ryan couldn't miss the ship's name painted in peeling, cursive letters across the stern: *Tempest*. Bolted to the top of the stainless-steel stern rail was a canvas-shrouded longblaster on a swivel mount. It had a massive box magazine.

Shooting back wasn't what was on Tom's mind.

"Cast off the lines!" he shouted at Ryan and Jak, then he disappeared below the coaming.

Ryan did better than that, whipping out his panga he slashed through the two-inch braid on the crane cleat with three hacking blows. Beside him, the ship's auxiliary diesel engine started up with a burbling rumble. Gray smoke puffed from exhaust ports just above the waterline.

From the bow cleat Jak waved and shouted to Ryan. "Longblaster! Up here! Quick!"

Ryan dropped the end of the severed line. Sheathing his panga as he ran, he unslung the Steyr. Kneeling next to Jak, looking under and around the bowsprit, he saw a rowboat crossing the harbor mouth about one hundred yards away. The seated men at the oars were working in unison and stroking hard. Two others stood bent over the stern, dumping a barrier net over the side. From the floats bobbing on the surface, they had already blocked more than half the entrance.

Ryan tossed his backpacks onto the sailboat's foredeck, then scrambled over the rail himself.

"Get aboard!" the captain hollered as he put the engine in gear and the ship started to slide away from the moorage.

As the gangway glided past, Jak jumped the widening gap, onto the port deck, and scrambled into the cockpit.

Bullets rattled the deck, shattering the fiberglass and skipping off the brightwork. There were definitely more than two sources of fire now. Shooting was coming from the dock, as well.

Ryan flipped up his scope's lens covers as he moved behind the skimpy cover of the anchor chain locker.

Clear of the other trader ships, but still broadside to incoming fire, Tom redlined the diesel and the vessel surged forward.

Bullets whining overhead, Ryan lined up his shot on the closer rower. Holding the center post low, he tightened down on the trigger, taking up the slack. After a last second adjustment of his lead, he applied an ounce more pressure and the trigger crisply broke. The Steyr roared and bucked.

Downrange the rower was struck center body mass as he leaned into a backstroke. He kept on going backward, losing his grip on the oar.

Ryan cycled the action, chambering a fresh round. They were closing fast on the rowboat. Peering through the scope, he saw the other rower frozen on the thwart, staring down at his dying comrade.

The one-eyed man held the sight post lower still and fired again.

Struck high in the belly, the second rower twisted sideways and was thrown half over the far gunwale.

Two men in the stern stood stunned, net in hands, as their boat rapidly lost momentum.

Ryan glanced back when he felt the ship veer to the right. He saw Tom's head poking over the ship's wheel. The captain had altered course, intending to ram.

The men in the skiff dropped the net. Pushing their wounded comrades out of the way, they grabbed for the oars and tried to row back the way they'd come. By then the bow of the vessel was bearing down hard. Realizing that they couldn't get away, they dumped the oars and reached for their AKs.

The much larger, much taller vessel was so close the rowers couldn't do anything but fire straight through the hull. Before they could get in position to do that, Ryan abandoned his longblaster and rolled to the starboard rail. Drawing his SIG, he leaned over the side, aimed down and rapid-fired, shooting them to hell right where they sat.

As the stern scraped past the dead boat and dying crew, and the end of the net, Ryan gathered up his treasured rifle and hopped down into the cockpit, which was lined with steel plate.

Bullets were still coming at them, but the ship was back end first to the enemy blasters, and therefore a much smaller target. When Ryan raised up his head and looked back toward the dock, he saw a flash of ignition. He recognized at once what it was from the madly spiraling a smoke trail.

A rocket-propelled grenade.

He managed to yell out a warning to Tom, but before the captain could cut the wheel hard over, the grenade whooshed past them, wide to the right. The rocket skipped on the surface of the water once like a flat rock, crow-hopped another 150 feet in the air, then nosed in and blew up, spraying shrap in all directions.

Ryan climbed out of the rear of the cockpit and shouldered the Steyr, using the top of the stern rail as a shooting brace. Through the eyepiece, he saw the fat man in the middle of the dock, his tree trunk legs wide apart for balance, still holding the RPG launcher, waving and shouting for his men to keep firing.

"What in radblazes are you doing?" Tom said, turning toward him. "They can't touch us. We're home free."

Ryan didn't answer. He held his sights steady and tightened down, doing his best to time the trigger break with the rise and fall of the distant dock. The Steyr barked and its butt punched back hard.

Three seconds later, through the scope he saw BoomT's head suddenly snap back, chins pointing skyward, arms flung wide. The gargantuan entrepreneur toppled over backward, spread-eagled, off the dock and into the water with a tremendous splash.

"Nukin' hell!" Tom exclaimed, clapping the one-eyed warrior on the shoulder. "Now that's what I call a shot!"

"Dumb luck," Ryan said.

"Call it whatever you want, but I'd like to see the fat cheating bastard get up from that one."

The big ship was rigged for solo sailing. In a matter of minutes, without any help from Ryan, Tom had the sheets up and full of wind, and they were skimming due south, away from Port A ville. When the captain ducked down to shut off the diesel, he called for the others to come up top.

"You've got a few bullet holes through the hull," Mildred told him as she took a seat on the cockpit's built-in bench. "They're all above the waterline."

"Then there's nothing to worry about," Tom said. "I'll check them after we get some distance from here."

"Isn't BoomT going to send ships to chase us?" Krysty asked.

"Mebbe in another life," Tom said.

"You took him out?"

"Not me," Tom said, then he nodded toward Ryan, who shrugged.

"It was either that or keep looking over our shoulders for the rest of our days. BoomT wasn't the forgiving kind, and we did pretty much wipe out his livelihood."

"'Pretty much'?" Mildred repeated. "All we left him with was his bedspread!"

"Yeah, and they can fish it out of the bay and bury him in it," Ryan said.

"All things considered, we didn't come out of this too bad," J.B. said, cradling his sore ribs with a forearm.

Ryan took a moment and introduced each of the companions to the captain. And when they were done shaking hands, he said, "What's your last name, Tom?"

"Wolf."

"And your ship's called *Tempest?*" Ryan asked.

"Wait a radblasted minute!" J.B. said, grimacing as he sat up straight on the bench. "You're *the* Harmonica Tom?"

Mildred said, "The who? The what?"

"Half the stuff you've heard is bull," Tom assured J.B.

"Well, I heard you singlehandedly repelled a boarding party off the Linas," the Armorer went on. "Then you trolled a wounded coldheart in your boat wake. Robber's crew regrouped and tried to rescue him in their own ship. You kept their man just out of their reach for better than a mile. Until something triple big and triple nasty swam up from below and cut him clean in two. You played a jig on your mouth organ the whole time, that's how you got the nickname."

"Well, that one's true," Tom admitted.

Then he turned to Ryan and said, "I knew who you were the minute I set eyes on you. No mistaking that missing peeper and scar. Know some of what you've done, too. Funny how quick word gets around who's chilled who. You took down Baron Willie Elijah and Baron Tourment. And you nailed that oversexed pile of pus, Captain Pyra Quadde, with a spear."

"Harpoon," Ryan said.

"If it was long and pointy," Tom said, "ol' Pyra probably died happy."

"Not particularly."

"You can bet the news about today's little shindig will spread along the coast like wildfire," the captain continued, clearly enthused at the prospect. "BoomT was widely known, but not widely admired. Trader might have set the benchmark for fucking with people's shit at Virtue Lake, but what you just did to Port A ville runs a close second."

"BoomT did it to himself," Krysty said.

"And that's what folks are going to be talking about for years to come," Tom said, shooting a grin at Ryan. "How you all set him up for a royal hosing, and how deep he swallowed the stink bait."

Ryan changed the subject. "How long is this trip to offload the C-4 gonna take?"

"The distance is 240 miles, plus or minus," Tom said. "How long it actually takes us is up to the wind and the tide. We could do it in less than a day, if we're lucky. That means sailing all night, of course. Which means round-the-clock watches. Got plenty of hands for that so we can all get some shut-eye. Round-the-clock watch is something we have to do anyway because of the competition."

"Who's the competition?" Cawdor asked.

"Pickings aren't what they used to be," the captain said. "Scroungers are having to dig deeper and deeper into the nuked-out places for spoils. The prime, top-quality goods are a hell of a lot harder to come by than they were even five years ago. But hey, you know all that. You saw the godawful garbage BoomT was selling. Got to figure that the decline in merchandise is something that's only going to get worse as time goes on. After all, they aren't making any new stockpiles. How many were there to start with, anyway? Who the fuck knows? How many haven't been looted? Who the fuck knows? Long and short of it, some of my seafaring brothers and sisters are gathering their cargoes offshore, by bushwhacking and raiding other traders. Seems like there's always a boat or two patrolling, looking for an easy highjack. The unlucky traders and crews just disappear, and their ships sail into port with fresh faces. Goes without saying that nobody asks where the goods came from, or where the previous owners went."

"Robbers robbing robbers," Krysty said.

"You mean, they've turned pirates?" Mildred said.

"Traders, pirates, it's always been hard to tell the two apart," Ryan said.

"And it's gotten even harder of late," Tom said. "Believe me, it's not like it used to be in these parts when there was plenty of the good stuff to go around. I don't suppose you've heard any tales about what's happening well to the south of here? Down the Lantic coast?"

"What tales?" Ryan said.

"Yeah, I didn't think you had," the captain said. "The stories have filtered up as far as Padre Island, but the traders working out of there have kept a lid on them. Nobody wants to start a stampede of newcomers. There's too many in the business as it is."

"Are you going to tell us, or what?" Krysty said impatiently.

"The details are sketchy, as you would expect," Tom went on, "but it sounds like the folks to the south came out of the Apocalypse better than we did up here. They didn't get any direct missile hits. Nuke winter wasn't near as hard for them as it was for us. They caught some badass tidal waves, though. I've heard rumors they're still making diesel in the predark plants. Other shit, too, you know, manufacturing stuff like before skydark. I was thinking seriously about sailing down there myself, just to see what's what. If things are opening up half that good, I wouldn't mind getting in on the ground floor."

"How far?" Ryan asked.

"Mex, and points south."

"We've been to Mex City," Cawdor told him.

"And?"

"It was just another shitheap. Not a nuked shitheap, though. It was shaken apart by earthquakes and volcanos blowing off their tops. Natives weren't all that friendly, either. Triple-crazy chillers if you want to know the truth. If you want to know the truth, it wasn't much different than here, except for the funny hats."

"How'd you manage to get all the way to Mex City?" the skipper asked.

"On foot," Ryan replied, lying without hesitation. The predark mat-trans system that allowed companions to jump between redoubts in seconds was too valuable a secret to give away.

"Sailing is a hell of a lot easier than walking," Tom said. "And there's more to the world than what any of us has seen. There's got to be."

"In terms of total landmass and population before skydark, that's a no-brainer," Mildred said. "What's left, of course, is anybody's guess."

"It has been said that travel broadens one," Doc added. "Of course, it can also get you beheaded."

"So, travel makes shorter?" Jak asked.

Ryan cracked a smile. Mildred and Krysty giggled.

"Two jokes in one day," J.B. said, shaking his head. "What's the nukin' world coming to?"

"We've all got to die some way," Tom asserted. "How I look at it, might as well be some way interesting. And a person has got to look farther ahead than just the next meal, or the next safe hole to crawl into at night. Got to look past what's here and now, to set a course, a proper course…"

Tom paused and gazed off to starboard, frowning as he seemed to consider something important, then he said, "I've got a business proposition for you folks. I've been thinking about it for a good long time. I don't make the proposition lightly, and this is the first I've mentioned it to anyone. We know each other by reputation. And I've seen what you can do, the kind of fight you put up, with my own eyes. My business proposition requires a sec crew. A heavy-duty sec crew I can trust to sail down the Lantic coast with me, mebbe all the way to Tierra del Fuego if need be. I figure you're just what I've been looking for. Got no back-down in you. We can supply *Tempest* from the Padre Island stockpiles, then head on south. We'll share the spoils of the trip equal shares. No telling the wonders and riches we might find."

"A journey of discovery?" Doc said, his interest piqued. "A reprise of the Lewis and Clark expedition, three hundred years after the fact?"

"I don't have a clue what you're rattling on about," Krysty told Doc.

Then to Tom she said, "You, either. You're talking about making an open-ended sea voyage through unknown waters based on gaudy-house gossip?"

"No risk, no gain," the captain replied.

"We're not shy about taking risks, and big ones at that," Ryan said. "But the gain at the far end has to be more than a pipe dream."

The captain shot Ryan an incredulous look. "Hey, correct me if I'm wrong," he said, "but when you sashayed into Port A ville, your butts were dragging mighty low. Tongues half hanging out. For adventurers you ain't exactly living high on the hog, are you? You're barely scraping by. My guess is, more often than not, you're hungry, thirsty, cold and low on ammo. At a point not too far down the line all the hellscape's prime booty will be gone and there'll be no more scraping by the way you've done. No survival except for those who don't mind stump clearing, rock chucking and shit shoveling. I'm talking dirt farmers. I'm talking goat milkers. I'm talking fighting off muties with wooden clubs and with blasters made out of iron pipe and bailing wire. And you all know I'm right. You can read the signs as well as I can. The awful day when the predark spoils run out is coming, sure as hell smells like sulfur. Nothing can stop it."

The captain's word were met with silence.

"Don't say no to my idea right off," he told them. "Think on it awhile. That's all I'm asking."

"We'll think on it," Ryan said.

"There's plenty of food and drink in the galley," the captain said. "Go down and help yourselves."

Ryan was the last to descend the steep companionway. He could stand in the rear cabin without bumping the top of his head, but barely. On the port side was an aft bunk; in the middle of the cabin stood a chart table. An open, locked back bulkhead door led into the main salon. On the right was the galley: propane cooktop, sink, counter. Hanging above the sink in a net were pots, pans and cooking utensils. On the left was a dinette table surrounded on three sides by a settee. Above the back cushions were two rows of densely packed bookshelves. The table was set with miscellaneous bowls, jars, jugs and bags of food. Forward, through another locked-open bulkhead door, Ryan could see another set of steps, and beyond them, V-berths at the bow of the ship. He assumed *Tempest*'s cargo holds were hidden belowdecks. The cabin was scuffed, chipped, but spanking clean. There was a faint smell of bleach.

The companions slid in around the small table and without fanfare plowed directly into the eats and drinks. There was salted hard tack for bread, shelled walnuts, ripe tomatoes bigger than Ryan's fist, melons, oranges, a variety of dried fruits and plenty of fresh water. The jars held pickled hard-boiled eggs and filets of small fish.

Except for the sounds of chewing and swallowing there was silence as they ate. They packed it in like there was no tomorrow, filling the voids.

"Not bad grub," Jak said at last, licking the tomato juice dripping down his snow-white wrist.

"This is just nasty," Krysty said holding up a piece of pickled fish on a knifepoint for Mildred to sniff.

"Gak," the doctor said, spraying hard tack crumbs over the tabletop.

Krysty plopped the tidbit back into the jar and screwed the lid down tight.

Their hunger finally sated, the companions pushed back against the settee's cushions and breathed deeply.

"Do we have to think twice about this offer?" Mildred asked the others. "It's our first real chance to see what the rest of the world is like."

"We saw Mex and we saw Baja," J.B. countered. "We saw other foreign lands. They were shitpits. Barely got out of some places in one piece, if you'll remember."

"My dear John Barrymore," Doc said, "you know other nations have survived. Entire predark nations, perhaps. Even cultures."

"Ever wonder why these advanced civilizations haven't paid Deathlands a visit in the last hundred years?" Krysty asked. "Sent rescue missions?"

"Maybe because they think we're all chilled," Mildred offered. "Perhaps they think there's nothing left to visit or save. Nothing but poisoned earth, air and water, and crazy-chiller muties. Maybe they've turned their backs on us for bringing on the end of the world. Any or all of those reasons could be valid."

"Or they could be bullshit," J.B. replied with venom. The pain of his injury seemed to have put him in a par-ticularly foul temper. "Deep down you and Doc still want everything to be back the way you remember it, before you got frozen and time trawled, before the nukecaust, and that's not gonna happen. The both of you are living in a dreamworld. You don't want to admit that what we have here is all there is. Mebbe even better than what's left of the world. We've seen some downright evil shit in parts of the world we visited."

"We know what we're up against in Deathlands," Krysty said, picking up the thread of J.B.'s argument. "The four of us were born and bred here. We've come up fighting muties, coldhearts and barons. We know how to survive whatever the hellscape throws at us. And we've got the mat-trans as our ace-in-the-hole. We can always get out of a hotspot in a hurry if we have to. Where this tub is headed there aren't going to be any redoubts, no mat-trans, no quick escapes, no telling what's going to be thrown at us. On this tub, if something goes wrong we're dead meat."

"Sailing south could be a suicide mission," J.B. summed up.

Arms folded across his chest, Jak grunted in assent.

"In case you haven't noticed by now," Mildred countered with heat, "life is a suicide mission."

"Wait a minute," Ryan said, raising his hands for calm. "Let's just look at the facts in front of us. Harmonica Tom's the real deal. We know that. If he's done a quarter of the stuff people say he's done, there's no better skipper."

"Okay, facts on the table," Krysty said. "How long could the trip take?"

"If the historic voyages of discovery are any measure," Doc said, "perhaps a year, barring accident. Perhaps longer. The distance spanned, round trip, is something on the order of 12,000 miles."

"Nukin' hell," J.B. groaned.

"Assuming we found something valuable," Krysty said, "how much of it could we bring back on this boat? Seven people and provisions for same are going to make it kind of cramped."

"That depends on what the valuables are," Ryan said. "Good things sometimes come in small packages."

"There's more to this than just a fresh vein of booty," Mildred said. "This could change all our lives for the better. If there's another world out there, an un-nuked world, maybe we wouldn't want to come back."

"Mebbe you wouldn't want to come back," Krysty said.

"If you've got big love in your heart for the Deathlands

because you were born in it, that's your business," Mildred told her. "From what I've seen over the years, I'd say all the hellscape does is kick our asses. But hey, maybe that's just me."

"And what if the captain isn't telling us the whole truth?" Krysty said. "What if he's holding something important back to get us to sign on? Figuring he'll break the bad news when it's too late for us to back out?"

"We kind of outnumber him," Mildred said drolly.

"A guy doesn't survive solo without having some neat tricks up his sleeve," J.B. said with confidence.

Ryan held up his hands again. Though he didn't show it, he was deeply concerned by the way things were shaking out. For the first time, he was facing the possibility that a fork in the road might permanently split up his crew.

"Look," he said. "I can see both sides of this. It isn't a matter of looking for new adventures. We've got plenty of that without shipping out. It's about the devil we know versus the devil we don't. The familiar, bad as it is, is still familiar. We can pretty much reckon how we're gonna die. Starvation. Thirst. Gutshot. Backstabbed. Ate by some mutie. I don't particularly care where I croak or how. But if there's a chance of never having to go hungry or drink my own piss again…"

"So you're for taking this pipedream trip and mebbe never coming back?" Krysty said, aghast.

Before he could answer Mildred said, "Are we going to put it to a vote, or what? Everybody in favor raise their hands."

"By the Three Kennedys!" Doc exclaimed. "Can we please set some ground rules before we proceed? Is this going to be a majority decision that we all agree in advance to abide with, or does the vote have to be unanimous?"

"There's not going to be a radblasted vote," Ryan told the others. "It's too soon to make up our minds about any of this. We don't have to decide until after we're paid for the C-4. Let's wait and see how the islander deal works out. Mebbe pick up some more information while we're there. Get a better feel for how the captain does business, and how he runs his ship."

His words hit home.

"Of course you're correct, Ryan," Doc said. "Your logic is impeccable. There is no need for haste in the matter. And a decision this important is best made by cool heads all around."

"So we're going to wait and see?" Ryan said, pointedly staring down the companions in turn.

Each of them nodded in agreement.

Not a victory. A temporary truce. Perhaps simply a postponement of an inevitable outcome.

Mildred turned on the settee and began reading out loud the titles from the spines of the shelved books and magazines. There were century-old *National Geographic* magazines, sailing and travel books, books on first aid and emergency surgery, marine engine repair and gunsmithing books, cookbooks, crudely printed volumes on creating homemade explosives and poisons and books that taught foreign languages. Spanish. French. German. Chinese. Japanese. Maori.

"Our host has acquired quite a broad collection of useful twentieth-century nonfiction," Doc said.

On the bottom shelf was a long section of dog-earred,

paperback, pulp science fiction and fantasy novels. The
gaudily jacketed *Slaughter Realms* books were sequen-
tially numbered from 157 to 241, and filed in order of pub-
lication. J.B. pulled one out and opened it. He scanned a
few random pages. The edges of the brittle, yellowed
paper crumbled at his touch.

"Listen to this," he said. Thumbing his spectacles up
the bridge of his nose, he read out loud.

"'Damn you, Ragnar! I'll soon cleave your fire-furred,
Norse wedding tackle from your groinal region!' The
Iroquois ninja princess hurriedly scythed her singing
katana around and around her head, making her firm, up-
thrusting breasts jostle beneath her buckskin doublet ever
more wildly with each rotation.

"'Uff da!' the Viking leader responded with a guttural
roar, ducking under the voracious windmilling attack to
snatch up his Martian-made brain armor from the castle's
basaltic flagstones. He clapped the filigreed silver meta-
plastic bowl down on his head, bending the tops of his
huge pale ears against his scraggly red pigtails, thus an-
ticipating and deflecting the cloud operatives' flanking
maneuver.'"

Krysty put a hand on J.B.'s wrist and gently forced
him to lower the book. "Stop, please," she said. "I'm
getting queasy."

A second or two later the ship turned forty-five degrees
and its speed increased markedly. The hiss as the hull
split water grew much louder, as did the resounding thud
and jolt of the bow pounding into and splitting successive
wind waves. The vessel heeled over hard to starboard,
sending the food containers sliding to that side of the
table.

Chapter Eleven

Phantoms cloaked in black bunting swirled in and out of the edges of Okie Moore's field of vision. Ashen-faced phantoms with huge heads reveled, grimacing and grinding their long teeth. Their mirror-polished black boots shuffled and scraped on the floor's planking; dust motes rose like smoke in the wedge of sunlight that burst through the hut's doorless doorway.

Okie lay on his back in a vile puddle, hallucinating. It was the middle of the afternoon, the hottest part of the day. He couldn't get up. He was so weak he couldn't lift a hand to shoo away the flies drinking his tears and blood. It took all his strength just to suck the next breath. He lay slow-baking in the hut-oven, amid the reek of decomposition, shit and piss. The bare mattress beneath him was soaked with all three.

On the fourth day of the sickness, his terrible fever had abated, leaving him shaken and drained. He had thought it was finally over. He was wrong. On the fifth day, the fever returned with a vengeance. And along with it, new and horrible symptoms: bleeding from gums, nose and ass. Bright red spots had popped out all over his body. Bathed in cold sweat, his pulse rapid and thready, he had collapsed.

That was yesterday. He hadn't moved since.

He was not alone in the hut.

His two wives lay on either side of him on their backs, dead; the babies in their protruding bellies, dead. Two of his six children had been taken to the *Yoko Maru* because they had shown no sign of the illness. Everyone who had come down sick had been left in the ville, abandoned there to die. Okie's other children lay around him, caught in the same awful grip as he. He couldn't tell if they were alive. Even if he could have turned his head to the side, he couldn't have seen them. The light spearing in from the doorway didn't reach into the corners where they lay huddled.

There had never been a sickness like this before. Not in anyone's memory. A sickness that struck so many simultaneously, like a lightning bolt, with blinding headaches, high fever, bone-breaking pain and vomiting. A sickness that dropped people squarely in their tracks. In less than two days, the social fabric of the island had come unraveled. Bodies lay unburied not only inside the ville's squalid huts, but in the winding, narrow lanes and along the Gulf shore.

Ghastly pale visages loomed closer to his bed of pain, pressing in on him from all sides, blocking his view of the hut's dim ceiling. Outsize noses and ears, too-large eyes and mouths mocked his suffering and his grief. The bunting that trailed from the phantoms' elbows brushed across his bare skin like an open flame.

Okie knew he was dying.

The how of it was an unsolvable mystery. Any one of the island's recent visitors could have brought the terrible sickness with them. The traders had all sailed away before the outbreak. The Fire Talker had fallen ill along with everyone else. In point of fact, who gave what to whom no longer mattered. It was done. "Why me?" The question he had asked himself over and over had no meaning, either. He had neither the strength nor the mental focus for outrage.

When folds of coarse, gauzy fabric grazed his forehead and fell down over his eyes, Okie did not struggle. Beaten, destroyed, he was ready to depart the world of flesh. Deep in his chest, he felt a stabbing, tearing, transecting pain, then hot blood gushed from his lungs into his throat, filling it. He coughed, and gore sprayed over his chest and drooled down the sides of his face and neck. His throat refilled at once as the massive hemorrhaging continued. There was no end to it. Buckets of his own blood choked him, and then drowned him. As his consciousness faded, long, powerful arms lifted him from the sodden pallet. To his horror, he was not carried up through the roof into the bright and open sky, but down through the floor into smothering blackness.

Into the pit.

DANIEL DESIPIO STROLLED around the perimeter of the vacated ville, his survivalist do-rag tied over his nose and mouth in a futile attempt to filter out the stench of death. There was no longer any need to pretend he was one of the stricken. He was the only person moving. Everyone else was either deceased or on the verge of same, or otherwise incapacitated. He guessed at least one hundred people, fully half the island's population, were down and out. Without his lifting so much as a finger.

The more things changed, the more they stayed the same. Body count was still a central focus in his life.

Unlike Typhoid Mary, his early twentieth-century pre-
decessor, Daniel didn't deny that he was the source of the
plague. What he did deny was that it was his responsibility.
After all, he hadn't asked to be turned into a living bioweap-
on, it was something that had been done to him. He saw
himself as the quintessential victim. If he had had any
sympathy for those he infected, he might have summoned
the courage to take his own life. Absent sympathy, he felt
only hate for his victims. He loathed them for their
weakness, blamed them for their susceptibility to the flavivirus, and saw them as the root cause of his predicament.
After all, if nobody got sick from the disease he carried, if
it hadn't made people die like flies, he'd have been a free
man.

To his left, a shallow pit had been opened in the beach
sand and bloated corpses tumbled in, their limbs tangled
together. He pulled the camouflage do-rag tighter over his
face. Shovels lay discarded at the verge of the hole. Panic
had set in, as it always did, when disease swept through
like a firestorm. The still-healthy had abandoned the dead
and the sick, taking shelter in the freighter. As if that could
protect them.

Part of Daniel, the needy, greedy core of who he was,
reveled in the avalanche of destruction he had wrought. He
dimly remembered sitting on a summer sidewalk in shorts
as a small boy, squishing a column of ants one by one with
his little pink thumb, and making up a story about himself
as a terrible god teaching lessons of fear and obeisance to
the helpless and insignificant. The meat of his earliest-
remembered power fantasies, the meat of his twenty-nine
published books, which were also power fantasies, had

come to life. He had become a force of nature, albeit uncontrollable.

A four-year-old with bigger thumbs.

Although that small, hidden part of him rejoiced as he took in the carnage, Daniel felt a growing sense of unease, of emptiness, even despair. Not because of the indiscriminate loss of innocent life, but by what the looming, one-sided victory presaged.

Reconfinement.

Daniel's liberty, such as it was, was about to come to an end. He had at most a few hours of freedom left. Like a trained bird of prey, again and again his masters released him to perform a single murderous trick, then when the trick was done, he was reeled back and returned to his cage. Literally. What he bore in his blood was far too dangerous for there to be any option but solitary imprisonment.

Why didn't he seize the opportunity to get away while he still had the chance? Why didn't he push a boat off the beach and head for the mainland as fast as he could row? What held him shackled when his overseers were miles away?

Daniel Desipio was not a bird of prey. He was not a hunter; he was not even a gatherer. He was a talker; even in his predark profession, he'd been a squawking parrot in a flock of same. He lacked the physical skills and training, and the inclination to exist as a solo predator. And he couldn't function as a social animal in close contact and cooperation with others of his kind. It was guaranteed that if he removed himself to some backwater ville, close to half the residents would be dead within a week's time. Those who recovered from the first round of illness would be taken in the second round, after they were reinfected by mosquitos. If he revealed his predicament in advance to those offering him hospitality, he could expect to be chilled on the spot, and his body burned to ashes. There was no way around it. The evil seed that lurked in his blood chained him invisibly to the jailers who fed, clothed and protected him.

The other reason he could not summon the will to flee was fear.

Fear of what would happen to him if he was caught running away.

Daniel circled wide around the antipersonnel-mined paths and headed across the littered dunes for the north-west tip of the island. He had watched the Claymores being positioned and armed, amused by the islanders' defense plan. There was no reason for the Matachìn to enter the ville proper before assaulting the freighter. The dying couldn't be saved; there was no treatment for the genetically engineered plague. Islanders in the ship with natural resistance to the virus—those who only came down with flulike symptoms, or the few who showed no signs of infection—would be pacified and then taken as part of the spoils, as slaves.

With the ville and its reek well behind him, he moved the do-rag from over his nose and mouth and retied it around his head. As he walked he sucked down the salt air blowing off the Gulf, felt the humid breeze on his face, the sun on his back, and heard the waves lapping against the shore. Daniel tried to soak it all in, to hold the experience, but he knew that every step took him closer to the door of his cage. And with every step, he grew more distraught. His lower lip began to quiver and his eyes brimmed with tears.

The heavy machine gun position on the southwest point of the island was manned, but only technically. The two gunners inside the bunker were slumped against the sandbags and steel plate, still conscious but clearly showing signs of the sickness. They moaned as he strode past.

There was no one to stop him, no one to challenge him.

Daniel walked to the tip of the point, to the edge of the water, and took a signal flare from his vest. He pulled the striker tab and held the tube over his head. The flare whooshed and sizzled, shooting high into the sky. The rocket exploded with a loud pop, flashing fluorescent pink and billowing pink smoke. He tossed the spent tube aside, squinting at the horizon line.

The pirate fleet waited just beyond the curve of the earth, watching for his signal. As terrible as they were, the Matachìn were the instruments, the familiars of something infinitely worse.

As was he.

More than a century ago, Daniel recalled reading some obscure scientist's theory about the nature of thought, which put forward the proposition that ideas operate like viruses, with no reproductive machinery of their own, spreading from brain to brain, mutating over the course of transmission. Like viruses, some ideas were harmless, others were anything but. The idea that now stalked the earth was an ancient legend. It had had 1500 years—and the assistance of Armageddon—to evolve and flower. Unlike *Slaughter Realms,* it was not cobbled together by a committee of English Lit majors from bits and pieces of crosscultural fables, a slapdash reassembly that diluted and eviscerated the underlying power. This legend was pure. It was complete. Much of what had passed for entertainment in predark popular culture was a pale imitation or parody of the basic concept: that the world was a shambles, the playground of insane demons.

This was neither imitation nor parody. Daniel had seen the truth of it with his own two eyes.

Chapter Twelve

An abrupt change in the pitch and roll of the ship woke Mildred and she couldn't fall back to sleep. She lay beside J.B. in one of the bow's vee berths, hanging on as *Tempest* pounded through rising waves. Outside a torrential rain was falling. It drummed on the top deck and sizzled on the surface of the sea. There was so much water vapor in the air it was hard to breathe.

Beside her, J.B. was oblivious to the passing storm. He snored softly, peacefully, as if nothing had changed.

Mebbe for him it hadn't.

But for Mildred everything felt different. Everything.

That's what hope could do, she thought.

Memories from her life before cryogenesis, before skydark had returned in a flood. Suppressed memories of who she'd been, what she'd done, her professional interests, her daily routines, her hobbies, her colleagues and friends. She vividly remembered the sense of safety a complex, organized, global society provided. She remembered the overwhelming amount of goods and services within easy reach. She remembered electricity, flush toilets, refrigeration, a hot bath whenever she wanted and the deluge of information: books, movies, music, Internet.

Virtually everything she had devoted her life to prior to Armageddon was for naught in Deathlands. There was no science. No real medicine. No search for knowledge. There was only the gun.

And using it to stay alive.

J.B., Krysty and Jak couldn't conceive of a world otherwise. A world where people depended on millions of others, but at the same time, within agreed-upon limits, had some independence. Where the public will produced mass transit, and mass food and energy. The companions' only experience of a higher social organization was the baronies, a corrupt, poisonous feudal system based on oppression and exploitation. The idea of government devoted to the common good was alien to them—they suspected it was simply the baronies all over again, only on a grander scale.

She had tried to talk to J.B. about it. But it was like trying to explain swimming to someone who'd never seen water.

What Tom had said about the future of Deathlands made perfect sense. The current level of culture, savage though it was, was propped up by artifacts from the highest point of human industry and civilization. If anybody in the hellscape knew how to rebuild or operate the machines that had made that explosion of mass production possible, Mildred had never met them or heard tell. The requisite skills in math and engineering had been lost in the century of chaos after the all-out missile exchange. To create those skills in the first place, society had had to evolve to the point where a separate techno-scientific class could flourish and develop.

How long had it taken for someone like Galileo to appear? Who paid his rent?

As Tom saw it, the devolution of Deathlands had been

postponed by the stockpiles and caches of predark goods
that had survived the nukecaust. Therefore, Deathlands
hadn't hit bottom, yet. Based on what Mildred had witnessed and endured so far, rock bottom was going to be
triple ugly.

The idea of leaving the others, perhaps never seeing
them again, was very painful for Mildred to even consider.
She owed her companions more than she could ever repay.
They had resurrected her from a cryotank tomb, they had
saved her life over and over. But what she felt more toward
them wasn't just simple gratitude. Though there was certainly friction at times, they were dear friends; her only
friends, in fact. More like family.

The differences between their life experiences and hers
were buried under the weight of the day-to-day fight for
survival. The captain's proposition had brought those dis-
parities front and center, reminding the others who
Mildred Wyeth really was; that part of her belonged to
another world. Because she had special feelings for J.B.,
his pulling away saddened her the most of all. But she
understood his reaction. If her world wasn't lost, he was
afraid he couldn't hold her.

Thrown over for a double-tall frappuccino?

Whoa, that was something she hadn't thought about in
a long time!

As fast as the memory appeared, she pushed it out of
her head. There was only one bright spot that she could
see: she and Doc still had a chance to change J.B.'s mind,
to change all their minds about the voyage south.

After an hour or so, the rain squall passed and seas flattened out a bit. In the wake of the storm the air temperature dropped and Mildred managed to doze off. Sometime

later, she awoke, drenched in sweat. The sun had come out again. It blazed through the portholes on either side of the bow.

Mildred carefully rolled out of the berth so as not to wake J.B., then timing her gait with the roll and heave of the boat, she climbed the forward companionway steps to the foredeck.

The wind whipping off the Gulf cooled her down at once. The flying spray was as warm as bathwater. On the landward side, the sea was stained the color of rust, and yellow custard foam topped the waves. The wind carried the smell of baking bread. It wasn't bread, Mildred knew. The odor was from volatile petrochemicals still seeping into the Gulf from ruptured tanks inland. Iridescent toxins, oils and tars had streaked *Tempest*'s white deck and coaming a nasty yellow-brown.

She looked back toward the stern and saw the captain and Ryan standing in the cockpit, talking. Over the wind singing in the lines and the hiss and slap of the hull she couldn't make out their words.

Mildred moved aft, holding on to the stays and starboard rail, and climbed down into the cockpit.

"Rough as a cob for a while there," Tom said to her. "Sorry, but I couldn't run around it. Too big a squall and it was coming too fast."

"No problem," Mildred said. She glanced up at the stern rail. The rail-mounted machine gun was still shrouded in its waxed canvas. "I take it we're still clear of pursuit?"

"Lucked out so far," Ryan said.

"The competition is probably laying further offshore to stay out of the weather," Tom said.

The two seemed to get along well, Mildred noted. That wasn't surprising. Both were products of the hellscape, and they were in many ways similar. Stoic. Determined. Battle-seasoned. Fearless. Men of legendary prowess who didn't give a good goddamn what folks said or thought of them.

It had already occurred to Mildred that Ryan might be more intrigued by the voyage of exploration than the other three Deathlanders. After all, he had been trawled to the shadow world, a parallel earth that had missed the nuke-caust and was by far the worse for it. That experience had forcibly opened his eye to other possibilities. To alternatives to the status quo.

Though he was a leader, Ryan was also very much his own person, a craggy promontory in the hellstorm. It seemed Harmonica Tom had touched a nerve; Ryan was taking his offer seriously, unlike the others. Mildred knew their hunker-down mentality could have been the product of exhaustion. All of them had expended strenuous effort in the preceding twenty-four hours, running and fighting while dehydrated and half-starved. If it was a temporary stubbornness, only time, rest and more food would tell.

Tempest soon left the rusty sea behind. The edge of the discolored water was a stark borderline where suspended rust turned to deep emerald green. Beyond it, the Gulf's swell became widely spaced and even. They were making excellent time, with a steady wind and clear sailing ahead.

"I'm nuked," Tom admitted, trying to work the kinks out of the back of his neck with his fingertips. "Got to shut my eyes for a little while. Can you handle the ship and hold course while I have a snooze?"

"Sure," Ryan said, taking over the helm.

"Keep the wind at your back," Tom advised as he started down the companionway steps. He winked at Mildred. "And don't run into anything big."

JUST AFTER NOON, with Tom back in command, they approached the eastern tip of what had once been North Padre Island. Stretching ahead of them to the southwest, as far as the eye could see, was a vast curve of intermittently breaking surf. Small waves crashed on the patchy, seemingly endless offshore shoal. Like an abandoned spiderweb, hummocks of barely submerged sand caught ships. There were derelicts as old as skydark: cadaverous tankers, freighters and shrimpers. Some of the wreckage was smaller, made of fiberglass, and far more recent—the shoal was still catching traders' ships. There were no lighthouses, no warning buoys marking the shallow water. The capsized, rusted-out hulks were a testament to the limits of dead reckoning.

"Another twenty miles to the ville," Tom announced. "Two hours mebbe, and we'll be there."

One by one the other companions stirred themselves from belowdecks. Jak beelined for the bowsprit, and there he sat, his ghostly face into the breeze, his long white hair flying behind his head. Doc and Krysty joined Ryan and Tom in the cockpit. J.B. was the last to come up for air. He climbed the steep steps slowly, like an old man. His ribs had really stiffened up during the night. He groaned as he took a seat on the padded bench beside Mildred, cradling his chest with a forearm.

"Want me to rewrap your ribs?" she asked him with concern. "Has the bandage come loose?"

"No, it's okay," he said. "The ship rolled and I caught

myself wrong. I'll be fine in a minute." With that, he tipped his fedora down over his eyes, settled into the seat cushion and seemed to go back to sleep.

He didn't want to discuss his pain, which from experience Mildred guessed meant he was hurting plenty. There was nothing she could do about that; she couldn't even offer him an aspirin. Barring compound fracture and lung punctures, rib injuries were customarily left to heal on their own. And at their own pace. J.B. was going to be hurting for a good long while.

Six miles away, on the far side of the shoal, was the mainland coast, the southernmost edge of the much-feared Dallas-Houston death zone. What Mildred saw was a dark green wall of mangrove branches and the sun gleaming off trapped backwaters. Above the treetops, skeletal structures protruded, some of them clearly industrial with cylindrical, four-story-tall holding tanks and latticework walkways; others looked like condo towers gutted down to poured concrete walls and floors. Everything was draped with verdurous creepers. Mosses and vines trailed down to the waterline.

At the base of the trees, where the beach should have been, lay an unbroken, miles long pile of rubbish. The partially submerged junk had been backwashed off the land as successive tidal waves receded. A peek through binocs revealed cars and trucks filigreed with rust. Disintegrating sofas and mattresses. Battered refrigerators, washers and dryers. On top of it lay the lighter stuff: heaps of splintered wood, plastic and aluminum.

Deeper in the mangrove swamp, dense black smoke boiled up through the canopy and blew inland. There were no visible flames, just smoke. A huge section of the backwater burned. Something floating on the water had caught fire, oil or gasoline, Mildred thought. Perhaps set off by a lightning strike.

"What are you looking for?" Ryan asked the skipper who was leaning over the port rail and scanning the horizon ahead, this while keeping a one-handed course a quarter mile from the edge of the breaking surf.

"Looking for the *Yoko Maru*'s radar mast," Harmonica Tom said. "We'll be able to see the top of the mast long before we catch sight of the island. Got to be four hundred feet off the ground."

From his perch in the bowsprit, Jak let out a cry. "Lookee!" He pointed to the horizon.

It wasn't a mast.

Tom cut the wheel hard over to starboard, giving everyone a full-on view of a brilliant pink light low in the sky, slowly sinking out of sight over the curve of the earth.

"Signal flare," Ryan said.

"From a ship?" Krysty said.

"Probably," the captain replied.

"How far off?" Mildred said.

"Hard to tell," Tom told her. "A ways."

"May we assume that some unfortunates ran their vessel aground?" Doc asked.

"Could be," the skipper said. "Take the helm, Ryan."

Harmonica Tom pulled the waxed shroud off the stern-mounted blaster and tossed it into the cockpit. The Soviet-made PKM light machine gun sported an unfluted barrel, and a skeletonized rear plastic stock and pistol grip. It had no carrying handle atop the action; instead of a bipod, it pivoted 180 degrees on a stand clamped to the rail. Under the receiver like a gigantic, olive-drab sardine can on its side, a 100-round-belt, boxed mag rode horizontally. The action and barrel glistened with protective grease. The business end of the ammo belt was already in the feedway. After removing and pocketing the muzzle plug, Tom dropped the selector switch from safety to fire, then charged the cocking handle. With a crisp clack the first 7.62 mm round chambered. Ready to rip.

"Would traders-turned-pirate use an emergency SOS flare to lure another ship in close?" Mildred asked.

By way of answer Tom said, "Mebbe a couple of you should go below and stock up on ammo for everybody. There's a hatch under the rubber mat in the forward cabin. Pull out the big plastic tubs. It's all boxed and clearly marked caliber and load. You should find everything you need."

Jak and Doc went below to gather up the requisite ammo and J.B.'s shotgun and Ryan's scoped longblaster. Everyone else watched the horizon for the ship that had sent up the flare.

Minutes passed. Jak and Doc returned with the bullets. They all reloaded their weapons and their extra mags. More time passed.

There was nothing in front of them but empty sea.

An hour later they caught their first glimpse of Padre Island through Tom's binocs. When it was Mildred's turn to look, she aimed the lenses at the dark blip on the horizon to the seaward, along the curve of shoal that divided the Intracoastal Waterway from the Gulf. She saw the top of the grounded ship's radar mast and the tattered, enormous Lone Star flag flapping against the bright blue sky.

Shortly thereafter, Tom shouted a warning to the passengers to mind the boom, then made an abrupt course change, steering toward shore. He ran the vessel through Aransas Pass, which had once separated Mustang Island and San Jose Island. Both landmasses were gone now, but the deep water channel between them still remained. *Tempest* entered the Intracoastal Waterway and continued southwest, pushed by a steady breeze.

As they steadily bore down on their target, more and more mast became visible. The top third of the freighter's towering rear smokestack was missing. The white bridge and wheelhouse atop the aft superstructure appeared. Then gradually, the whole ship came into view. It looked as if a giant hand had carefully lifted, then set the freighter down on dry land. It rested on its keel, slightly canted to port, on the highest point of the island. The top deck was still stacked three-high in places with cargo containers; some had tumbled over the side and onto the sand.

"How long since you been here?" Ryan asked the captain.

"Almost two months," Tom said. "After I arranged for the scroungers to get the C-4, I sailed away east. I've been all the way to the Linas and back since then. I had a shipload of islander goods to move. Shoes. Clothes. Ammo. You're not going to believe the predark stuff they've got in that freighter."

"Your ship's pretty much empty, though," Krysty said. "You traded the islander goods for what?"

"Small objects of big value to barons," Tom said. "Easily concealed. Gold and silver rings, bracelets, teeth."

"I don't get it," Mildred said, changing the subject. "What was the SOS flare all about? Is the ship that fired it farther to the south? Is that why we haven't come across it? Or did it sink without a trace before we reached it?"

"Neither of those things is likely," Tom said. "If the ship had been farther away, over the horizon, we wouldn't have seen the flare. If the ship had run aground on one of the sand bars, it would still be stuck there. I think the signal came from the island. The distance is about right. It was probably nothing. Just some of the kids playing around. The place is crawling with them. Islanders take their breeding serious."

As they scooted along the outer edge of Corpus Christi Bay, Mildred glanced over at the ruins of Corpus, itself. Aside from the skeletal skyline, there wasn't much to see. The city was derelict, flooded, abandoned and overgrown.

At the northeast corner of Padre Island, on the edge of a low bluff, was a partially buried gun position. The bunker was roofed and reinforced with layers of corrugated steel hacked from cargo containers. It was also heavily sandbagged. The firing port was a dark slit that ran the width of the emplacement. Mildred could make out the muzzle and ramp front sight of a heavy machine gun just inside the opening. No faces popped up as they glided by. And the MG's sights didn't turn and track them.

If there were guns on the freighter, she couldn't see them. The up-angle to the top deck was too steep. She could see through the underside of the radar mast's steel mesh platform. The flag was flying but nobody was watching the store.

Ahead was the ruin of the JFK Causeway bridge, which had connected Padre to the mainland. Only the footings on either end of the bridge remained intact; the deck had fallen into the channel. Tom steered *Tempest* to the deepest part of the waterway, then slipped between the jutting stubs of the bridge pilings.

The ship began to lose way as it swung into the island's lee. The captain cut in close to the shore, taking the shortest route to the protected anchorage.

The beach was deserted. There were no other ships in the bay.

"Where is everybody?" Ryan said.

"Is something wrong?" Krysty said.

"No," Tom assured them. "Ships come and go all the time. Sometimes the bay is packed, sometimes it's empty."

"What about the people?" Krysty said. "You said there were lots of kids."

"Dunno," Tom said, scratching the stubble on his chin. "Weird that there's no cook smoke rising from the ville."

He didn't seem worried, just a bit puzzled.

The rusting bow of the *Yoko Maru* loomed above the ville's clustered shacks, cresting an immense wave of sand. Mildred could imagine the next instant, the Lilliputian hovels squashed flat under its weight. There were maybe a hundred ramshackle dwellings built along the slope that led down to the anchorage, separated by winding, narrow lanes.

It was hardly an impressive trading center, even by Deathlands' minimal standards. The residential shacks were not much bigger than the outhouses. And there was debris everywhere. Paper, metal and plastic.

"So the islanders are all in the freighter?" Mildred asked.

"There's no place else for them to be," Tom said. "Mebbe they're taking inventory. Mebbe they're counting their kids. They ain't all run off, that's for sure. Wouldn't leave their pot of gold."

With that, Tom dropped his sails and coasted into the

middle of the anchorage. As the ship rapidly lost speed, he hopped out of the cockpit and ran forward to lower the anchor. The chain rattled off, then the hook struck bottom. Momentum carried the ship forward. Tom continued paying out more chain until he had the proper scope, then he locked it off with an eyebolt.

As *Tempest* swung around at anchor, the captain stared at the deserted beach, hands on hips. Without a word he walked back to the cockpit and furiously rang the ship's bell.

The clanging echoed in the distance.

Nothing stirred on the land.

"That should have brought out the camp dogs," Tom said.

There was no evidence of dogs, not so much as a bark.

Mildred suddenly got a creepy-crawly feeling. Not just that something wasn't right; that something was very wrong. She wasn't alone.

"Perhaps, dear friends," Doc said, "we should rethink our plan of action. Perhaps our going ashore this afternoon isn't such a good idea, after all. Perhaps a better course would be for us to move on while we can. Surely the East Coast barons will pay well enough for the explosive—"

"We're already here," Tom said.

"He's right," Ryan said. "We've come a long way in the wrong direction to sell the plastique to the East Coast barons. Least we can do is check it out. If it doesn't look right, we'll make tracks in a hurry."

"Leave the C-4 belowdecks for now," the skipper told them. "It'll just slow down the recce. We can come back for it if everything's okay."

Ryan and Doc helped the captain swing and lower a gantried twelve-foot raft over the side.

"Mebbe you'd better stay behind," Tom said to J.B. "You're gonna have a hell of a time getting in and out of the dinghy."

"I'm fine," J.B. said through clenched teeth.

"You might be able to carry that scattergun," the captain went on, "but shooting it is going to cause you a world of hurt. No reason for you to take the chance of injuring yourself more."

"I'll be just fine."

Ryan and Tom helped the others down into the boat, then they climbed in themselves. Seven people made the dinghy mighty cramped, but the distance to the island was short, no more than seventy-five yards.

When everybody was seated and as comfortable as they were going to get, Tom put out the oars and, leaning his back into it, began rowing them to shore. Ryan sat on the bow, his longblaster at the ready, scope lens uncapped. Just in case.

As the inflatable raft skidded up onto the beach a smell enveloped them. Rank. Fecund. Eye-watering.

Unmistakable.

"That ain't home cookin'," J.B. said.

Chapter Thirteen

Daniel Desipio shielded his eyes from the sun with the flat of his hand, searching the horizon to the southwest for a sign of the oncoming Matachìn miniarmada. The pirate ships first appeared as a row of dark dots in the seam between sea and sky, then vanished one by one as they slipped into the trough of the offshore swell, reappearing again as they climbed the crest. Disappearing. Reappearing.

As the vessels crept closer and closer to the island, with his naked eye Daniel could distinguish three low, squat shapes, which he knew were oceangoing tugs. No plumes of dark brown smoke pumped up from their stacks. To save precious fuel, the tugs were under "people power" until they closed on the target. There were plenty of able-bodied rowers to choose from, former residents of Browns and Matamoros villes conscripted into service at blaster and blade point. The Matachìn had all the time in the world to reach their destination. Their quarry wasn't going anywhere, and for damned sure reinforcements weren't on the way.

Sweeping in front of the trio of tugs, four sailing ships beat back and forth to make headway against the breeze. They were the fleet's pursuit and interdiction craft.

Though the hour of slaughter grew near, the Texas sky

showed no hint of turning black; nor the Gulf of turning red as blood. The Vikings and Martians of Daniel's fireside tale were artifacts of *Slaughter Realms,* figments of an anonymous cumulative imagination; they were not the pirates' closest allies. The Matachìn relied on their own mythic savagery—and mortar barrage—to put the fear of death into intended victims. The predark tugs carried more than enough ordnance to dismantle Padre's stationary defenses. They carried enough HE to flatten the place, end to end. And the master of the fleet was no stranger to excess.

Under the command of machete-wielding Commander Guillermo Casacampo the venerable nautical catch phrase "All hands on deck!" took on a grisly literal meaning. Post-conquest, the hands of the defeated lay severed and scattered along the scuppers of his flagship while their former owners bobbed like corks in the armada's wake, waving bloody stumps.

When the ships came within ten miles of the island they started to spread out to their assigned attack positions. Although there were no sounds of alarm from the *Yoko Maru,* the surviving islanders had to be able to see what was coming; they had to be getting nervous. Daniel was starting to get nervous, too. This part of the operation always gave him butterflies. He had seen things go sour before.

Matachìn cannon crews in a chill frenzy tended to lose focus and get swept up in the moment. The really big worry, however, was Casacampo, himself. His ships could only carry and feed so many slaves, and stow only so much booty. They already had gathered more than enough of both from the previous two sackings. Under the circumstances the commander was free to take even wider liberties with human lives.

Including Daniel's.

After all, he wasn't the only plague vector at their disposal.

Disposal being the operative word.

He hurried away from the shore. It was time to relocate to a nice, safe place.

The job of disease vector was no cakewalk. Accidents happened in the heat of battle; shrapnel was indiscriminate, as was automatic weapon fire. Sometimes dengue carriers infiltrating a new ville were murdered just because they were strangers, or for some other reason unrelated to the threat they posed. Not all of them were Fire Talkers. Some were whores, some were traders, some were mercies. Or combinations of same. The key was sociability. Making new friends.

Daniel climbed to the top of the dunes and jogged along the ridge to make better time. He had already scoped out the best spot, in the center of the island as far as possible from the machine-gun emplacements, the ville and the grounded freighter—the main targets of the Matachìn gunners. While the folks abandoned in the ville struggled in their death throes, he had dug himself a deep, narrow foxhole in the sand.

At times like these the freezie saw himself as Faust, selling his soul not once, but to a succession of ever more fiendish devils. The first mortgage was given to the publisher of *Slaughter Realms* in return for the warm glow of seeing his very own words in print. To escape the bottomless sink hole of wage slave-hood that was series publishing, he had thrown himself at the mercy of scientists by answering an ad in the back of an alternative throwaway newspaper for "medical research subjects, some foreign travel required, top pay and stock options."

The initial interview and physical exam had gone well; he had been offered the job of human lab rat, which paid close to ten times his current annual salary. The details of the research program were skimmed over with platitudes about "saving humanity," "ending suffering" and promises of "virtually no personal risk." All Daniel could see were the dollar signs and the opportunity to uncover something exciting to write about, something worthy of his talent and devotion, something that would bring him the acclaim and reward he deserved. It seemed like a win-win.

The moment he arrived at the remote Panamanian research site, a former maximum security prison in the heart of an immense rain-forested island, he realized he'd made a frying-pan-into-the-fire mistake. As it turned out, the ultrasecret Project Persephone was black box military. Not only was it underfunded and undersupervised, the grave dangers to participants had been purposefully concealed. Once boots were on the ground, there was no way to back out of the deal, either.

In the first six months of captivity, close to ninety percent of his fellow volunteer test subjects had died from the biological weapon experiments. That Daniel had survived the agonies of infection was a double-edged sword. The experience had turned him into a carrier of weaponized, hemorrhagic dengue flavivirus. He was a walking disease factory. He couldn't return to civilization without spreading the bioengineered plague. He was stuck in the stinking, sweltering jungle.

So much for spending all the money he'd been promised.

So much for dreams of using the experience to become a bestselling writer.

Eventually, the Project Persephone scientists had convinced him that his only hope was cryogenesis, that some point in the future a cure would be found and he'd be free to rejoin humanity.

A little more than a century later, thawed out in a time that still offered no cure, he had signed the third Faustian pact, this one with the worst of the lot, the Lords of Death, also known as the Xibalban.

The other options on the table were death by torture and suicide.

Atapul X, the highest ranking of the Lords of Death, made Commander Casacampo look like Mother Teresa. He was living proof that evil, along with eye and hair color, resided in the genes.

Daniel remembered Atapul X's distant ancestor most vividly. When he had first arrived at the decaying compound's helipad, Atapul Suarez-Denizac had been one of the prisoners held over from the Noriega days, still incarcerated because he was too dangerous to transport. The last surviving inmates of Panama's Devil's Island were glue- and gasoline-sniffing, brain-damaged mass murderers and rapists. They had been sold as a job lot to the Project Persephone scientists, part of the shabby furnishings of the moldy concrete prison, to do with whatever they pleased.

While Daniel was enduring the scientists' experimentation, Suarez-Denizac, a homicidal maniac with delusions of grandeur, had led a violent prisoner escape into the bush. Living in dense forest among the crocodiles, Bushmasters, vampire bats and packs of feral dogs, the escapees had turned cannibal, waylaying and devouring the military police who tried to track them down. By the time the ringleader was recaptured by prison authorities Daniel was already in cryostasis, locked away in the bowels of the main structure. As the legend went, Suarez-Denizac had renamed himself Atapul the First after Armageddon and the fall of the whitecoat compound.

By an unhappy and tragic twist of fate, the psychotic delusions of Suarez-Denizac turned out to be pretty much on the money, as five generations of subsequent history would attest.

Daniel was about to jump down into the hidey-hole he'd prepared when out of the corner of his eye he caught a blur of movement. He turned and through the long strands of dune grass, saw the top of a three-masted ship, sails furled, as it glided to a stop in the otherwise deserted anchorage.

A seagoing trader arriving late to the party. And the skipper and crew couldn't see what was bearing down on the other side of the island.

The unlucky fucks, he acknowledged, were about to get the surprise of their lives.

Chapter Fourteen

The companions fanned out on the empty beach with weapons drawn. Nothing moved along the shore; nothing moved upslope, from the direction of the huts, either. Mildred and the others advanced on Ryan's signal toward a long, low berm of recently turned sand about seventy-five feet above the waterline. The odor of death was coming from that direction, as was the droning of flies.

Neither boded well.

Four shovels lay discarded on the berm.

Covering her nose and mouth with a hand, Mildred looked over the verge of the excavated pit. The open grave was five feet deep and about eight feet across. It held corpses of all ages: men, women, children, babies, piled on top of each other in a tangle. All with bloodied faces and clothes. Some of the dead were horribly bloated.

Mildred saw scurrying movement in the pit: black shadows, long-tailed blurs scattering, darting among the bodies.

Rats.

Krysty groaned through her cupped hand. "There's got to be more than thirty people in there," she said. The prehensile tendrils of her red mutie hair had drawn up into tight ringlets of alarm.

"Massacred." J.B. spit.

Mildred watched the captain's face as he took in the victims. The youthful light went out of his eyes for a second. It just winked out. He looked suddenly as old as the creases in his face.

"What the hell happened?" he exclaimed.

"It doesn't appear they were gunshot," Mildred told him.

"Then what killed them?" Tom said.

There was no way of telling without taking a closer look.

Mildred quickly tied a kerchief over her nose and mouth and then leaned over the edge of the mass grave. She could see petechia on exposed skin everywhere. The red spots stood out against fish-white bellies and backs, every place the sun hadn't browned in life. Although Mildred was a medical doctor she wasn't a diagnostician; she had been a researcher in a specific field—biochemistry related to resuscitation problems in cryogenesis. Med school and residency were more than a century in her past. She wasn't exactly sure what the markings signified, or whether they were connected to the cause of death. Petechia and high fever often went hand in hand.

"Could be any number of things," Mildred said, pulling back. "Some kind of influenza. Bird flu. It could also be a mass poisoning. Red tide. Cigatura. Paralytic shellfish poisoning. Or a predark chemical that somehow ended up in their water or food supply. There's no way to tell for sure without drawing blood and tissues samples from the deceased and putting them through a toxicology lab. And we all know that isn't gonna happen."

"How long have they been dead?" Ryan asked her.

"In this heat? Your guess is as good as mine. Ten hours. Five hours."

"Why did the grave diggers not complete the interment?" Doc said, glancing over at the dropped shovels. "Why did they not cover the bodies?"

"Mebbe they took sick, too," J.B. suggested.

"Could they all be chilled?" Krysty said, looking up at the rows of shanties. "Could the whole ville be wiped out?"

"Perhaps we should take this for a sign," Doc said. "A Biblical visitation of plague is by definition random and puts wayfarers such as ourselves at grave risk. I hasten to remind everyone that the ship awaits…"

Then the sound of moaning wafted down to them from the ville, high-pitched, desperate.

"Not all croaked," Jak said.

Nobody made a move.

"There were a couple hundred people living here," Tom told the companions. "I did a lot of business with them. I liked them. Some were my friends. If anyone's still alive on the island and can be saved, we need to find out. And get them out of here. Mebbe they can tell us what happened."

None of the companions said anything in response.

The moaning continued. Whomever it was, he or she was in terrible agony.

"You can wait here," the skipper told them, "or go back to the *Tempest* if you want, but I'm going ahead."

"I'll come along," Mildred said.

"We'll all come along," Ryan told him.

With Tom on point and weapons up, they moved cautiously toward the first of the shacks. When they looked up the narrow lane that led deeper into the ville, they could see bodies on the ground, left where they fell.

"Biblical," Doc muttered.

Mildred and Tom followed the moans to a one-room shack on the right with delaminating plywood walls and a sheet-metal roof. Beside the doorless doorway, in the shade of the rusting eaves was a black-enameled, knock-off Weber kettle and a pair of white plastic lawn chairs.

Mildred entered first with her ZKR 551 blaster in a two-handed grip. The skipper backed her up with his .45-caliber Smith. There were no windows in the hut. The only light and air came from the doorway and the cracks in the wall seams. The heat and the stench—the coppery smell of blood mixed with fleshy decay and expelled bodily fluids—in the enclosed space was paralyzing. The sauna from hell. The concentrated stink burned Mildred's eyes and the lining of her nose and throat.

The moaner was a woman in her late twenties in a gauzy, badly stained, Hawaiian print dress. She lay on her back on a pallet on the floor. Her dirty blond hair was matted to her skull with sweat and oil.

Mildred knelt beside her, taking in the deathly pale cheeks and chin crusted with dried gore and vomit. She was bleeding from her nose and blood oozed from the corners of her mouth. Every time she exhaled, a rattling sound came from deep in her chest. Her eyes were wide open, but she didn't seem to be aware of Mildred's presence.

Tom leaned over Mildred's shoulder, his blaster lowered to his side. "Oh shit," he said.

"Stay back," she warned him, beads of perspiration rolling down her face.

Glancing around the hut, Mildred counted four supine bodies on the floor. One adult and three children. Only the young woman was still alive; from the distention of their bellies and the ghastly swelling of their limbs, the others were long gone. Was the woman the children's mother? Had she looked on helplessly as all her babies died? Mildred's brain automatically made those tragic connections, although there was no way to tell if they were accurate.

"I can't examine her in here," Mildred said. "It's too dark and the smell's too awful."

"Is it safe to move her?" Ryan said from the outside the hut's doorway.

"Safe for her, or safe for us?" Mildred asked.

"Both," Ryan said.

"I doubt it's going to matter as far as she's concerned," Mildred told him. "It's safe for us if we don't get her blood or other fluids on bare, broken skin. Be very careful picking her up."

Using her clothing, the hem of her skirt and the back of her dress collar, Ryan and Tom hoisted the sick woman up like a sack of grain and lugged her limp form toward the doorway. As they stepped into the wedge of hot sunlight, she jolted awake, then went berserk in their grasp, kicking and thrashing, fighting to get away. Maintaining control with difficulty, Ryan and Tom rushed her into the lane; as they did, blood trailed out from under her skirt in a thick, crimson ribbon. They set her down on the hard-packed sand and stepped well back.

She lay there, eyes open, hands trembling, breathing shallow and fast. The brief, violent struggle seemed to have taken everything out of her.

Doc took in the pale, tortured face, the smeared gore and vomit, and murmured, "Dear sweet Lord."

Holstering her weapon, Mildred knelt again. She back-handed the sweat from her brow to keep it from stinging into her eyes. She noted the petechia on the woman's exposed upper chest and throat, and the facial pallor and cyanosis—blueness—around the mouth. She gently touched the woman's extremities and found them cool and clammy. With difficulty, she found a pulse at the wrist. It was rapid and thready.

Mildred summarized the symptoms in her head: agitation followed by prostration and collapse; evidence of high fever, vomiting and diarrhea; facial pallor and cyanosis of the lips; profuse sweating; bleeding from mouth, nose and gastrointestinal tract. Her pulse was dangerously weak.

"Based on the symptoms she's presenting," she said, "I think it could be some variety of hemorrhagic fever. Yellow or dengue. There's no evidence of redness of the tongue or jaundice to the skin, so that eliminates yellow fever. As I recall, there were four serotypes of the dengue virus, none of which was fatal. But any of the four varieties can escalate into Dengue Hemorrhagic Fever or Dengue Shock Syndrome, which are both very bad news. Without oral and intravenous fluid replacement and supplemental oxygen, the predark mortality rate for DHF and DSS was close to fifty percent."

"You sound somewhat less than confident, my dear," Doc said. "Is there a remaining question regarding the diagnosis?"

"Afraid so," Mildred said. "A real big question. Back in the day only one out of a hundred infected with the virus advanced to the hemorrhagic form of the disease. Based on the body count I'm seeing, it looks like everybody here caught it and most of them have died."

"Can you help her?" Krysty said.

"There's nothing I can do," Mildred said. "Not even with a plasma drip, if I had one. Her platelet count is probably so low at this point, she'd bleed out at the intravenous site. She's in the final stages of circulatory collapse." When Krysty gave her a blank look, she explained further, "Her heart isn't pumping hard enough to move the blood through her body. She's dying."

"Can we catch whatever she's got?" J.B. asked.

"Dengue is a blood-borne virus," she told him. "Infection requires blood-to-blood transmission."

"What means?" Jak asked.

"Mosquitos are the primary vectors of dengue fever, that's how it's spread from person to person," Mildred said. "Look around this place, there's puddles of standing water everywhere. We need to be long gone from here before the skeeters come out."

"Can you hear that?" Tom said. "Can you hear that?"

From around the bend in the lane, from deeper in the ville, came the sounds of feeble groaning.

Multiple groaners.

The skipper didn't wait for the others this time. This time he forged ahead, full speed up the path.

As Harmonica Tom disappeared around the winding turn J.B. grumbled, "He knows we can't sail the radblasted ship without him."

"Then we'd better hurry up and get this over with," Ryan said, urging the companions onward.

Mildred didn't immediately follow her friends deeper into the ville. She remained by the stricken woman's side. She couldn't do anything to help the poor woman, but she was unable to walk away and desert her in her final moments. She had lost everything—everything except her pain. Mildred reached down and put a hand to the clammy forehead. There was no way of telling whether the woman could hear her, but hearing was one of the last senses to fail.

The doctor leaned closer and gently, slowly, stroked the crown of the woman's head. Softly she said, "It's okay for you to give in to it now, honey. It's okay. It's over. It's okay to stop fighting. It's time for you to let go. To float away and be with your darling babies again. It's okay. It's okay…"

As Mildred stroked and reassured, the woman's body relaxed, head to foot. Then the trembling of her hands stopped, as did the shallow, frantic rise and fall of her chest. And she was gone. Gone like a shot to wherever she was bound. Mildred carefully brushed closed the lids of her blankly staring eyes.

Mildred had seen hundreds of people on the verge of death since her reanimation. Despite her extensive medical training, she'd been able to help few if any of them. That experience had not inured her to the death or suffering of others. Death and suffering had always touched her heart before, and she was touched now. The first time Mildred had "died" she'd skated on the experience: she had been unconscious and on an operating table. When the next time came she knew there would be no anesthesia, no oblivion; there probably would be intense pain; and she hoped that someone, even a complete stranger, would be kind enough to tell her goodbye.

Mildred scooped up a handful of sand and as she hurried to join the others, used it to clean her fingers.

After wiping off her hand on the leg of her BDU pants, she unholstered her Czech wheelgun.

Around the bend, she could see more dead people. They were collapsed across the thresholds of the wall-to-wall huts and facedown in the lane, which was no more than fifteen feet wide.

The others had fanned out to either side of the path, and were leapfrogging, checking bodies and looking into the shacks for the source of the continuing moans.

"Hold it! Everybody freeze!" J.B. suddenly shouted. "Don't take another step!"

Everyone stopped and looked at J.B. for an explanation. Standing in the middle of the lane, he reached out with the barrel of his scattergun and pointed to a thin black metal wire running just along the surface of the sand. It was stretched perpendicularly across the path between a pair of ramshackle structures.

"Trip wire," he announced. "This place is mined."

"More wire, over here," Jak said from twenty feet farther up the slope.

"And here, too," Ryan said, staring at the ground in front of him.

Mildred watched Ryan as he looked from trip wire to trip wire, following them to their respective end points.

"It's a radblasted triangle," he said. "Three antipersonnel mines. From the looks of it, they've been rigged in unison. One blows, they all blow. Anything inside the killzone is guaranteed chilled."

The low moaning suddenly got louder. And it was accompanied by a rustling, scraping sound. Mildred looked up the lane, past Jak and Ryan, beyond the trip wires they had located. The noise seemed to be coming from one of the shacks on the left, a hut higher on the hill that they hadn't searched yet.

"We need to back out of here right now," Ryan said in an even voice. "Back out the way we came, very carefully in the same footsteps if we can."

Before they could retreat even three yards, a disheveled man crawled out of a hut on the left. His face was crusted with dried gore, and fresh blood oozed in a wet, red stripe from his nose down over his lips and chin.

Heaving himself forward into the lane, crawling in their direction, the man howled, "Wait! Wait! Help me!"

"Stay where you are!" Tom shouted at him. "Don't come any closer!"

The man kept coming.

Mildred's heart sank as she watched Jak raise his Colt Python and take careful aim at the poor delirious bastard who was about to kill them all.

Before the albino could fire, Tom's stainless-steel Smith & Wesson barked. The gunshot echo resounded up the hillside. The .45 slug kicked the man's head hard to the right, his brains exited in a puff of pink mist mixed with bone fragments. He dropped to the sand, his twitching hand lay six inches from the trip wire.

Mildred saw a wave of dismay and disgust cross the skipper's face as he looked down at the cratered mess he had made of the man's skull.

"Stupid, stupid, stupid…" Tom hissed down at the dead islander. He didn't look happy with himself, either.

There was more moaning and more rustling from the ville above them. Before they could resume their retreat down the path, two very sick men staggered into view.

Raving with fever, coughing, bloody, but still on their feet, they lurched downhill.

"Stop where you are!" the skipper cried, his weapon half raised. There was an edge of desperation in his voice.

Perhaps they couldn't hear him. Perhaps they were hallucinating and didn't understand the words. Perhaps they didn't want to understand.

"Back up!" Ryan shouted to the others. "Everybody back the fuck up!"

Seeing companions in full retreat made the sick men come even faster, wobbling down the lane, straight for the wire.

"Hit the deck!" Tom shouted over his shoulder as he bolted to the right.

The companions split up, diving for cover on either side of the path.

Mildred and Krysty barreled through a doorway shoulder to shoulder. They hit the crude floorboards hard on palms and knees, almost skidding into a trio of bloated human forms.

The trio of deafening explosions overlapped, shaking the ground beneath them. Ball bearings blasted through and splintered the plywood wall like a volley of grapeshot, whining over their heads before slamming through the far side of the shack. Dust and rust rained down from the underside of the corrugated steel roof. Down on the open eyes of the hut's former occupants.

As Mildred and Krysty backed out of the wretched hovel, a dense smoke cloud hung over the lane. As it lifted, all that was left of the two sick men were their legs from the shins down and bloody rags flung against the scorched and partially collapsed fronts of the huts closest to the combined blast.

"Claymores in tight quarters," the Armorer said, shaking his head in disgust. "Nukin' awful."

Ryan turned to the skipper and said, "Have you seen enough?"

Half question. Half accusation.

Tom nodded grimly. "It's too risky to go farther," he said. "The ville's a lost cause. The last time I anchored here there were a lot more people than what we've seen. The others must have taken shelter up in the ship."

"Could they all be dead, Mildred?" Krysty asked.

"From the way this dengue variant seems to operate, dead or dying are both distinct possibilities," Mildred said.

After they had backtracked to the edge of the shantytown, Krysty voiced a question. "I don't understand the connection between the sickness and the laying of the Claymores," she said. "The islanders wouldn't rig their ville with booby traps unless they thought they were about to be overrun, and unless they were leaving it to the invaders."

"The unfinished grave and the discarded shovels imply a hastily diverted purpose," Doc speculated, "as do the strewed corpses and the abandoned dying. I am afraid there is only one logical order of events here. The plague came first, the booby trapping second. No one in full command of their faculties would trip wire a ville that was still inhabited. I think we can assume that circumstances beyond the islanders' control forced them to stop dealing with the outbreak of disease and its aftermath—tending the stricken and burying their dead—in order to lay explosive traps for their enemies and then withdraw to the relative safety of the grounded vessel."

"But that would mean…" Krysty began.

"We're in deep shit," Ryan finished.

As if in confirmation of that fact, a heavy machine gun on the far side of the dunes opened fire with a sudden, furious clatter.

Somewhere in the distance out to sea, huge engines bellowed to life.

"Come on!" Ryan shouted, waving the others after him as he turned away from the ville and stormed toward the slope opposite, beelining for the top of the island's sandy spine, an elevation that would give an unobstructed view of the southwest and the source of all the racket.

Mildred fell in behind J.B., scrambling up the steep, shifting, boot-sucking grade. No one questioned Ryan's decision to recce. They needed to know what they were up against before they could craft a response.

Cresting the top of the dunes, the companions had their answer.

Seven vessels approached the southwestern tip of Padre Island. The fleet was about two miles offshore, and closing. Four large sailing ships. Three massive tugboats with black smoke pouring up from their diesel stacks. The sailboats had all their canvas unfurled and were beating against the wind in a staggered formation, moving to the left for the Gulf side of the island while the tugs bore straight in for the point, three abreast.

At the edge of the island below them, automatic fire continued. Mildred could see the gunsmoke pouring over the top of the low, makeshift, fortified emplacement.

Engines roaring, the three tugs abruptly changed course, splitting up to divide the gunpost's effective fire.

"They're out of range," J.B. said, grimacing as he

adjusted the weight of his M-4000 on its shoulder sling. "That gunner is just wasting ammo."

"Mebbe he's trying to warn them off," Krysty said.

"If he is, it's not working," Ryan said. He passed the minibinocs to the captain. "Do you recognize the ships, Tom? Do you know what's going on?"

"Not a clue," the skipper admitted after he had a quick look-see. "Especially about those diesel-powered boats. Where the hell did they get enough fuel to run them? How did they get so close to the island without starting them up? They don't have masts for sails. One thing's for sure, if those ships were friendlies, the islanders wouldn't have started shooting at them unprovoked."

"It would appear the islanders aren't all incapacitated," Doc said as the machine-gun clatter continued. "A show of a defense is better than no defense at all."

Without warning, in a blur of pale hair and limbs, Jak jumped backward a good three feet, bumping into the long-legged Victorian before he could shuffle out of the way. Inexplicably, the albino aimed his .357 Magnum Colt Python at the empty ground directly in front of him.

"For nuke's sake, Jak, what is it?" Ryan said.

"Something under sand," Jak told him without taking his red eyes off the target. "Not right. Something moved."

His pistol in front of him, Jak edged forward. He carefully dropped to one knee and brushed the surface of the sand with his palm, revealing the top of a fractured-off piece of plywood. Around the ragged edges, the grains of sand funneled away, like through an hourglass.

Into a big hole beneath.

Ryan signaled Jak to stand and take a step back. Then looking over the sights of his SIG, he said, "Whoever you are under the board, you've got seven blasters pointed at you. If you've got a blaster and it's in your hand when we pull the lid off, we're going to shoot you to shit."

"Don't fire. I'm not armed," said a thin, muffled voice from the underside of the board.

Using the tip of his sheathed swordstick, Doc deftly flipped the plywood hatch out of the way.

All the blasters drew a bead on the diminutive figure cowering in the narrow, neck-deep pit.

Camouflage do-rag askew, the man looked up into the muzzle of J.B.'s 12-gauge and whimpered. Slowly he raised empty hands. There were angry skeeter bites on his face and bare arms. Dozens and dozens of them.

"Are you sick?" Mildred demanded at once. "Are you sick like the others?"

"N-no. I feel fine."

"Get the fuck out of there, and be quick about it," Ryan said.

As the do-ragger scrambled from the pit, J.B., Doc and Krysty moved well out of the way, giving Jak a clear background for a close range chill shot with his .357 Magnum.

Soft-looking, big brown eyes and too-long lashes undercut the effect of a square, clefted, beard-stubbled chin.

Mildred's immediate impression was *mama's boy*.

"I've never seen you here before," Tom said. "Who the hell are you?"

The machine gun below stopped chattering, either because its magazine was empty or because the gunner had finally realized the enemy was too far away to hit.

"I'm Daniel Desipio. I'm a Fire Talker," the man told them. As he spoke he again raised his hands in submission. "A lot of people in the ville came down sick. I was trying to help them…"

"You were helping them down that hole?" Ryan said sarcastically.

"Islanders saw the pirates coming and those what could still walk hightailed it up to the freighter. Because I wasn't of their blood, the bastards wouldn't let me in there, so I had to find my own place to hide."

"How do you know they're pirates?" Tom said.

The machine gun on the distant point opened up again, at a steady, rip-roaring 600 rounds a minute. There was still no response from the oncoming tugboats.

"I don't know for certain that's who they are," Daniel said. "But it sure seems like a safe guess."

"What about the sickness that killed all those people down in the ville?" Mildred asked.

"A crewman off a trader ship came down with it first, right after I arrived," Daniel said. "Then just about everybody else came down with it. And then they started dying off. All in the space of three or four days."

"I hasten to remind everyone that we could have easily avoided this unpleasantness…" Doc said.

"Oh shut up, Doc," Krysty said.

"What's done is done," Mildred agreed. "What we need are some viable options to either dying from the fever or dying from gunshots."

"We can still escape," Tom assured them. "There's still time. If we weigh anchor and continue south we've got the wind behind us."

"You mean, run straight into the bastards, and not away from them?" J.B. said dubiously.

"I can scoot *Tempest* along the edge of the mainland

shore, right past those tugs but far enough away so they can't cut us off. The pirate sailboats will be on the other side of the island by then. They won't see us leaving the bay and when they do finally see us we'll be on the horizon line. We'll have such a lead they'll never catch us. My guess is they won't even try."

"I don't like the looks of that," J.B. said, nodding seaward.

The three tugs had stopped their forward movement, and with idling engines, had taken up stationary positions roughly a mile and a half offshore. They were spaced more than seven hundred yards apart in the lee of the island, on water that was flat and glassy.

"Me, either," Ryan said. "We'd better get cracking."

"What about him?" Jak said, gesturing with the Python's muzzle to indicate the hands-up Fire Talker.

Their bug-bit prisoner looked woeful and desperate. There was something practiced about his pathetic, pleading expression. When he batted his eyelashes, it made Mildred's skin crawl.

Nobody else was buying it, either.

"He's still got his hidey-hole," Ryan said. "Let him jump back in it."

A bright flash and big puff of smoke from the forward deck of the middle tugboat caught Mildred's eye. Ryan and Krysty saw it, too. A fraction of an instant later similar flashes and puffs of smoke appeared on the bows of the other two tugs. Before anybody could shout a warning, a full four seconds before the hollow whump of the reports rolled over them, mortar shells were already screaming down on the island.

A trio of HE explosions rocked the ground. The detonations were thunderclap loud, and Mildred felt the concussions in the center of her chest, like the beats of an alien heart. Two of the mortar hits fell one hundred feet to either side of the distant machine-gun emplacement, their blast rings overlapping; the third landed a fraction of a second later, in the middle of the roof, blowing out the sidewalls and collapsing the ceiling.

Needless to say, the machine-gun fire abruptly stopped.

"Shit!" Tom said. "Shit, come on!" Then he took off running back the way they had come.

The companions followed him, triple time. Mildred brought up the rear, keeping tabs on the injured J.B. who, despite her concern, seemed to be moving along just fine. Behind her, the roar of the tugs' engines grew louder and louder as the ships advanced on the now undefended shore. She and the others skidded, stumbled and slewed down the loose sand of the dunes, scrambling to reach the beach and harbor.

When the mortars resumed firing, the explosions started walking north, taking giant steps up the island's spine, toward the ville. The first three explosions fell behind them. The second three leapfrogged the dunes and landed ahead and below, between them and the shanty-town. The shells detonated on the flanks of the slope with brilliant flashes and plumes of flying sand and smoke. The concussions that rolled uphill felt like snapkicks to the gut. Even though Mildred ran with her stomach tensed, they almost knocked the breath out of her. Hot shrapnel sizzled and whined all around, snicking into the sandy hillside, and the acrid stink of burned Comp B filled the air.

There had to be more than just the three bow mortars firing, Mildred thought as she struggled to keep up with

J.B. There had to be at least a half dozen cutting loose simultaneously. The companions were caught between the dunes at their rear and the high explosives in front. There was no cover ahead, but there was no going back.

They couldn't stop running.

More mortar shells screamed overhead, raining down on the ville. The pirate gunners had it zeroed in. The shantytown came apart before her eyes, pounded by a concentrated barrage of HE. In the wake of blinding flashes, sheet-metal roofs and plywood walls cartwheeled skyward, as did an ever-widening column of dust and smoke. The explosions started triggering the Claymore booby traps, which unleashed thousands of ball-bearing projectiles.

They were running straight into a meatgrinder.

The route to the *Tempest* was cut off.

"We'll never make it to the beach!" Ryan shouted at Tom's back. "Go right! Turn right!"

Tom led them away from his ship, and their only hope of escape, away from the harbor and certain death. He raced along the lower slopes of the dunes, heading for the grounded freighter. It was the only way open.

Then the explosions in the ville suddenly stopped. The pirate mortars went silent for a moment.

Hearing a grunt of effort behind her, Mildred glanced over her shoulder and saw the Fire Talker was right on her heels.

Chapter Fifteen

Chewing the stub of an unlit cigar, barefoot Commander Guillermo Casacampo leaned out over the rail of the bridge deck of his flagship, called the *Ek'-Way* in Mayan—the *Black Transformer,* in English. Casacampo's dreadlocks stood piled atop his head in a ten-inch-high, lopsided beehive. The stacked coils of felted hair were interlaced with gold bracelets and necklaces, and his long beard had been braided into stiff, six-inch-pigtails, which were bound at the ends with close wraps of brightly colored thread. Ground-in dirt and oil blackened his cheeks and forehead; the eyeliner that rimmed his eyes gave them a sunken, raccoon-like appearance. The commander of the Matachìn fleet wore red longjohns with a sewn-on chest pocket, and a parrot-green scarf knotted at the side of his very short, very thick neck.

The steady, rhythmic beat of the coxswain's drum drifted up to him from the stern, and thirty oarlocks creaked in counterpoint as human power inexorably levered the massive ship forward.

Looking down the starboard flank of the flat-black–painted tug, Casacampo couldn't see the conscripts from Browns ville and Matamoros ville. They were hidden from view beneath a crude, corrugated steel awning that ran over the scuppers, fully two-thirds the length of the one-hundred-foot boat; a similar structure shaded the port side of the ship. The awnings protected the bare-headed, bare-shouldered captives. The Matachìn didn't give a damn about the comfort of their galley slaves; the slaves just lasted a little longer if they were shielded from the sun and rain.

If the commander couldn't see the tightly packed ranks of rowers below him, he couldn't miss their long oars, dipping and stroking in unison to the metronomic beat of the drum. There were fifteen oars on either side of the ship, and three rowers were assigned to each.

A total of ninety prisoners working in chains.

Sleeping in chains.

Eating in chains.

Shitting in chains.

All of them doomed.

Two members of Casacampo's crew paced along the inside edge of the awning, closely monitoring the performance of the starboard "propulsion unit." Because they were mere grunts and not line officers, their dreads weren't piled high. Instead they hung like nests of flattened snakes to the middle of their wide backs. What gold the crewmen had glittered and flashed around the ankle tops of their heavy-soled boots, garlands of chain that had been taken from nameless, faceless victims as trophies of conquest. The crewmen's hands rested on the pommels of scabbarded machetes and on the butts of hip-holstered, knock-off Government Colts—.45-caliber Obregons and Ballester-Molinas—relics from Mexico and Argentina, respectively. Braided leather quirts, short but effective motivational tools, were tucked under their belts.

As the commander watched, the third oar from the

stern suddenly seemed to lose its steam. Because it didn't move forward quickly enough, its paddle hooked on the shaft of the oar behind. Instead of immediately untangling and reestablishing the stroke rhythm, the two oars remained locked, which tipped the balance of thrust to the port side and caused the ship to veer off course to starboard.

The problem was easily fixed.

As easy as changing a fouled spark plug.

The commander hand-signaled the coxswain and the drumming stopped. When the drumming stopped, the slaves on both sides of the ship stopped pulling on their oars. Break time.

The Matachìn crewmen quickly unchained an exhausted rower from the third starboard oar and dragged him out from under the awning. The slave didn't fight them. He was a spent force, his shoulders welted and bloodied from strokes of the lash, as weak as a kitten after so many nonstop days of effort. As the crew manhandled him aft, toward the stern's low transom, he made shrill and unpleasant noises, pleading for his life.

Commander Casacampo took the cigar stub from his mouth, then hawked and spit a viscous yellow gob a remarkable distance downwind.

In the grasp of the crewmen, the slave craned his neck around, looking up at the pirate leader. His expression communicated his mortal fear: he knew what was coming.

There was no thumbs-up or thumbs-down from the bridge deck.

Show no mercy was a given.

The Matachìn threw the slave belly-down across the stern gunwhale. While one held him pinned from behind in a double armlock, the other unscabbarded a machete. The top of the sixteen-inch blade ended in rear-pointing hook, a crescent moon of razor-sharp steel. Originally designed to facilitate the cutting of sugar cane, the hook was even more efficient at unzipping human guts.

Wielded by a powerful arm, the machete caught the sunlight as it flashed up, then fell in a blur. There was no hesitation. No "would you like a blindfold?" No "do you have any last words?"

If anything, it resembled the killing of a chicken.

In a single strike of the blade's main edge, with a precise application of force, the pirate hacked open the back of the slave's neck, stopping short of completely severing his spine. The horrendous blow energized its helpless target. It set the still-living man to squealing and kicking as the gaping wound spouted geysers of blood. The two Matachìn held him trapped and bent over the stern while his rich red ch'ul—his "soul stuff"—poured over his face and head and into the hungry sea. After no more than minute, the piercing cries faded to silence and the slave went limp in their grasp. His chillers then grabbed him by the ankles and launched him headfirst into the water.

The body floated away spread-eagled and facedown.

The coxswain rolled aside his timekeeper's drum and raised the hatch in the stern deck. It opened onto the wide, windowless hold where the replacement slaves were stowed until needed. Kneeling on either side of the hatch, the other two pirates bent over, reached down, and hauled up a blinking, dazed and terrified slave by the armpits.

The man was in his early twenties and had a wispy brown chin beard. Already stripped to the waist, his sun-tanned arms, face and neck were a stark contrast to his fish-white belly. Before the crewmen chained him to the oar, they used their quirts on his back, to make sure they had his attention.

Although the replacement rower looked plenty strong and reasonably well nourished, there was no telling how long he would last pulling an oar. Sometimes the strongest-looking ones died first, and the weaker-looking ones kept going and going.

The coxswain glanced down into the hold. Pointing with his finger he counted its occupants, one by one. He held up his hand to the bridge.

The commander pulled a little leather-backed notebook from the chest pocket of his longjohns. As he chewed the butt of his cigar, he corrected the tally with a pencil stub. One down, five to go. He was pleased at the attrition rate. They were running out of replacements just as they prepared to take on a new batch from Padre Island. When the island was theirs, his crew would evaluate the remaining survivors from Brownsville. Those who weren't worth feeding and watering would be dispatched by machete. The entire process was very well organized. It had to be due to the nature of the expedition. Limited space onboard a relatively small number of ships meant that stores were restricted, which created a balancing act between acquisition and consumption and miles traveled.

Because the Matachìn had been employing slave galleys for almost a century, and had used them extensively in their northerly expansion up from the Lantic side of the Panama Canal, the basics of care and feeding had been worked out by trial and error, what in the twentieth century would have been called a cost-benefit ratio. How many days did galley slaves actually have to be fed? What was the minimum amount of water required to sustain them at peak efficiency? A precise schedule dispensed food and water, and the dispensation was scrupulously kept track of in a logbook. Of course there were no rowers on the sailboats, which meant there was room for the stowing of fleet supplies, and of course, the accumulated booty.

New slaves were the best cost-benefit: they brought their own energy reserves with them, which could be drained for days without replenishment. The number of arms and backs necessary to move the tugs depended on wind and tide, as well as the combined strength of the rowers. But generally speaking, if there were fewer than twenty-five rowers to a side it overtaxed the entire system, simultaneously providing meager headway and wearing out the individual component parts too soon. A full complement of healthy, minimally fed slaves could last as long as a couple of weeks, again depending on natural factors: wind, tide and sea state.

The commander put the dog-earred notebook back in his longjohn pocket and waved at the coxswain to resume his drumming. When the beat started up, the oars dipped lively, in time, and in perfect unison. They were soon making excellent speed against the light wind. Close to ten knots, Casacampo guessed. There was nothing like a summary execution to put the slaves in the mood for exercise.

Every once in a while they needed a graphic reminder that they were an expendable commodity.

If for some reason, the commander wasn't able to find replacement slaves en route, he did have a quantity of diesel to burn. But he watched his fuel gauges with as much care as his food stocks. Unlike the case of food, there was nowhere to get more diesel in the six hundred miles of coastline the search and destroy expedition had covered. If he'd been able to fill up the *Ek'-Way*'s three thousand gallon tank before he'd left port, his range under engine power would have averaged somewhere close to five thousand miles. But a fill-up was not in the cards. Accordingly, he saved his precious store of diesel for maneuvering during battle and for emergencies. The three tugs under his command had a total fuel load of just under a thousand gallons. Enough to get them all the way home from Tierra de la Muerte, but if they returned to Veracruz on fumes, the fuel burned would deduct from the success of the expedition. The Lords of Death valued economy in all things, except of course human life. People were a self-generating resource.

Casacampo turned away from the stern and looked into the wind, toward the low island. His four pursuit craft were streaking away hard to the southeast under full sail. Soon they would be looping around the far end of the island with the wind behind them. They would contain any attempts at escape by ship to the north.

A cluster of distant, muffled explosions made him look in the direction of the island. He watched as a column of smoke coiled up from the other side of the ridge of dunes. Before the smoke could climb high in the sky, the prevailing wind bent it horizontal and sent it scudding toward him.

Casacampo grinned around the gooey stump of his cigar. It was clear whose side the gods were on.

Without haste, the commander ducked into an archway

in the steel superstructure. Directly ahead was the riveted steel door leading to his quarters. He climbed the short, steep flight of metal steps on the right, up to the pilothouse on the third story above the tug's main deck. Standing at the helm of the *Ek'-Way*, in front of the windshield and wraparound instrument panel, was his second in command, Captain Roberto Dolor.

The tall, leanly muscled, caramel-skinned man turned as Casacampo entered and gave him a respectful nod of greeting. Dolor had a wandering left eye that never tracked with its opposite number. At times—when he was either very happy or very angry—Dolor look utterly and dangerously insane. Because he was a Matachìn officer of lower rank, his pile of dreads was less spectacular. Three coils of felted hair, instead of Casacampo's seven. And it was laced with fewer golden trinkets.

Dolor had already donned his ribbed black, chest, hip and shin-boot top armor. Back in the day it had been made in Tampico from Kevlar and tempered steel trauma plate.

The final touch of Dolor's battle dress, a seam-split garment stained with blood, semen and tears, lay draped over the back of the navigator's armchair. Into every fight the captain wore the dead woman's shift. He wore it pulled over his chest armor; it was so short on his body that it looked like a long shirt. To his opponents in combat its feminine cut and faded floral print, and its awful stains were animalistic obscenity. To the pirate captain, the ruined dress was yet another badge of status, symbolic of having seized and taken the sustaining and nourishing spiritual force, the *itz*, of a defenseless victim.

The Matachìn had their own set of standards. They

were judged not by the heights of their good deeds, but by the depths of the bad.

Tucked into niches and crannies in the low, pilothouse ceiling, in the niches and crannies between the clusters of exposed power conduit and electronic cables were a wide assortment of Central American fetishes. There were amulets made of feathers and human small bones stripped of flesh and sinew and bleached dead-white. There were brightly beaded pouches of copal incense. And dangling by their ornate little head dresses, flesh-colored, molded plastic statuettes of the Lords of Death.

Fanged.

Snarling.

Squatting like pink toads over the hieroglyph for *yol,* the secret gate of Xibalba, the Place of Awe.

In their left hands the Lords brandished ceremonial stone cleavers, which dripped hand-painted, enamel blood down their forearms. In their left hands they held severed human heads by the hair; the ragged neck stumps were also hand-painted red. The doll collection represented Atapul the First through Atapul the Tenth. The statuettes were virtually identical, except for the raised Roman numerals on their gold-painted breastplates that identified them individually.

The Mayan legend of the Lords of Death was older than recorded time. From their kingdom in the Otherworld of Xibalba, rumored to exist somewhere beneath the earth, they held dominion over human sickness, starvation, fear, destitution, pain and ultimately death. The other residents of the Otherworld—spirits, ghosts of ancestors, goblins— were compelled to rise up and carry out the will of these dark gods on the surface. According to the ancient myth, the Hero Twins, Hunuhapu and Xbalanke, succeeded in tricking and killing all twelve of the Lords of Death. Which left their avatars of sickness and disease stranded and without direction in the mortal plane.

In the Mayan legends, resurrection was not unheard of; indeed, the promise of same was how the Hero Twins fooled and destroyed the Lords of Death. After watching the Twins restore life to a dead dog, a person and themselves with their magic dance, the Lords asked the Twins to kill them, too, then bring them back. The Twins slaughtered the Lords, all right, but they left them dead. For five thousand years the Lords of Xibalba stayed that way, until the Armageddon of *El Norte* resurrected them.

Through the pilothouse's front windshield, Padre Island loomed large.

Casacampo referred to the crude, hand-drawn map that lay atop the control console. A captured resident of Browns ville had been convinced under torture to set down the major features of the island, including the hardened blaster emplacements, and the position of the harbor and the ville, neither of which could be seen from a southwesterly approach. Based on the map, the smoke had to be coming from the ville. It gave his Matachìn gunners something to aim at.

The commander picked up a laser range-finder and took aim at the nearest point of land.

Reading the LED display, he told Dolor, "Another three hundred yards and we'll be well within range."

The commander checked the row of gauges that measured the status of the ship's electric power, which came from solar panels on the pilothouse roof when the engines were not in use. The batteries were fully charged.

He took the cigar out of the corner of his mouth, raised the microphone to his lips and pressed the transmit button on the ship-to-ship radio. "Attention," he said. "Attention. *Xibal Be* and *White Bone Snake*. This is *Ek'-Way*. Take positions twelve hundred meters from target one. Prepare your mortars."

As he released the transmit button, waiting for acknowledgment from the other two tugs, a distant clatter from the shore rolled over them.

"Machine gun," Dolor said.

"I can hear it," the commander said, popping the stogie back into his mouth and squinting at the island's southwestern point. "Is it shooting at us? I can't see where the bullets are landing."

He picked up a pair of high-powered binocs from the console and scanned the water ahead. It took a moment for him to find them. The slugs were riffling the surface like a school of tiny bait fish some four hundred yards away. Despite coming up that short on its target, the machine gun continued to fire. Shaking his head, Casacampo passed the binocs over to his captain.

Roberto peered through the lenses and then laughed out loud. *"Pitigallos,"* he said, snickering as he lowered the binocs.

Casacampo spoke into the radio microphone again. *"Xibal Be* and *White Bone Snake,* start your engines. Advance to your attack positions at once. Await my command to begin firing."

Dolor cranked up the *Ek'-Way*'s powerful twin diesels, which set the entire ship vibrating.

Turning the switch on the radio from ship-to-ship to loud-hailer, the commander addressed his crew through speakers mounted fore and aft. "Ship oars," he said. "Ship oars. Break out the mortars and prepare for firing."

Through the pilothouse's rear bank of windows, past the davited inflatable rafts they used as landing craft, the commander had a clear view of the aft deck. While four of his crew saw to the stowing of the oars, four others unshackled eight slaves and set them to work on the artillery. They broke out two XM252 mortars from the lockers behind the superstructure. It took two slaves to carry each set of separated launch tube, mount and aluminum base plate. And another four to carry the metal crates of stacked HE M374A3 ammunition.

Casacampo walked around the wheelhouse windows, following as a pair of slaves headed for the bow with their disassembled mortar. There, at the direction of the Matachìn gunner, they fitted the base into one of the steel keyhole fittings inset in the foredeck. Then the mount was secured on the base and the launch tube to the mount.

A second mortar was positioned amidships on the tug's port side.

As the crates of 81 mm HE shells were laid close to hand, Dolor eased back on the throttle and took the engines out of forward gear. He said, "That's twelve hundred meters, Commander."

"Hold us steady."

The water was as flat as a pancake, not even a slight rise and fall. The breeze was a constant six knots. Perfect conditions.

Through the loud-hailer Casacampo said, "Lorenzo, line up your shot!"

Sighting on the MG post through the mortar's M53 elbow telescope, the Matachìn gunner took his distance measurement, gauged the speed of the headwind, then quickly adjusted the angle of the launch tube to drop a shell on the target. When he was satisfied, he gave the pilothouse a wave.

Back on the ship-to-ship, Casacampo said, "*Xibal Be, White Bone Snake,* are you ready?"

Both tug captains reported that they were in their designated holding positions and ready to open fire.

"Fire away," Casacampo told them. He leaned forward and gave his waiting crewman the hand signal to drop one on the target.

The bow gunner slid the shell down the pipe, aluminum fins first, ducking to the side and covering his ears as the round whistled away. The tugs a half mile on either side of them fired their mortars, as well. All three rounds flew in high looping arcs toward the beach.

The commander watched through binocs as the gunpost was bracketed, then vanished in a flare of orange and black. It took a full second for the sounds of the explosions to reach the tug.

So much for that.

It was impossible to tell which of the three shells hit the target. Down in the *Ek'-Way*'s bow, the gunner Lorenzo was thumping his chest, grinning from ear to ear, and nodding like he *was* the man. The nice shooting wasn't a surprise to the commander. It wasn't luck, either. Casacampo's mortar crews practiced endlessly, firing ship to shore in varying seas and wind conditions.

"Pull in closer, five hundred meters," the commander told Dolor. Then he repeated the same order into the radio microphone.

There was always the remote possibility that the island-

ers had something with more range and punch—a cannon
or recoilless rifle—and they were holding it back for a
surprise. If they missed with their first cannon shot, the
target tug would be off and running under engine power,
making an accurate second shot impossible, this while the
other two stationary ships zeroed in on the gun's location.
The Matachìn had practiced that maneuver, too.

From what he'd seen in Matamoros ville and Browns
ville, Casacampo didn't think much of the Deathlanders'
ability to mount a defense or turn back an attack. The
measure of a civilization, in his opinion, was the skill and
bravery of its warriors, and the fighters of Deathlands
were clearly overmatched. They had no style, no technology. No prowess. No ingenuity. All their glory was in
the dead past.

It amused him that more than a century ago, *El Norte*
had destroyed itself with its own terrible weapons, essentially committing suicide by proxy, and at the same time,
by the same means it had managed to release the Lords of
Death from five thousand years of limbo, of nonexistence.

Casacampo returned to the windows overlooking the
stern. Some of his Matachìn were sitting on the gun-
whales, sharpening their machetes' gut hooks with files
and whetstoning the long edges. Others were in the
process of putting on their body armor or setting out the
weapons and ammunition for the coming assault.

As the other two tugs approached the second firing positions, their complements of Matachìn marines were
doing the same thing.

Casacampo had a total of sixty seasoned fighters under
his command. Thanks to the intercession of the Lords of
Death, that was more than enough for the task at hand. The

Lords' invisible weapons were their *duendes*, their *enanos*, dwarves and goblins who took the terrible sickness with them wherever they went. An invincible strategy. It lowered the odds to insure victory, weakening the opposition to the point where it could easily be subdued by a small Matachìn landing party and the survivors then enslaved. A certain percentage of those stricken by the Xibalban disease were only mildly impaired; a smaller percentage were completely unaffected. They were the ones harvested to make up the galley crews.

The Lords had used its goblins and its dominion over human suffering and fear to great effect over the past hundred years, building an empire of city states along the Atlantic coast of Central America. In terms of *enanos,* the current expedition had been costly. Between the battles for Matamoros ville and Browns ville, five of the six he had brought along on the voyage had been lost. It was only a temporary set back, though. The Lords of Death could always make more.

Looking down on his fighters, the commander knew he felt exactly what they felt.

Exhilaration.

He sensed what they sensed.

The smell of blood.

The Matachìn were demons in the service of greater demons. In return for their allegiance the Lords of Death promised everlasting pillage in life; in death, everlasting delight. Their savage spirits would reside among the towering pyramids and vast acropolises of Xibalba.

"Five hundred meters, Commander," Dolor said to his back.

It was time to close the trap.

"Bring us broadside to the ville," Casacampo said.

As the *Ek'-Way* came about, through the loud-hailer he ordered Lorenzo to adjust the bow gun's launch tube ninety degrees, this to bring the mortar to bear on the new target.

Switching over to ship-to-ship, he gave the same commands to the other captains and gun crews.

When he received confirmation from the other tugs that everything was ready, he ordered the mortars to drop seven rounds a minute on the target for three minutes, then hold fire and await his further orders.

The firing began at once.

Six rounds per volley.

There wasn't much to see as the shells rained down on the ville. The target was hidden behind the high dunes. As the erratic booms of the barrage rolled over the water, black smoke billowed over the crest of the ridge.

Casacampo turned to his own preparations for combat. From a locker in a corner of the pilothouse, he took out his personal firearm. The Brazilian-made LAPA had an M-16-style carrying handle that housed its flip-type rear sight; the front sight was an elevated, protected post. Very stubby from pistol grip to muzzle, it looked like a handgun with a fixed, plastic shoulder stock. The LAPA was chambered for 9 mm Parabellum rounds and held thirty-two bullets in its curved mag. The commander checked the clip to make sure it was topped off, then reinserted it into the weapon and collected six more full mags from the locker.

At the bottom of the cabinet was his machete, pearl-handled and scabbarded in black ballistic nylon. He unsheathed the gleaming blade, which was engraved on both sides with the hieroglyph of the Black Transformer, the symbolic gate of Xibalba. At the tip was a cruel steel horn, razor sharp on its inside edge—the Matachìns' signature gut hook.

Setting the machete aside, Casacampo took out his custom-fitted, black chest and back plates, and black leg and shin guards. After stepping into and lacing up his steel-toed boots, he began buckling on the ribbed body armor, all of which had been blessed by the Lords of Death.

He was dressing for a very short, very one-sided war.

Chapter Sixteen

Even though the mortar shells had stopped falling, Ryan could still feel the aftereffects of the too-close explosions. The soles of his feet tingled down to the tips of his toes, there was a high-pitched ringing in his left ear, and a slight numbness to that side of his face. He ran on with grim determination, knowing there was nothing ahead for him and the companions but a bit more breathing room, mebbe some time to think, time to come up with another escape plan—if they made it to the freighter before the barrage resumed.

He had seen the north end of the island on the way down and he knew it didn't offer an obvious way out of their predicament. The waters were a jigsaw puzzle of shallow, sandy reefs. There was no protected moorage, so there were no boats tied up offshore. There weren't any boats beached there, either.

The grounded freighter above them had all the makings of a death ship. Based on what he'd seen in the ville, he figured it was likely filled with sick people and corpses. Once the companions ventured belowdecks, there was a better than even chance they would never come out. The ship was like a box canyon, only man-made and with a steel lid. The ear-splitting concussions and the flying shrap and ball bearings hadn't offered them a choice in the

matter. Even if they could have reached it, the channel sep-
arating the island from the mainland was far too wide to
try to swim.

With the *Tempest* cut off, there was no place else to go.

The moment the shells started pounding the ville Ryan
guessed what the pirates were up to. Their strategy was
designed to drive everyone who could walk or run out of
the shantytown, up the hill and into the grounded ship.
Otherwise they would have shelled the shit out of it, too.

With an effort of will, Ryan pushed a premonition of
disastrous defeat out of his head. They had been in worse
spots, he reasoned, or at least nearly as bad, many times
before and they'd always found a way to pull through. At
least this time they were still all together, they had their
blasters, they had plenty of bullets, and the route to the
freighter was temporarily open.

Running behind Harmonica Tom, Ryan and the others
started up the flank of the immense dune on which the
vessel sat. Above them, an even steeper ramp, about
ten feet wide, and sculpted of hard-packed sand, led all
the way to the top deck and the gate in the freighter's rail
amidships.

If Tom knew where he was going, he also knew the immediate danger they faced. As soon as they hit the base of
the compacted ramp, he started yelling up at the ship and
waving his arms, "It's me! Don't shoot! It's me!"

As Ryan started up the ramp he saw the reason for
Tom's concern: rows of irregular, vertical slits had been
hacked or blowtorched into the freighter's steel hull plates.
They were maybe five inches wide and two feet high.

Blasterports.

From all the bullet impact dimples and spawled paint

around them, this wasn't the first time Padre Island had
come under attack.

Ryan couldn't see a rifle muzzle behind every slit, and
most of the muzzles he did see weren't tracking them as
they climbed. They were stationary. That all the blasters
weren't manned didn't matter. More than enough moved
to do the job. Once an enemy boarding party started up
the ramp, there was no escape, nowhere to jump, nowhere
to hide. The entire length of the ramp was a kill zone.

Tom still was yelling and waving his arms as he cleared
the gate at the top of the ramp. Ryan stepped onto the ship
beside the skipper. Looking back, he watched as the others
rushed through the gate, one by one.

Only after Mildred reached the deck did he realize
they'd picked up some unwanted baggage.

"I thought I told you to jump back down that radblasted
hole," he said to the Fire Talker.

The tagalong was out of breath—or pretended to be—
and didn't respond. He shuffled to the far side of Doc, as
far away from Ryan as he could get and still remain under
the companions' protection.

"Where is everybody?" Krysty said as she looked up
and down the vast, 250-yard-long top deck.

There was no movement anywhere, but the line of sight
was blocked by rows of rusting cargo containers stacked
three high in places. Crude ladders made of lashed-
together iron pipe leaned against the open doors of some
of the topmost boxes. As the vessel's cargo booms had
been torn away, there was no way to lower any of the
massive containers to the deck to get at the contents. The
islanders had to climb up to them using the ladders and
carry or rope-lower the goods.

Ryan looked down a long, canyon-like aisle between the stacks to the stern. Looming over everything, still flying the tattered Lone Star flag, was the bridge tower. It had looked more or less intact from the water; up close it was an absolute ruin. The six-story structure was laced with a million rust holes. Ryan could see light all the way through it, front to back. Every window frame was empty of glass. It had taken a terrible beating on nukeday, and the beating had continued for a century after.

"We need to do a quick recce of the situation," Tom said, waving the others after him as he headed for the bow, which rested on the peak of the dune and stuck up higher than the stern.

Ryan kicked through ankle-deep piles of rubbish: discarded packaging from the contents of the containers, and dunnage from the holds: plastic, cardboard, pieces of broken wooden pallets, foam pellets. The trash collected in drifts along the scuppers and around bases of the lowermost containers.

Some of the bottom container doors were open.

There were no bodies evident, outside or inside the boxes.

From the ship's bow, they looked almost straight down on the ville. Black smoke poured off the flattened ruins. Low fires still burned. Ryan guessed that more than a hundred mortar rounds had been dropped on it. Between that and the Claymores, there wasn't much left.

Tom directed their attention in the opposite direction, to the sailboats scooting northeast, past the island on the Gulf side. "The bastards are heading for Aransas Pass," he said. "They're going to circle around the line of reefs and come down the waterway to the harbor, same way we did."

"That's bad?" Mildred said.

"Good and bad," Tom replied. "Good because it gives us more time to reach the *Tempest*. They've got to beat against the wind to make the pass. Bad because they're going to have the wind at their backs once they one-eighty and bear down on us. If we don't have a big head start, we're in trouble."

Much closer in, the trio of tugs was moving north under engine power, to about a half mile off the beach, directly opposite the stranded freighter.

"They're tightening the noose, dammit," J.B. said.

"Can we fight them off?" Krysty asked. "Do we have a chance?"

"Depends on what they do next," Ryan said.

"Do you not mean what they *value?*" Doc said. "If these brigands intend to take whatever's in all these containers as spoils of war, they're unlikely to turn their mortars on the ship."

"If they don't want what the islanders have," J.B. said, "this is going to be a piss poor place to mount a defense."

"We need to find out where the other islanders are and how many are in shape to help us fight," Ryan said.

"This way…" Tom told them, turning back for the stern.

"Keep your blasters holstered," Ryan warned the others. "Let's not give these island folks the wrong idea."

"Or an excuse," J.B. added.

They proceeded down the deck alongside the stacks of rusting containers. The narrow aisles with towering stacks on either side were made to order for a cross-fire ambush from above. But no ambush materialized.

Tom stopped them opposite a bollard on the right. The

massive steel stump had been originally used to secure the eye of the waist-breast mooring line after it passed through a large opening in the port rail. Now the bollard back-stopped a machine-gun position. Its bipod legs heavily sandbagged in place, a well-worn M-60 overlooked and controlled the southern approach to the island. Or it would have if anybody was home. Connected to an ammo satchel by a belt of 7.62 mm cartridges, the weapon had been abandoned.

"Over there," Doc said, pointing fifty feet aft and to the left where on the ground the sole of a white basketball shoe peeked around the corner of a deck-level container. They moved quickly but cautiously in that direction.

The islander wearing the shoe was belly down and newly dead. Perhaps he had been the machine gunner; there was no way of telling. His face, neck and exposed arms bore the same red marks they had seen in the ville, and there was dark, congealed blood around his nose and mouth.

"Another victim of the virus," Mildred said.

"A disease that appears to be relentless," Doc said. "Relentless and merciless."

"Live one!" Jak announced to the others, reaching for his holstered Python, but stopping just short of the butt.

Ryan turned to confront a blond boy of no more than fourteen who had popped out from a narrow gap between the containers. He wore a gaudy short-sleeved shirt and shorts, and high-topped basketball shoes like the dead gunner, only his looked three sizes too large. His hair had been shaved to stubble, and there were deep circles under his blue eyes. He didn't look sick, just exhausted. He was haggard, but hard focused, and he seemed entirely comfortable holding the full-stock AKM in his hands.

Apparently, a fourteen-year-old was the only one defending the freighter's deck.

Not a good sign.

"Who the fuck are you?" the boy demanded in a hoarse voice, leveling the assault rifle to fire from the waist.

Ryan could see the selector switch was set on full-auto. At the present range, there was no way the kid could miss. Gesturing for calm with both hands, he said, "We're not with the bastards who shelled your ville, so you need to put down the weapon."

The boy showed no sign of doing that. Just the opposite. His mouth tightened into a narrow seam, and his fingertip curled around the trigger as he braced the metal shod butt hard against his right hip.

The teenager looked from person to person, first the eyes, then the hands, clearly noting the fact that although their weapons were not drawn, they were within easy reach. The expression on his face was defiant and murderous.

"I know I can't chill you all," he said, "but I can mess up most of you before you git me."

"We're not the enemy," Ryan said.

The AKM's muzzle swung to the left, locking on Ryan's midsection. "Git down on your knees, Eye Patch," he said.

"That's not likely to happen," J.B. told him. "You need to take a deep breath and settle down."

"Fuck your advice, mister."

"We've all got the same problem," Ryan said. "Look over there." He indicated the three tugs, which had stopped five hundred yards off the beach and were holding position, parallel to the freighter's deck.

"Matachìn," the teenager snarled.

"Who?" Krysty asked. "What did he say?"

"Matachìn, murdering pirate scum that come up the coast from Mex," the boy said. "We heard they already burned Matamoros ville and Browns ville to the ground. If you don't believe me, ask him…" He gestured with the AKM, pointing out the tagalong who was still keeping well back of the rest, pretending to be Doc's shadow. "He's the one who told us about them."

"Funny, he didn't mention it to us," Ryan said.

"Mebbe it slipped his mind," J.B. said, turning on the man in the do-rag. "Is that what happened?"

Daniel Desipio didn't say a word. He looked like he wanted to become invisible.

"Not very talkative for a Fire Talker, is he?" Mildred said.

"Not now mebbe," the teenager said, "but you should have heard him when he first got here, before everybody took sick. He was on and on about all this triple-stupe shit from Mars, and how it was part of the Mex pirates' plan to take over the hellscape. There was more bullshit about other people that he said came from the moon. Some of them were these giant mutie vegetables that could talk, drink whiskey and shoot blasters.

"Nobody with norm brains could make sense of his Martian-moon crap-a-roo. The only ones on the island who paid him any mind were the droolies. He had them fuddle nuts eating right out of his hand. They followed him like baby ducks everywhere he went, even to the shitter. Everyone norm wanted to shut him up permanently. Either by stringing him up by the neck from the radar mast or by making him swim buck-naked for the mainland through a chum slick."

The intensity and personal nature of the attack made Daniel speak up, if not step forward. But it wasn't in his own defense, as Ryan would have been expected.

"Why do they hate me?" he asked, his voice breaking.

It was a rhetorical question.

And it had the opposite of the desired effect. It engendered expressions and exclamations of disgust, not sympathy from the companions.

"Hey, don't I know you?" Tom said to the boy. "Sure I do. You're one of Nelson Reed's kids."

"I'm Garwood Reed," the teenager said. "Pa's dead. So's Ma. So's most everyone. Or else they're so damned sick they can't hold a blaster."

"We're all in for it, Garwood," Tom told him. "You need our blasters to help defend the ship. We've got to pull together. You need to take us to the others. There's no more time to waste."

"He doesn't even have a blaster," the boy said, nodding at Daniel. "Why does he have to come with us? Why can't he just stay out here on deck?"

"I can help the sick ones," Daniel countered meekly and without much in the way of conviction.

"Nose and butt wipe," Garwood retorted, "that's all he's good for."

"Enough!" Ryan said. "We don't have time for this. Move it, kid!"

Garwood shut up and sulkily complied with the order. He slung his AKM and turned for the bridge tower on a dead run. The companions followed him through a doorway at the base of the superstructure and onto the tower's ground floor. Ryan could see through the huge, rusted-out gaps in the ceiling to the story above. The steady breeze whistled through countless holes in the cheese grater tower.

The teenager made a beeline for a metal staircase leading to the ship's lower levels. On the landing wall was a row of burning torches in crude stanchions. Garwood snatched one of them and started down the steps. The flame threw a weak light down the pitch-dark stairwell. Ryan and Doc each grabbed torches and held them high, lighting the way for the others as they descended, single file.

Over the sounds of their footsteps, Ryan heard moans echoing up the stairs. Sounds of disembodied pain and suffering. As they passed the second landing, he smelled the sickness wafting up from below. Vomit sweet and triple foul.

When they reached the Upper Tween deck, Garwood exited the staircase and led them onto an all-metal corridor that extended into the dim distance, apparently the full length of the ship. The boy slipped his torch into a empty wall stanchion; Ryan and Doc followed suit. Torches weren't necessary. Sunlight streamed through the blaster-ports cutting narrow, vertical wedges through the gloom.

Most of the weapons Ryan had seen coming up the ramp were propped up on crates and unmanned. They had been positioned to look like there was an army lying in wait. The islanders had plenty of blasters, all right, but they were big-time short on gunners. Every fifth or sixth assault rifle had an actual person behind it. A couple were kids four or five years younger than the companions' guide, and thirty pounds lighter. Ryan found it hard to believe that the first jolt of recoil wouldn't put them square on their skinny little butts. There were a total of fifteen adults on the entire firing line.

"This can't be everybody," Tom said in disbelief.

"In here," Garwood said. "They're in here." He unlatched, then strained to open a bulkhead door into a main hold. As the door swung back, it was clear the hold was where all the moaning was coming from.

And the smell.

The hold had no opening to the sun. It was lightless except for torches flickering in stanchions along the walls, airless and stiflingly hot. The metal walls steadily dripped rivulets of condensation, which had pooled on the metal deck. Cargo containers were stacked three-high inside the hold. They created canyons of darkness where no light penetrated.

The Upper Tween deck hold was part hospital and part morgue, but mostly morgue. Islander bodies lay uncovered among the rubbish drifts of splintered wood, cardboard and burlap sacking. At a glance it was impossible to tell how many people were still alive. A dozen or so were on their feet though, and moving here and there around the hold, trying to help the stricken.

With the smoke from the torches, the weak, erratic light they threw, the looming walls of the stacked containers, the incessant moaning and the smell of sickness and decay, it was like some lower pit of hell.

Tom shouted into the hold, "Who's in charge?"

A jut-jawed woman straightened from tending one of the moaners. "Who the fuck's askin'?" she snarled back. Wide across the hips, she had hugely fat and doughy upper arms. The pockets of the birdhunting vest she'd somehow managed to squeeze into bulged to bursting with high brass shotgun rounds. Sweat plastered her thin brown hair to her skull in stringy plaits. Slung on a canvas strap over her right shoulder was a sawed-off 12-gauge pump shotgun.

"It's me, Tom Wolf," the skipper replied. "Is that you, Brenda?"

Recognizing him, the woman looked surprised, then she smiled. "Dammit to hell, Captain Tom, you sure went and picked yourself a shitty time to pay us a visit."

"Spilt milk, Brenda, I'm here and that's the truth," he said.

"You seen what those Mex pirates done to our ville?"

"You don't have a ville anymore, Brenda," he said flatly. "And those same bastards are gonna be climbing up our butts shortly. I don't get the feeling they're in a merciful mood today. It's gonna come down to chill or be chilled. How many of yours are well enough to stand and fight?"

"Mebbe twenty-five total. Some of the girls are too little to hold a rifle, let alone shoot one. But what we've got to do first off is to blow up the access ramp, make 'em use ropes and grappling hooks to reach the top deck. That can't wait. The charges are already set. Someone has to go out and light the fuse."

The sick man she was tending to suddenly lurched up into a sitting position. "I'm okay," he said, his upper body weaving from side to side. "I can do it. I can do it. I'll blow up the ramp…"

It was obvious that he was not okay. He coughed from deep in his lungs, and he sprayed blood mist out of his mouth all down his shirtfront. A fresh coat. It was obvious he was dying.

"Jimbo, right now you couldn't blow up dogshit,"

Brenda said, firmly taking hold of his shoulders and pushing him back down.

Then she told Tom, "Mebbe we'd better take this out into the hallway."

"Send the Fire Talker," Garwood suggested as they stepped over the bulkhead's threshold.

"I don't know anything about explosives," Daniel protested. "I'm a storyteller. A fabulator."

"All you got to do is light the fuckin' fuse," Brenda said.

"Nukin' hell," J.B. muttered, "you can't trust someone like him to do it right, or at all."

"Even a droolie could light a fuckin' fuse," Brenda replied.

"Yeah," Garwood said, "even a droolie. Make him do it. Make him go out there and do it."

Ryan watched Jak move to one of the unmanned blasterports and press his face against the opening, looking across the water at the parked tugs. Only a couple of seconds passed before the albino spun away from the blasterport and shouted at the top of his lungs, "Incoming! Incoming!"

Before anyone could react, mortar rounds screamed down on the ship, detonating one after another on the main deck above them, a nonstop roar of explosions and tremendous concussion waves. Everything began to shake and roll. Ryan was staggered from one side of the corridor to the other. He swung the Steyr around on its shoulder strap, trying to protect its scope against his chest.

He hit the exterior wall with his back and then was thrown forward. He crashed to his knees.

Better stay down, he thought as shock waves flexed and rippled the floor beneath him and overlapping concussions pounded inside his skull. Fearing his eardrums might burst, he covered his ears with both hands and yelled as loud as he could to equalize the pressure.

If anyone else was yelling he couldn't hear them.

He couldn't even hear himself.

Another volley of shells blasted the main deck, bow to stern. Dust and pulverized rust cascaded from the ceiling, obscuring the hallway in a boiling cloud. It even choked out most of the light pouring in through the gun ports.

Ryan turned his face to the inner wall and raised a forearm across his brow to protect his one good eye from the debris fall. The pressure of the nearly continuous explosions was like a giant boot stomping him, head to toe. The world kept going white inside his head. Wall-to-wall white then black, as his consciousness winked in and out. Somewhere in the back of his mind, in the middle of it all, he managed a crystal-clear thought. He was aware, as never before, of the limits of his own skin, of his own being.

Of his own fragile life.

Doc had guessed right, he told himself. The pirates didn't give a damn about the cargo. They were blowing the islanders' booty all to hell, blasting the stacked containers apart, sending the topmost ones thundering down onto the deck. From the screeching against the outside of the hull, steel on steel, some of the huge boxes were sliding over the side.

As the shells continued to land on target, Ryan lost count of them. He kept telling himself that it couldn't get any worse. That if it did get worse, he'd be chilled and it wouldn't matter.

The pirates proved him wrong.

A rocking boom almost directly above his head was accompanied by the shriek of tearing metal followed by a resounding crash on the hold side of the corridor wall. The impact jolted the floor under his knees and a column of light suddenly speared through the roiling dust, through the open door of the makeshift sick bay. Successive blasts ripped open the top deck, uncapping the hold's roof and penetrating it.

Through the cloud of dust Ryan saw the able-bodied islander ministers to the sick frantically lurching, stumbling and spilling out of the bulkhead doorway as they tried to escape falling metal.

Some of them made it out, but not in one piece.

The tugboat mortars dropped more rounds right down the hole they had just blown through the top deck, dropped them into the middle of the Upper Tween deck hold.

A tight cluster of explosions from behind blew the runners out of their boots, out of the doorway, sending their bodies and severed parts of same slamming into the inside of the hull.

A tremendous rush of searing hot explosive wind momentarily blasted away the dust and Ryan got a glimpse of Brenda, who was on the far side of the ajar hold door, pulling herself up to her feet by the handle. As another shell detonated, sending shrapnel flying out the doorway and into the hall, she used the back of the door as a shield. Throwing her considerable weight against it, she slammed it shut and dropped the latch.

Before she could jump away, multiple shells exploded inside the hold. The corridor's steel walls bulged, popping out rows of rivets, and the concussion knocked her off her feet. She hit the floor hard and stayed down.

As the explosions continued to pound the wreck, the floor under Ryan undulated like it was made of liquid.

There was nothing to hold on to.

And there was no escape from what was coming.

Ryan was certain that the next volley would take out the buckled wall, the hallway and everything in between.

But when more shells rained down on the freighter, the explosions didn't blow out the corridor walls. Instead, they bowed up the floor, which suddenly became too hot to touch. Ryan realized as he scrambled to get his boot soles under him that the muffled blasts had come from the deck below. A tightly grouped barrage had opened a hole in the Upper Tween deck, allowing HE to fall even deeper into the ship.

Again and again, the mortars dropped shells on the same bull's-eye. Again and again explosions in the ship's very bowels shook the floor.

The pirate gunners were coring it like an apple.

Then the shells stopped falling and everything went deadly quiet. The floor stopped undulating. It was finally over.

Coughing and choking, Ryan used the buttstock of the Steyr as a crutch. He pushed himself to his feet, then staggered around a heap of broken, unmoving bodies, to the nearest blasterport. Through the churning dust and smoke, over the barrel of an AKM, he could see one of the tugs had already swung a pair of rafts into the water and the heavily armed landing parties were rowing for the beach.

The other two tugs had launched their rafts and were loading them with men and gear on the far sides of their pilothouses.

Up and down the hallway, the survivors of the mortar attack were stirring.

"Get to the blasters! Get to the blasters!" Ryan shouted at them.

Twenty hostile targets were approaching the shore, with about twice that many about to debark the other tugs. It was a situation that called for firepower, not finesse. He carefully set the bolt-action Steyr on the floor.

Before he checked the AKM's mag, he brushed the dust and grit off the top of the receiver and ejection port. Under the dust there was wet stuff. When he looked at his fingers in the light, they glistened pink, blood mixed with serum. He wiped them off on his pants. The clip was full, and there were six more on the deck at his feet. He picked up a couple, checked the round counters, then stuck them into the back of his belt. Before he reinserted the rifle's mag, he looked down the bore to make sure it was clear.

As he charged the actuator handle, chambering the magazine's first bullet, there was movement all along the firing line. The survivors were stepping up to the blasters. Because of the smoke he couldn't see very far down the corridor, but he could see Krysty and Doc on his left, hunched over their own assault rifles. They looked unhurt.

He bellowed first in one direction, then the other, "Everybody, this is Ryan. Check in! Check in! Let's hear you."

One by one from either side there came answering shouts. Each affirmative sent a surge of relief coursing through him. Mildred, Jak, J.B. and Doc were all okay. So was Harmonica Tom.

There was no way of telling how many other people had lived through the barrage; however many it was, it was going to have to do. Ryan knew he couldn't count on any of them having fired an automatic rifle before, let alone be able to hit moving targets at long range.

"Don't shoot until they come ashore!" Ryan called out through a cupped hand. "Wait until they're on the ramp. Then they won't be able to use the mortars without hitting their own troops. We've got to sit tight and let them come to us. Wait until they're so close we can't miss. Check your actions and barrels, make sure there's nothing stuck in them. Make sure you've got extra mags close to hand."

Ryan used the hem of his T-shirt to wipe his eye, which was tearing profusely, trying to rid itself of dust. When his vision cleared, he looked out the blasterport again. The two rafts were moving at a rapid clip, four sets of oars dipping in unison, rowers really putting their backs into the strokes. The pirates knew until they reached the shore they were dangerously exposed.

Four hundred yards. Three hundred yards.

Having recovered their senses and their wits, the islanders manning the blasterports were venting at top volume. They cursed and yelled insults at an enemy that couldn't possibly hear them; they promised revenge to the corpses that littered the hallway. Their understandable fury was on the verge of boiling over.

Way too soon.

"Hold your fire," Ryan cautioned them. "Don't shoot, yet. Let all the pirates land. Let them get close."

Two hundred yards.

The closer to shore the Matachìn rowed, the more agitated and vocal the islanders became.

Ryan shouted over the rising noise, repeating his warning to hold fire.

The other companions picked up his refrain, passing the word up and down the hallway for the shooters to wait.

One hundred yards.

Off to Ryan's right, out of sight in the gloom, an AKM opened fire. And once that happened, there was no stopping the rest of them. Assault rifles cut loose all up and down the ship's port flank.

"Shit!" Ryan snarled. There was only one thing left for him to do: join the turkey shoot. He snugged into the AKM's buttstock and dropped the fire selector to full-auto. As he looked down the iron sights, he shouted over the din of sustained autofire, "Aim low! Aim low."

Downrange, over the AKM's sights, he could see the bullets fall. No one had heard him, or if they had they didn't understand that he was warning them to compensate for their elevation and down angle. A mini-hailstorm was hitting the water between the rafts and the tugboat that had launched them. The others were shooting way high. At least six of the AKs would be on target—his and the companions'.

Ryan dropped the sight post a good five inches below the bow of the first raft and cut loose a short burst.

Too low.

The bullets splashed sixty feet in front of the bow. He raised the sights, cutting the low hold in two, and pinned the trigger. He let the muzzle climb walk the stream of slugs right up the middle of the boat. The vibration of the autofire from both the recoil and the clattering bolt, and the distance to target made it hard to see exact hits, some seemed to go wide on either side of the pontoons, but the hailstorm had definitely found the pirates.

As Ryan stripped out the empty mag and reached behind his back for a fresh one, the combined firepower of twenty or so AKMs finally locked on the invaders, more or less. The water around the two craft was whipped to a froth by hundreds of 7.62 mm rounds.

The pirates in the rafts didn't attempt to return fire.

Those that hadn't already abandoned ship were too busy dying.

Under the squall of bullets, both boats' pontoons took multiple hits, burst and immediately started to deflate. Without flotation, there was nothing to keep the plywood floors from sinking beneath the weight of the dozen or so bodies they each supported. And sink is what they did, leaving some of the corpses drifting on the blood-slicked surface. Even though the enemy was facedown and out of the fight, the islanders continued to hammer their backs with blasterfire.

Other gunners along the firing line tracked the pirates who'd jumped ship and were trying to swim for the beach. The accuracy required was too far and too fine. The pirates dived under the water to avoid being hit.

"Hold your fire!" Ryan said as he slapped the mag home and racked the actuator handle.

Again, no one was listening to him.

Buoyed up by their success, the islanders started strafing all three tugs, fanning at them with lead. They were burning up ammo like there was no tomorrow.

Ryan shouldered the assault rifle, but this time didn't fire. Five hundred yards was at the extreme limit of an AKM's range. Accordingly the hit ratio on the new target set was even lower, the spread of bullet fall much wider.

Some of the slugs were landing on the boats, though.

They had to be, based on sheer volume and concentration. The three tugs had low metal awnings along the sides of their top decks. Because of the down angle, Ryan's view was completely blocked. He couldn't see if anything of importance was being hit.

The second fusillade was pointless, except in celebration of a temporary victory. The other four rafts were protected by the ships' hulls. All the pirates had to do was move to the far side of the wheelhouses to avoid the autofire.

As simple as that.

After another minute or so of melee, the islanders stopped shooting and started whooping it up, cheering and congratulating one another.

Turning back the pirates had been a piece of cake.

Way too easy, as far as Ryan was concerned. He knew something triple bad was coming. Before he could snatch up his longblaster and gather his companions it was on top of them.

Mortars flashed from the bows and decks of all three tugs. The screeches of the shells were shrill—and short.

The world went white again, white and blistering hot, and the outside wall seemed to jump into Ryan's face. He bounced off the AKM and the blasterport, bounced backward onto his side on the deck, facing the stern.

Tremendous explosions rocked the hull again and again. Blinding orange strobe light flashed the length of the corridor and the exterior wall imploded, sending steel plates and shrapnel flying down the hall, ricocheting off and gouging through the opposite wall.

If people were screaming as they were hit, their cries were lost in the roar of the detonations.

The floor and the walls slammed into Ryan. He was

rattled like a marble in a jar as waves of skin-melting heat washed over him. He tried to crawl to where he'd last seen Krysty, but he couldn't make headway, and all he could see through the smoke and dust and screaming shrapnel were the brilliant flashes of igniting HE.

The pirate mortars were firing at low angles into the side of the ship, blowing apart sections of the hull and the gunners behind it.

Death stormed up and down the passageway.

Mindless.

Senseless.

Indiscriminate.

A heavy, warm body crashed into Ryan from behind, landing across his legs. He turned to push it off. In a flash of HE light, he saw the islander man reach up to grab the end of a jagged spike of steel that protruded from the side of his neck.

"No, don't, don't pull it out," Ryan said as the shock wave, the heat wave, the air blast slammed them and then everything went black again. He wasn't sure if he had actually spoken, or if he'd just thought the words.

Two seconds later another explosion lit the hallway.

And Ryan saw that it was already too late.

The islander had yanked the dagger of steel from his throat. Bright arterial blood was jetting out of his neck, squirting well past the tip of his shoulder. The man looked puzzled at the outcome; and he tried to staunch the unstoppable flow with his fingers.

Blackness slammed down.

Ryan felt the man's weight fall back across his legs. As he kicked himself free, the explosions stomped away from him, toward the stern. It was as though the pirate mortars were trying to cut the ship in two, lengthwise.

Realizing that he had a window of opportunity, Ryan forced his arms and legs into motion. Ignoring the sharp debris that covered the floor, he started crawling as fast as he could toward the last place he had seen Krysty. He wasn't thinking; he was acting on instinct and emotion. If this was where the two of them were going to buy the farm, he wanted to be by her side.

He couldn't see for the smoke.

He couldn't think or hear for the roar of shelling.

Then even crawling was beyond him.

The side of the ship opened up not fifteen feet away with a boom so powerful that it didn't even register as sound. It was pure, instantaneous, incomprehensible force. Orange light. Intense heat. A blast wave lifted him sideways and slammed him headfirst into the interior wall.

Everything went black.

And this time, it stayed black.

Chapter Seventeen

Casacampo observed as his second in command positioned the *Ek'-Way* broadside to the new target, the
grounded Texican freighter. His flagship's powerful
engines throbbed at low thrust, making every horizontal
surface vibrate and buzz.

On either side of them, the *Xibal Be* and *White Bone
Snake* had taken up their respective firing positions.

All was in readiness.

With a curt order into his radio and a hand signal
through the pilothouse glass, Casacampo began the precision shelling of the freighter's top deck. The three tugs
launched their first mortar rounds almost simultaneously.

Unlike the shelling of the ville, this was an attack on a
visible target, a spectacle to be enjoyed and savored.

The commander watched through binocs as the mortars
began to land down range. The explosions were impressive—colorful, loud and powerful. Orange balls of fire
blossomed, tearing the stacks of cargo containers apart,
blowing open the boxes on top, sending aloft a confetti of
debris. Destruction rained down on the *Yoko Maru*'s main
deck, from bow to stern. Under the merciless pounding,
huge containers fell three storys, crashing to the deck.
Some fell over the side.

Then the Matachìn gunners turned their attention to the

bridge tower, which commanded the deck and all access to it. It was the perfect high ground for snipers to hole up.

The first shell's explosion cut free the Lone Star flag, and took out the top twenty feet of the radar mast. As the huge flag fluttered down through the black smoke and fire, mortar rounds deconstructed the tower. Held together by little more than paint and rust, it came apart even more easily than the cargo containers. Successive explosions, laid one on top of the other, blew out the center of the tower, took it down story by story, leaving a yawning, smoking chasm between the port and starboard outside walls.

Meanwhile, the contents of the burst containers were feeding the fires scattered all along the main deck. Flames leaped into the sky and oily black smoke poured off the bow in a river, blown hard downwind.

Casacampo didn't need binocs to see the deck burn. He adjusted the soggy butt of his cigar in the corner of his mouth. To him the conflagration was a beautiful sight. For the enemy hiding in the ship, it had to be a demoralizing shock. If the Matachìn weren't interested in looting their precious predark stores, then those stores couldn't be used as a defense, essentially as a hostage to forestall all-out attack.

As the shelling continued, the commander tried to imagine what it was like being trapped inside that ancient steel can, with giants pounding on the roof. His already weakened opponents, if they weren't blown apart, would be prostrated by the combination of sound and concussion, unconscious, disoriented. No trouble for the assault teams to mop up. He anticipated easy pickings just like Matamoros ville and Browns ville, an appropriate end to a glorious and victorious campaign.

Picking up the microphone and hand-signaling his own crew, Casacampo called off the mortar barrage. It was time to get face-to-face, hand-to-hand. As the last echoes of the shelling faded in the distance, he gave the crew of the *Xibal Be* the honor of setting foot on the beach first.

Looking out the pilothouse's rear window, he saw the second of the *Ek'-Way*'s rafts being lowered from its davit into the water. His crew was loading weaponry in the other dinghy, which had already been launched, and which they held tethered on the tug's starboard side.

He raised his binocs again and watched as the *Xibal Be*'s rafts headed for shore. His pirates were stroking hard on their oars, eager for the coming slaughter. A thrill coursed through him. His own blood pounding, Casacampo reached up and rubbed the belly of a dangling Atapul X icon with the ball of his thumb.

For luck.

The first Lords of Death had been imprisoned and tortured by secret elements of the northern government. Because of the horrors that had been done to their ancestors, subsequent Lords felt a particular hate for all things Deathlands. But until recently they hadn't been in a position to make their hatred felt. Only recently had it been in their interest to expend military assets to that end.

Casacampo knew the *Yoko Maru* had been bound for Brazil before Armageddon swept it off course. He hadn't seen a copy of the ship's manifest, a copy no longer existed, but he had an idea of what was in it. The contents of the *Yoko Maru* might have been valuable to the Brazilians of the period or to the Deathlanders, neither of which had anything better, but to the Lords of Death and their minions, the Matachìn, it was just century-old, second-rate crap.

Casacampo's pirates would, as was their custom, help themselves to whatever gold and jewels they could find, and to the various orifices of the survivors at blasterpoint, but as to the other stuff, the cargo of the *Yoko Maru,* the treasure of Padre Island, it was only good for burning.

The destruction being wreaked was savage, but it wasn't mindless.

There was strategic, long-term gain in it for the Lords of Death.

The sooner the predark stockpiles were gone, the faster Deathlands would revert to the Stone Age. Stone Age people couldn't hold territory against automatic weapons and artillery. And ultimately, it was all about territory, about having room to expand, resources to exploit. It was about spending as little of your own capital as possible to get the most return. Six hundred years before, Casacampo's progenitors, dressed in loincloths and armed with clubs, knives and magic spells, had tried and failed to repel an invasion by a more technologically advanced civilization.

Now the shoe was on the other foot.

A sudden clatter of autofire broke his train of thought. At first he couldn't tell where it was coming from. There was nothing for his men to shoot at. Then he looked across the water to the grounded ship and saw the muzzle-flashes winking all along the side of the hull. He quickly focused the binocs. The blasterports, so narrow he had missed them, were now all too obvious, lit up as they were by blasterfire.

The bullets weren't aimed at him.

Casacampo's stomach tightened as he turned the optics on the landing party. Between the *Xibal Be* and its rafts, the water was being churned to a froth by bullet fall. The Matachìn in the dinghies stroked harder, trying to row away from the autofire and make it to the shore.

They weren't going to make it, the commander could see that. It was too far. They were moving too slowly, and it was too easy for the enemy to walk their blasterfire onto the boats.

As he watched, a hail storm of lead swept over both of his rafts. The inflatable pontoons were instantly torn to shreds. Some of the Matachìn managed to jump or pitch themselves over the sides. Most couldn't get out from behind their oars. Trapped on the thwart seats, the concentrated rifle slugs chewed them to pieces.

Without the pontoons, there wasn't enough buoyancy to support the plywood decks or the rowers. As the rafts rapidly sank, bodies floated free.

The survivors swam hard for the beach, targeted by autofire.

Casacampo shouted into the microphone for his gunners to resume shelling. "Aim for the side of the ship!" he said.

As the Matachìn lowered the angle of their launch tubes, bullets began raining down on the port side of the flagship tug, pelting the roof of the slaves' sun shade. The blasters were too far away for accuracy, but the rowers couldn't get out of the way. They tried, pulling on their shackles, taking cover behind their seats and one another.

Blood sprayed the deck and men screamed.

Then the port window of the pilothouse imploded, sending glass flying. Casacampo turned his head to avoid being cut in the eyes and face. He snarled a curse, then shouted into the microphone. "Fire! Fire!"

Gamely standing their ground, the mortar gunners let fly.

The shells looped over the water at low angles, with muzzle climb compensated.

Bright orange explosions lit up the flank of the ship. The incoming fire shut off in the same instant. Casacampo watched through the binocs as cavernous holes opened up in the hull. Along the row of blasterports, chunks of steel plate flew off like they were made of cardboard. Entire sections of the interior hallway were exposed to view, and hit over and over again. Smoke poured from within.

It wasn't enough for payback, the commander thought, but it was a start.

He spoke into the microphone, addressing the mortar crews, "Keep firing until we hit the beach. *White Bone Snake,* launch your assault teams."

Casacampo picked up his LAPA and headed for the stairs. Dolor left the helm, grabbed his own submachine gun and ammo belt, and followed.

When they reached the deck, Dolor ordered one of the crew to man the helm and hold position.

The commander stepped into the bow of one of the rafts, already loaded with men and gear. Dolor got into the other.

At Casacampo's command, both dinghies pushed off and the pirates began rowing around the starboard side of the tug, heading for the shore. Fires raged on the main deck of the freighter, and flames licked out of the holes blown in its flank. There would be no more unpleasant surprises from that quarter.

The commander waved his men to the right, to where the half-sunken rafts lay, where the corpses floated. He counted the bodies. They had lost nine of the twenty men in the two rafts. Some had died swimming to shore.

A disaster.

He barked an order to his crew and Dolor's. They shipped oars and began recovering the corpses. There were too many to pull into the rafts, so they tied loops of line to ankles, necks, wrists and towed their dead to the beach.

When the bow of Casacampo's raft slid up on the sand, the *White Bone Snake*'s landing party was already there. They had taken up firing positions on their bellies, aiming up at the ship. There was nothing to shoot at. The eleven survivors from the *Xibal Be* dinghies were there, too, machetes and pistols in hand.

With great care and reverence, the Matachìn pulled their dead from the water and lined the bullet-riddled bodies up on the shore.

Casacampo could sense their speechless fury. He shared it. This was the voyage's greatest loss. It would be repaid a hundred times and in the most horrible ways, before they left the island.

Under the cover of blasters from the beach, the commander led the charge up the dunes to the ramp. They met no resistance en route, and looking over the edge of the ramp as he ascended it, Casacampo saw nothing stirring among the ruins. The hallway exposed by the mortars had been turned into piles of rubbish, as had the enemy.

The commander climbed onto the burning deck, moving out of the flow of black smoke. His mortar crews' handiwork was evident. The roof of the central hold had been caved in by successive shell hits. Fire billowed up from within. The bridge tower had been reduced in height by half and nearly cut in two vertically; it was also on fire.

Whatever resistance remained, it had been driven belowdecks, just as Casacampo had planned.

Dolor touched his arm and directed his attention to the
harbor and the tall sailing ship anchored there. It was the
only escape from the island. It was too late to secure the
ship, now. His diminished number of marines was already
committed to the freighter assault. He couldn't risk splitting up the force. There was only one option: keep the survivors from reaching it.

Casacampo called over three of his Matachìn. He
ordered them to go around the bow, to the north side of
the freighter and watch for any escapees in that direction.
They were armed with submachine guns and M-79
grenade launchers.

"Gas anyone who tries to run away," he said. "If that
doesn't stop them, use lead."

As the pirates set off, the commander stepped to the
gate in the rail and signaled down to the beach for the rest
of his force to mount the hill and join them. They triple-
timed it. The ascent of the other thirty or so pirates took
about three minutes. When they were all on deck, he led
his men toward the stern. They leapfrogged around the
burning, toppled containers, covering each other, but the
enemy was nowhere to be seen.

At the base of the ruined bridge tower, Casacampo had
his crew clear the entrance to the stairwell, which was
blocked by fallen debris from the shelled storys above.
When the path was opened, smoke poured from the stairwell. He gave the order to put on gas masks and switch
on headlamps.

As they prepared for the assault, he paced up and down
their ranks, roaring words of encouragement, passionate

words straight from the heart. "We will make them pay," he assured his crews. "We will teach them what pain is. We will teach them to raise their hands against the Matachìn!"

With that, Casacampo pulled on his own gas mask, donned and switched on his headlamp.

The commander was the first down the steps into the smoke and the darkness.

Chapter Eighteen

Ryan awoke with a start from a horrible dream, a nightmare of his own suffocation and violent dismemberment. He coughed and tasted blood. He was on his back under a weight that pressed the full length of his body, pinning his arms and legs to the deck. Something lay across the scarred, eyeless left side of face. He blinked the lid of his functional eye to remove the grit clinging to it and his lashes. Directly above him, the hallway's ceiling had ruptured. Broken, multicolored wires, loops of gray conduit and disconnected ends of cylindrical aluminum air ducts hung from the breach.

Looking down, he could see the debris mounded on his chest. He was half buried under ceiling tiles and pieces of the imploded hull and interior walls. With the tip of his tongue he felt a long cut inside his mouth along his left cheek. The bleeding had pretty much stopped. Then he realized that he couldn't hear anything. Not even the beating of his own heart.

But he hurt. He hurt all over, all at once. It seemed like the tips of a thousand knives were sticking into him.

Every time he breathed in, the pain got worse by a factor of ten.

There was something he knew he had to remember.

He knew it was something important. Urgent, even. But

his brain seemed to have lost its ability to recall recent events. The harder he tried to remember, the further away they slipped. A very strange feeling. An anchorless feeling. He closed his eye and forced himself to concentrate on simple, direct questions. Where was he? How had this happened? Who was responsible?

Asking himself the right questions led to the answer he was after. Although the answer wasn't pretty or pleasant.

Recent events came back to him in a rush of images and recalled sensation. The island. The freighter. The sickness. The pirates. The shelling. And somewhere around him, amid the ruins of the grounded ship's corridor, his companions lay trapped, perhaps dead, perhaps dying.

Ryan tried to get up, but he couldn't move arms and legs hidden from sight under the heaped debris. He couldn't make his fingers move, either. Nor his toes. Mebbe they were just numb from shock like his ears, he told himself. Then other, more dire possibilities occurred to him. He wondered if he'd been hit by shrap and was paralyzed from the neck down, or whether, recalling the grisly details of his blackout dream, his arms and legs had been blown away.

Panic rose in the back of his throat.

If his heart was pounding in response, he still couldn't hear it.

He squeezed off the downward spiral of thought, then crushed it under a mental bootheel. He had never given in to fear before, and he wouldn't let himself do it now, with the last train west in sight.

Ryan stopped fighting the numbness and forced himself to breathe deeply and slowly, to gather himself. He noticed there was a lot more light coming into the corridor now. Even though the hall was still wreathed in smoke, the pall of Comp B was rapidly thinning. There was a breeze, too. Steady but slight. He could feel it gently brushing against his exposed cheek.

After a minute or so, Ryan managed to turn his head a little to the right and saw the holes in the plating. Four-foot-wide sections of the corridor's exterior wall and the ship's hull were missing. Those yawning gaps left the deck open to the air and the elements, floor to ceiling. Where mortar shells had directly hit the blasterports, nosing into the five-inch-wide gaps, the steel was peeled back into jagged crowns. From the scorch patterns across the ceiling, some of the shells had shot through and through into the Upper Tween deck hold, sending explosive backwash and flame into the hallway as they detonated.

Like thawing ice, from his shoulders down his arms to his elbows, from his hips down his legs, the feeling started to creep back. It was accompanied by a burning, rippling, electric sensation and intense localized pain.

He knew it might be ghost pain, imagined sensation in limbs that were no longer there, and he had to find out if he was whole or not. If he wasn't, he would crawl to find the others and somehow, some way get them moving to safety.

The pirate attack wasn't over.

Not by a long shot.

When Ryan commanded his right arm to move, the progressive thaw worked its way to his fingers. The backs of both hands burned like they were being blowtorched. He could feel his individual fingers, though. They were heavy, wooden, but he could feel them. With an effort, he pushed his hand up through the pile of dropped tiles and then swept them off his face and chest.

When he rose to an elbow, soot and metal dust fell away from his face and T-shirt. The burning sensation coursed down his legs to his toes. Hurting like hell was a good sign, he decided.

Ryan kicked the rubbish off himself and saw the rear stock of the Steyr laying across his left hip. He pulled it out from under the tiles. Bracing the butt on the deck and gripping the barrel, he used it to regain his feet. He felt an odd, constant pressure, a tightness at the base of his spine. When he reached back he found the loaded AKM mag, still tucked under his belt. He left it there.

Nothing moved in either direction down the hallway. Wisps of smoke hung just under what was left of the ceiling. Debris was everywhere, but it lay mostly heaped against the foot of the interior wall. More smoke, only black and oily, poured through massive holes blown in that same wall.

How could anyone have survived? he thought as he stared at the destruction. How had he survived?

Over the sustained hiss in his ears, he could hear the scrape of his bootsoles over the metal floor. But just barely.

Ryan looked out through a missing section of hull. Down on the shore he saw four beached, intact rafts. In front of them, bodies were lined up in a row. At least a dozen. Presumably pirate bodies, those chilled by the islanders' massed rifle fire. Between the shore and the ship there was no sign of the invaders. There were no pirates on the ramp. Ryan realized with a jolt that the enemy was already aboard.

"Get up! Get up!" he yelled down the ruined hall. "The bastards are coming! Get up!" It felt like he was screaming his throat bloody, but he couldn't tell how loud his voice was.

Loud enough, it turned out.

Here and there along the interior wall low piles of wreckage started to shift, then dusty heads, hands, arms began to appear.

Ryan launched himself in the direction he'd last seen Krysty and Doc. Slinging the Steyr, he started frantically turning over the large debris. He found Krysty behind a lean-to of hull plate, curled up with her back pressed to the foot of the interior wall. She wasn't moving.

Don't be dead, he thought. Don't be dead.

Then he saw her chest rising and falling. When he tipped the section of steel plate over and let it crash onto the floor, she stirred.

Her eyes opened and she blinked up at him, dazed. Her mouth moved, forming a single word.

He wasn't a lip reader but he could tell what she said. "Gaia."

There was blood on her face and hands.

He helped her to her feet, quickly checking her over for major injuries. She seemed to be okay. The blood was from shallow shrapnel cuts, one along her jawline, one above her right eye, several on the backs of her hands.

"They're coming!" he shouted at her. "The pirates are coming! Find the others!" He pointed her toward the bow.

Whether she could hear him or whether she read his lips or whether she just figured it out for herself, she nodded. After shaking the dust from her tightly coiled red hair, she rushed off and began searching the rubble.

Being in a hurry was a good thing, Ryan decided. There was no time to dwell on the uncovered legs, arms, heads that were no longer connected to live persons. As it turned out, quite a few people had lived through the attack, but only a handful hadn't suffered grievous injury. There was nothing to be done for the wounded. Ryan could see that from just looking at them. Even if their bleeding could have been stopped, the protruding hunks of shrapnel successfully removed, the injuries they suffered were terrible. Not only were they massive and internal, but packed with soot and rust. Infection was almost guaranteed. Infection and slow, agonizing death.

Ten feet away from Ryan, a section of blown-inward hull suddenly tipped away from the interior wall and crashed over onto the deck. Doc, coated with dust, and bleeding from his nose and ears, unfolded himself from the floor. When he saw Ryan standing there, his expression brightened and his lips moved.

All Ryan heard was muffled, garbled sounds. It didn't matter. He waved for Doc to follow him.

Together they found Brenda, Garwood and J.B. All three were alive. All three could move. Brenda was alert and immediately stood and cleared the action of her pump gun. The boy seemed to be in a state of shock. J.B. was in even worse shape. Clutching his ribs with an arm, squinting behind dusty spectacles, his lips moved in the same pattern, over and over.

Inaudible but again easy to lip-read: "Oh, fuck. Oh, fuck. Oh, fuck."

Doc put a hand on Ryan's shoulder to get his attention, then pointed toward the bow. Krysty was waving urgently at them. Harmonica Tom was at her side. He was waving, too.

Ryan broke into a run, and the others followed. As they approached Krysty and Tom, he saw the Fire Talker standing behind the skipper. Daniel appeared to have come through the barrage dirtied but unscathed; his survivalist do-rag was canted at an odd angle, over one ear. Then Ryan saw Mildred. She was on her knees, leaning over a still form on the deck. A still, pale form.

Ryan groaned.

It was Jak.

The one-eyed man knelt on the other side of the albino teen. There wasn't a mark on him. Not anywhere. Not a drop of spilled blood on the dead-white face. But his chest wasn't moving. For a second Ryan thought for sure Jak was chilled, that the concussions had done him a fatal internal torso or brain injury.

Mildred hadn't given up, though. She quickly rubbed the colorless hands between hers and lightly slapped Jak on the cheeks.

The stimulation worked. After a second, his ruby-red eyes opened. He blinked and gasped a deep breath of air.

Ryan was relieved when Jak pushed away Mildred's hands and rose to his feet, albeit shakily.

"Can you hear me?" Ryan shouted to the others.

There were nods all around. Even from the boy, Garwood. His eyes were bloodshot, but clear and focused. He had shaken off the shock.

"Hearing's coming back," Mildred said into Ryan's ear.

He could understand her, although there was a delay. It took a fraction of a second for his brain to interpret the still muffled sounds.

"Collect your blasters and ammo," he said in a voice

somewhere below a shout. "We've got to regroup with the islanders, make a stand." He pointed back down the corridor to where Brenda and the other survivors stood huddled, checking their weapons and ammo.

There weren't very many defenders left. Of the original twenty-five, only seven remained, counting Garwood. The rest lay in pieces or splattered over the walls and ceiling. Or dying in the rubble.

As the companions passed the bulkhead door to the Upper Tween deck hold, Garwood headed straight for the latch.

"You don't want to see what's in there," Krysty said.

Garwood ignored her. He cracked open the latch, yanked the door ajar and looked inside. What he saw froze him in place.

Ryan looked in over the boy's shoulder. The destruction was absolute and there was plenty of daylight to view it, despite the haze of rising smoke. A jagged, thirty-foot-wide hole had been blown into the roof of the hold. An even bigger hole had been blown into the center of the deck—three times as big as the cargo container that had fallen into it. Oily black smoke was pouring up out of the breach. The hold's metal walls were scorched to the ceiling and slashed by fragments from exploding shells. Nobody, nothing was alive in there.

Ryan gently moved the boy aside and stepped over the threshold. Standing out of the flow of harsh smoke, he looked over the edge of the central hole. The deck of the hold one story below had been penetrated by HE, as well. He could see all the way down into what looked like the ship's engine room. He could just make out the tops of massive engine blocks. That's where the fire was burning.

As he stepped back through the door, Ryan took Garwood by the shoulders and tried to turn him away from the entrance, away from the spectacle. The teenager dug in his heels and resisted.

"Come on," Ryan said, looking the boy straight in the eye. "They're all gone. It's done."

Garwood wiped away tears with the back of his hand. His lower lip quivered as he choked back sobs. He let Ryan steer him toward the stern.

Before they could move more than a few feet from the doorway, Brenda and the other four surviving islanders joined them. The big-armed woman pushed past Ryan and stared into the hold. Her face visibly sagged as she took in the mess. The Upper Tween deck was blast blackened all the way up the walls. All that was left of her people was bloody rags.

"There's nothing we can do for them," Ryan told her.

"Yeah, there is," Brenda said, her face suddenly beet red. "We can kick the asses of the bastards who did this."

She was really, really pissed off. She waved the other islanders over to look.

"The pirates outnumber us, big time," Ryan told her. "Mebbe four to one. We don't know what kind of armament they have. We need to make a fighting retreat to someplace we can defend."

"He's right. You know he's right," Tom said.

The other islanders, three men and another woman, came away from the doorway with faces contorted by blind fury.

"You and yours can do whatever the fuck you want," Brenda informed the skipper. She racked the slide on her pump gun, chambering a round. "But for us Texicans, it's time for some bloody fuckin' payback."

As the big-armed woman stormed off in the direction of the stern stairwell, which was about two hundred feet away, the islanders followed, their weapons up and ready.

"Dammit, Brenda, don't do this…" Tom called to her back.

Brenda didn't respond. She kept on walking away, shoulders hunched, head lowered. They all kept on walking for the stairwell.

Ryan could partly understand their decision. They were crazy with grief over the loss of their loved ones, crazy because everything generations of their people had worked for and protected was in the latrine, and gone forever. The islanders thought they had nothing left but their pride. And pride demanded vengeance at all costs. They were dead wrong. They still had their own lives, but in the heat of the moment no one was going to make them see that. It put the companions in an even more desperate situation.

The odds against them had just doubled.

When Garwood hitched himself up and started to go after Brenda, Tom reached out and grabbed him by the arm.

"No way, boy," Tom said. "You're coming with us, and we're getting the hell out of here."

"I want to fight them! Let me go!"

Tom wouldn't release his hold. "We all want to fight them and chill them, and we will," he said. "But we don't necessarily have to commit suicide doing it."

Garwood tried to throw a roundhouse punch at the skipper's face but missed when the larger man easily and adroitly pushed him off balance. From there, it degenerated into a stand-up wrestling match. While they struggled, the islanders disappeared up the stairs, heading for the top deck.

Ryan and Doc moved in to separate Tom and the boy.

As they pulled them apart, a blaze of blasterfire from the stairwell froze everyone. Automatic weapons chattered and a 12-gauge boomed over and over. The shotgun blasts were spaced a mere fraction of a second apart. Ryan recognized that frenzied chain of sound, as did his companions. Trigger pinned, the shotgun's firing pin snapped every time the pump action slammed shut.

Ryan drew his SIG-Sauer and stepped to the left, giving himself a clear firing lane. Krysty, Mildred, Doc, Jak and Tom whipped their pistols out, as well. Garwood dropped to a knee on the deck in front of them, shouldered his AKM and aimed at the stairwell entrance. J.B. couldn't shoulder his scattergun, so he held it braced against his hip, his face twisted in a grimace of pain.

The Fire Talker hung well back of them all, empty-handed, Ryan noted. Though there were a lot of islander weapons hidden under the debris, he didn't try to find one for himself. In fact, Daniel had a kind of wild look in his eye, like he was on the verge of making a solo break for it while the companions held the fort, but he didn't bolt. He didn't move a muscle.

The fabulator was too spineless even to hightail it.

It didn't matter, though. Ryan turned his attention back to the stairwell. They had enough blasters. Any pirate who stepped down onto the landing was going to be shot to pieces in a heartbeat.

Amid the savage, back-and-forth sawing of the continuing gunbattle on the stairwell came a series of loud pops in rapid succession. They weren't gunshots. And they weren't frag grenades. After a moment the intensity of shooting faded, turning into short bursts of autofire. One-way autofire.

Screams echoed in the stairwell. Bullets zinged down the stairs. Then an olive-drab cylinder bounced off the last step, onto the landing. It was spewing dense white smoke as it rolled into the corridor.

"Gas gren!" Ryan shouted, waving the others back.

The hissing canister was followed by Brenda. The big woman wasn't moving under her own power. She slid on her back, headfirst down the steps. Gravity dumped her at the foot of the stairs, but she wasn't dead. She struggled to her feet, bleeding heavily from a shoulder wound that had already soaked one side of her birdhunting vest. Tear gas from the canister billowed all around her as she lurched, half-blinded, for the hallway. Then from the steps above came more autofire. Before she could clear the landing, she was chopped down by multiple impacts to the head and chest. She hit the floor sideways and, rubbery limp, stayed there.

The screams up the stairwell continued until a pair of widely spaced single shots rang out. To Ryan they sounded like coups de grâce. Then came the tramp of many sets of heavy boots descending the metal treads. Light beams speared through the caustic chemical fog, crisscrossing wildly.

"Warn them, son," Ryan said, putting a hand on Garwood's shoulder.

The teenager cut loose a withering burst with his AKM. The flurry of slugs slapped the far side of the landing and sparked, gnawing chunks of metal from the edge of the entry arch.

While the pirates were thinking twice about taking those last few steps to the deck, Ryan waved the others away, toward the bow. He knew they couldn't hold the corridor against a tear gas attack. Even with the outer wall blown and a breeze coming through the holes, the chemicals would hang in the air, blinding and incapacitating them, making them triple easy to chill.

Two more canisters bounced down the steps and onto the hallway. The grens pinwheeled, spurting clouds of cottony smoke.

Garwood raised his assault rifle to his shoulder to lay down more covering fire, but Ryan stopped him with a hand on the still warm barrel. "We need a way off this deck," he said. "And then we need a way off this ship."

Jak bent and picked up an AKM from the rubble. Tapping the flash hider against the side of his boot to clear any debris from the barrel, without even checking the mag, he took aim at the landing.

Either the nukin' thing was loaded or it wasn't.

It was loaded.

The AKM clattered in his grip, spitting spent brass from its ejector port. Jak ripped off all thirty rounds in the space of four seconds.

"Get us out of here," Ryan told the boy as the blaster-shot echoes faded.

"This way," Garwood said, running for the bow.

Daniel was right behind him, almost a shadow.

Ryan grabbed the AKM from Jake, holstering his SIG-Sauer. "Go on! Everybody go!" he said, stripping out the empty mag and reaching behind his back for the clip he had stashed there. As the others ran past him, following

Garwood, he slapped in the full magazine, snapped the actuator and took rear guard.

Even though the three canisters were hissing a good two hundred feet distant, he could already feel his eye starting to sting and burn. The slight wind was carrying the CS smoke his way.

Before he was blinded by tears, Ryan fired from the hip, sending half a clip through the archway, then he turned and chased after the others. The freighter's hallway was close to six hundred feet long, a hell of a sprint, made more difficult because it was over an obstacle course of exploded rubbish. When Ryan saw the companions ducking through an arch at the far end of the corridor, he whirled and emptied the AKM down the hall. Tossing the rifle aside, he raced for the landing of the forward, portside stairwell.

As he stepped onto the landing, return fire from the stern clanged all around the bulkhead, spitting fat sparks as they ricocheted every which way. The pirates' window of target opportunity was a second at most, then he was around the corner and triple-timing down the stairs. The stairwell was wreathed in smoke, and after a dozen steps it got so dark that he had to reduce speed or risk taking a header. The smoke was even thicker at the next landing. He could feel radiating warmth against his face and arms.

Whatever was burning, it was plenty hot.

When he heard the hiss, he thought it was the ringing in his ears, then he realized it was too loud, that it was coming from the blaze, filtering up through the passages of the derelict ship.

As he continued down the stairs, he saw a yellow, flickering light below, too small and too weak to be the source of all the smoke. It was a torch. Ryan heard coughing and saw dim shapes on the Tween Deck landing, waiting for him.

Garwood had ignited a torch.

"They're coming," Ryan said as he joined the companions. "Mebbe three minutes behind me."

"Can you get us out of here?" Tom asked the teenager.

"Through the bilges," Garwood said. "There's a breach on the other side of the ship. It's real low on the hull, near the keel. You can't see it from the water. The sand dunes hide it."

"If we go out that way, can we get around the ville and make it down to the shore?" Krysty asked.

Tom answered for the boy. "Hell, yes! We can skirt the ville's backside, straight down to the water. Clear shot from the beach to the dinghy."

"We've got to go through the engine room to get to it," Garwood said. "And the engine room's back that way…" He indicated with the torch the direction they'd just come. The direction where the smoke got thicker.

"Nukin' hell," J.B. moaned, stifling a cough. His smudged spectacles reflected the yellow flame of the torch.

"No other way to the engine room?" Mildred asked the boy.

"Nope," Garwood said. "Not from here."

"If the Matachìn went down that aft staircase, the one Brenda tried to go up, then they've already got us cut off," Mildred said.

"If they didn't, then we've got a chance," Ryan said. He grabbed a pair of unlit torches from the wall and gave one of them to Jak. "We need more light."

As they touched the ends of their torches to Garwood's, grens popped on the stairwell above.

"Don't get too far ahead. Don't lose us," Ryan told the teen. "Without you to guide us we're running blind in here." Then he clapped a hand on Garwood's back and said, "Go, boy! Go!"

They ran single-file back toward the stern, another six-hundred-yard sprint. There was less debris on this deck, for sure, but it was harder to see it through the dense smoke. In the lead, Garwood picked his way around the scattered obstacles. Everyone followed his path, more or less.

J.B. was having a hard time keeping up. He gradually dropped back in the line, until he was running right in front of Ryan.

It was the cracked ribs, Ryan knew. J.B. couldn't suck in enough air, and the smoke was making things worse. He was a hard little son of a bitch, though. He wasn't going to give up.

They had traveled about half the distance to the stern when the smoke began to ease off and the heat got a whole lot worse. And there was a kind of red, throbbing glow up ahead on the left.

Automatic fire roared from behind, and bullets sprayed over the corridor, zipping past Ryan's head. The pirates had gained the lower deck, but the shooting was wild. Mebbe they were firing as they ran, he thought. Mebbe they were too anxious for the chill, or mebbe they were spooked by the enclosed space, the darkness, the smoke and the fire.

As another burst of slugs whined by him, Ryan could visualize the enemy's target picture: running figures silhouetted by the madly shifting red-orange glow. Stopping and returning fire was not an option for the companions. Speed was their only hope. Once they got past the glow and slipped into the darkness beyond, from the pursuers' point of view they would simply disappear.

The air was so hot it felt like daggers stabbing deep in Ryan's lungs every time he inhaled. J.B. was wheezing badly and staggering a bit, but he still had his eyes on the prize. Like Ryan, he knew the glow of the fire would hide them. If they were going to shoot back, it would be from the cover of darkness on the other side, where they had the advantage.

The glow was coming up fast on the left, and the air was getting much hotter. Ryan's clothes were soaked through with sweat. Even the shortest possible breaths seared the inside of his nose and the back of his throat. The firing from behind suddenly dwindled, then stopped altogether. He assumed the pirates were concentrating on their running, trying to close the gap and overtake them before they vanished.

Fifty feet in front of them, a torrent of flame shot sideways out of the left-hand wall, floor to ceiling. At the head of the file, Garwood veered wide right to avoid being cooked in his own skin. And it wasn't just direct flame he was dodging. Ryan could see the steel wall around its exit point was what was glowing red.

Suddenly there came another burst of blasterfire; not from behind, but from in front this time.

That the pirates had cut them off was Ryan's first dismal thought. If that was the case, there was no way out. They were going to be sandwiched in the hallway. Sandwiched and chilled.

The crackle continued, rapidly gathering in intensity.

He couldn't see muzzle-flashes down the corridor ahead of them for the light of the leaping flames. But bullets weren't flying from that direction.

When J.B. darted away from the source of the scalding heat, running next to the exterior wall, Ryan followed in his footsteps. Twenty feet away and rapidly closing, he saw fire blasting out through the doorway of what had to be the Upper Tween deck hold. The door was open, locked back against the wall.

Up close, the roar of the flame was so loud it made the air vibrate. And there was suddenly a hard wind at Ryan's back as the fire greedily sucked oxygen through every hole and crack in the hull, feeding itself.

Holding his breath to keep his lungs from being scorched, Ryan got a brief glimpse through the doorway.

Everything inside looked like it was burning. It was wall-to-wall fire.

From the hold, dozens of rounds went off at once, and bullets cut through the interior wall, angling up into the ceiling. Wild volleys of slugs chewed up the tiles overhead and dropped them on top of the companions as they ran.

Then he was past the door and the seething red glow, and running for the darkness ahead, although momentarily blinded by the afterimage of the glare. The blistering heat shifted from his face and left side to his back.

No one had been hit by anything but falling tiles and dust.

The blasterfire from the hold continued to rage as the companions put distance between themselves and it.

The Matachìn couldn't be in there, Ryan told himself. If they were, they'd be beyond staging an ambush; they'd be roasted meat. Even as he thought that, the din of the blasterfire behind him grew in volume and intensity.

Hundreds, perhaps thousands of rounds were going off at once. More and more of it was slashing through the wall, whining as it ricocheted against the inside of the hull.

If it wasn't the pirates shooting at them, he reasoned it had to be the islanders' ammo stockpile, stored in the Upper Tween deck hold, cooking off from the heat of the fire. Probably most of it was stashed inside a steel cargo container, which explained why more rounds weren't flying around. It was a situation that could change at any second if the container walls gave way.

The discharging ammo was going to be major obstacle for the pirates to negotiate. It might even turn them back.

The air felt cooler against Ryan's face, but there was noticeably more smoke and the light thrown by his torch was dimmer.

The cook-offs behind them continued to rage.

Up ahead, Garwood's light had stopped. He knelt at the arch in the wall that led to the aft staircase landing, then poked his AKM around the corner and upward. Tom moved to the other side of the entrance, aiming his big Smith downward.

"We're clear," the skipper called back to the others.

"I've got the rear," Ryan said, placing his torch on the deck and drawing his pistol. "Keep moving."

With Ryan covering the retreat with his SIG-Sauer, the companions hurried down the staircase. He strained his ears to hear the sounds of other footfalls, either from the steps above or from the hallway in the direction of the fire. But he couldn't hear anything over the noise of the cook-offs and the sizzle and pop of the fire. He sure as hell couldn't see anything for the smoke. When Krysty shouted up to him that they were in position, he holstered his weapon, picked up his torch and followed.

As he descended the smoke got thinner and thinner, and there was light coming from below. After another landing and another short flight of steps, the stairway ended on the engine room's steel floor.

Everyone had their blasters out—everyone but the Fire Talker who had retreated deeper into the room and was taking cover beside a steel-cabineted bank of gauges and dials. The companions, Tom and Garwood were stationed to pour withering blasterfire onto the foot of the staircase. They lowered their weapons momentarily, allowing Ryan to step into their midst.

The ship's engine room was low-ceilinged and cavelike, about one hundred feet long and half that wide. Its four engines were enormous, easily thirty feet long, and mounted in side-by-side pairs. The great rusting hulks dominated the center of the space. They had pipe railings around them and catwalks above them.

Torchlight was hardly necessary.

The intense blaze erupting from between the pairs of engines threw a bright, if wavering light over the room.

To Ryan it looked like mortar rounds had ignited some remnant of diesel in the freighter's tanks or fuel lines.

It was as hot as hell, but not nearly as bad as it had been on the deck above. The heat from the fire and most of the diesel smoke was being sucked upward through the irregular gap blown into the ceiling. The holes in the decks above acted like a huge chimney.

The noise from the exploding ammo stores above had gradually lessened; there was just the occasional firecracker string of discharges. The stockpile had apparently burned itself out.

"Which way?" Ryan asked the islander teen as he redrew his pistol.

Without a word, Garwood headed for the stern end of the engines. The riveted deck and walls were covered with peeling white paint, which was stained with streaks of rust and dark, fuzzy blotches of mildew.

"Good grief!" Mildred exclaimed, pointing down the deck, toward the bow.

Low, black blurs were circling around and around, almost too quickly to follow. There were dozens of them, and they were squeaking in panic.

The ship's trapped and terrified rats were going crazy.

Garwood put down his torch and his assault rifle and bent over a circular hatch set low on the wall, just above the join with the deck. It had a wheel-lock on the engine-room side, which he managed to turn without help. The hatch opened onto a black hole. Air whooshed in through it, smelling like rotten eggs.

"The bilges," Tom said.

The teen gathered up his weapon and torch and disappeared through the hole, backward. His torchlight flickered in the opening, growing fainter by intervals.

Steps, Ryan thought. There had to be steps, maybe a ladder on the other side, leading down to the keel.

One by one the others slipped through the circular hole.

The entrance was small and the steps into the dark were hard to negotiate backward. It was taking what seemed like a long time.

Too long.

"Keep moving!" Ryan urged them. He could hear the

tramp of boots on the steps leading down from the Upper Tween deck.

J.B. got past the opening, but with difficulty because his range of arm motion was limited by his rib injury.

Then it was Ryan's turn to descend.

After holstering his SIG-Sauer, he backed through the low hole. He found the steps of a stationary steel ladder with the toes of his boots. As he started down, bracing one hand on the inside of the hatch, blasterfire roared from the other side of the engine room. Bullets banged against the hatch as he slammed it shut. He felt the impacts of the slugs all the way up his left arm, into the socket of his shoulder.

There was no way to dog the hatch from the inside.

Twenty feet below, torchlight danced in a ring where the companions waited for him. The dome of light that was cast revealed a gleaming, black, velvety liquid spreading out all directions. The perimeter of the enclosure was invisible, too wide across for the weak light to reach its edges.

Ryan hurried down the ladder. The lake of black stuff was a remnant of the freighter's supply of bunker oil, he guessed. More than a century ago, when the huge ship had been driven aground, its ruptured fuel tanks had bled down into the bilges. Diluted with sea water, the remaining oil was worthless as fuel, but even after the passage of all that time the stench of sulfur was still overpowering.

By the time he reached the bottom of the ladder, Garwood was already leading the others across the shallow lake on a makeshift walkway. It was constructed of rough planking laid down on top of metal boxes and crates. The footing was wobbly at best, and in places it was slicked with oil; it wasn't meant for a mass, high-speed exodus.

Walking ahead of Ryan, J.B. lost his balance as the planking shifted underfoot, and he plunged in, up over his shins in the gunk.

"Shit!" The Armorer's comment echoed and reechoed in the yawning space.

Ryan quickly helped him back up onto the walkway.

On the starboard side of the ship, directly in front of them, Garwood had set the butt of his torch in a hole in one of the I-beams. It illuminated a half sheet of grubby plywood that rested against the hull, half in, half out of the bilge water. When the teenager slid the barrier aside, bright light streamed into the bilge through a jagged horizontal breach.

Ryan looked up over his shoulder, back the way they'd come, and saw a crescent of light above where the ladder started, where the hatch was. He whipped out his SIG-Sauer, turned on the plank and cut loose, rapid-fire.

The stuttering reports were punctuated by the clang of full metal jackets plowing into the inside of the hatch.

The crescent opened wider, and this time autofire sprayed down into the bilge.

Ryan stood his ground and, with a two-handed grip, put three tightly spaced rounds into the gap between the hatch and the wall.

Boom-clang! Boom-clang! Boom-slap!

Last sound was a 9 mm hitting flesh.

The hatch stayed open.

Ryan turned and quickstepped along the planking to the breach in the hull. There was no longer anyone in front of him. Everyone else had already ducked through the break and was out the other side. When he looked back one last time to check for pursuit, the SIG-Sauer up and ready to fire in his right fist, grens spewing clouds of gas were falling from the hatch into the bilge. They plopped into the bilge water, their caustic fumes boiling from the greasy surface like steam.

Too little, too late.

He crawled through the opening, out into sunlight so bright it hurt his eye. It took a couple of seconds before he could see his surroundings. At his back, towering six stories or more above him was the rusting hull of the freighter; in front of him was the dished-out back of a low sand dune.

Harmonica Tom had the point. He was already cresting the top of the dune and the others were scampering after him, single-file. Mildred had hold of J.B.'s arm on the un-damaged side of his ribs, helping him up the slope. Blaster in hand, Ryan brought up the rear. When he got to the summit of the dune, he looked down on a 150-foot-long, unprotected stretch of sand. It was all that stood between them and the backside of the burning ville.

Running hard, they'd gone about fifty feet down the hill when from the side of the ship behind them somebody let out a loud shout.

And kept on shouting.

It didn't sound like English.

Whatever the hell it was, it was bad news.

Chapter Nineteen

Daniel Desipio sprinted down the broiling hallway, with bullets from behind zinging past his head.

He wasn't just running scared.

He was running scared shitless, weak in the knees with terror as he approached the red glow and its incinerating heat. Forty feet away and it was scalding his bare arms and legs. He could visualize the skin sizzling and withering like steak on a grill. It hurt when he inhaled, too, an awful dull, burning pain in bottom of his lungs that forced him to breathe shallowly, to take tiny sips of air.

Daniel couldn't pull a sudden U-turn and head back for the oncoming Matachìn, yelling in Spanish that he was on their side—in the dark, under these circumstances, no matter what he yelled they'd shoot him for an islander. He didn't want to continue in the direction he was going because he was afraid he was going to be cooked alive. He kept on running because the shooting by his masters was guaranteed, and the frying was not. Sweat poured down his face, down the sides of his chest, the middle of his back and into the crack of his butt.

The red glow was fifteen feet away, then ten.

This was a bad idea, he told himself. A very bad idea.

He instinctively threw up his left arm, shielding that side of his face as he hurtled by the superheated section of wall. Flame rushed out of the hold's doorway like a giant anaconda snapping for his head, and coming up short, it made do by frizzing all the hair on his arm, turning it into little puffs of dust.

His sense of relief as he ran past it was almost hysterical. He suddenly had wings on his heels. Every stride took him farther away from a horrible death. On the fifth step a flurry of blasterfire and dozens of bullet blasted through the wall on his left and up into the ceiling above his head, startling him out of his wits.

In that instant, Daniel felt his bladder release. He hadn't even realized he needed to pee. And to pee massively at that. He kept running as the wetness traveled down the inside of his leg and into his boot. His toes squished every time his foot hit the deck. He didn't care. A little pee in the shoe was much preferable to being burned alive.

As he raced deeper into the darkness and the thickening smoke, he felt the fever pitch of his anxiety level drop a little. Perhaps there would be an opportunity to split off from these strangers ahead, he told himself. It was something he knew he had to do, and soon if he wanted to survive. The man with the eye patch and his six pals were going to continue to fight back, of that he was confident. The Matachìn tended to blast armed opposition first and ask no questions afterward. If you were caught in the wrong place with the wrong people, you were fair game.

He was pretty sure the one they called Ryan wouldn't shoot him without provocation. The islander teen was another story. Garwood's open hostility and aggressiveness toward him had made him flash back to more than a century ago and one of his rare, *SR* book signings. The incident Daniel recalled had taken place in a tiny independent bookstore in a suburban strip mall. It hadn't involved a machine gun, but there were certainly balled fists and physical threats. Something to do with "continuity."

In another life, the idea of sailing away from trouble would have had considerable appeal to him. But in this life, Daniel couldn't run away from what lurked in his blood. It belonged to him, and sadly, he belonged to it. Besides, knowing the Matachìn as he did, he seriously doubted that his temporary saviors could pull off the dash to the waiting ship, let alone the escape by sea.

The pirates had a knack for outthinking and snaring would-be runaways. In fact, they took great pride in it.

If escaping was a lost cause, why had he thrown in his lot with Eye Patch and crew in the first place? The answer was simple. He was more afraid of being blown to shit by shells lobbed onto the island from the tugs. He had witnessed "friendly fire" incidents in Matamoros ville and Browns ville that had taken out his fellow disease-carrying infiltrators. Mortars in the hands of the Matachìn were at best unpredictable. He would have gone into the freighter to hide if the islanders had let him.

The savagery of the current attack, and fresh memories of what had happened before, had sucked him into a kind of panic vortex. In retrospect, he would have been better off if he'd jumped back in his hole in the sand and pulled the lid over the top. But he hadn't been told in advance about Casacampo's battle plan. Information like that was never shared with the lowly *enanos*. He had assumed, like the islanders, that the Matachìn were after plunder, either in the form of select goods or human beings. He was as surprised as the Texicans when that turned out not to be the case.

At the end of the smoky hall, they came upon another set of stairs. The islander boy and the guy with the handlebar mustache checked for hostiles on the staircase. Temporarily at least, there didn't seem to be any. There didn't seem to be any escape route for Daniel, either. Going up the stairs wasn't an option, nor was going back. And for the same reason: the combination of the dengue and the shelling hadn't left the Matachín with a lot of lively targets, they would be itching for something, anything, to chill.

Eye Patch held the fort on the landing while Daniel and the others descended into the bowels of the ship.

It was much lighter, if not cooler, in the freighter's engine room. Even so, Daniel found the place oppressive and deeply disturbing. The fire raging out of control between the massive engine blocks was a force of nature. It hissed and howled and made the floor shake. It reminded him of something immensely industrial, something out of a predark steel mill or foundry. And the low ceiling seemed to press down on him, seemed about to crush him. The ship's rats had the same reaction. Sensitive to sound and vibration, terrified of fire, unsure of an escape route, they chased one another in endless mad circles on the deck.

The black woman gave him a look as he slinked past her, empty-handed. It was much the same look Eye Patch had given him on the deck above after the second shelling when he hadn't bent down to pick up a gun.

"Are you a pacifist, or just some kind of weenie?" she asked him point-blank, revolver in fist.

He didn't respond to the question. He kept on slinking, putting distance between himself and potential trouble. He had learned in his second incarnation that it was usually safer to pretend to be deaf.

These Deathlanders didn't understand his deep moral dilemma. How could they? They had no inkling of his secret identity, of his terrible, unasked-for powers, his lifelong curse. Even if they understood everything and had command of all the scientific detail, he doubted that they would empathize with his plight. From what he'd seen of them so far, their propensity for violence, their unsophisticated code of justice, he was pretty sure they would shoot him in back of the head.

There were two very good reasons why Daniel hadn't picked up a gun from the rubble of the Upper Tween deck corridor. First, he didn't fancy having his hands cut off with a machete. That's exactly what would have happened if he was caught bearing arms against his masters. He had seen too many of the ritual hand-loppings close up. And sometimes he had been forced to gather up the vile things from the scuppers, no longer quivering, but still warm.

The second reason had nothing to do with dire consequences. Though Daniel had made a meager living for years writing about firearms, he didn't know how to use one. He had never shot an automatic weapon. He wasn't sure of the correct way to hold one and certainly couldn't load one, not if his life depended on it. The only "gun" he had ever fired shot BBs, a Daisy Red Ryder carbine, and even that wasn't his. It had belonged to his cousin Arthur Junior. He hadn't loaded or cocked the Red Ryder. Cousin Arthur had insisted on doing that for him, so he wouldn't screw it up. Shooting the BB gun at pop bottles hadn't impressed the young Daniel. Also, and more to the point, he hadn't been able to hit anything, no matter how close the range. Cousin Arthur Junior's cruel ongoing commentary on his marksmanship, or the lack thereof, undoubtedly contributed to his lack of enthusiasm for gun sport as an adult.

The red-haired beauty called up the stairs to Eye Patch, letting him know they were in position.

Daniel had trouble keeping his eyes off her. She was definitely hot: great body, long legs, gorgeous green eyes. The others in Eye Patch's crew he found less appealing. The runt with glasses, the long-haired albino, the tall geezer with nice teeth, the mustache man, the hostile black woman with beaded plaits—to him they seemed like a cross between a rogue military unit and a renegade biker gang. They certainly lacked the style and sensibilities of the heroes of *SR*. Their language was coarse and brutal. They smelled unpleasant, too.

He caught Garwood glaring at him. The teenager had a lot of anger in him over what had happened to his island, his family and his friends. Understandable anger. He needed somewhere to direct that rage, someone upon whom he could vent his fury.

Daniel swallowed hard and averted his gaze. He carefully backed away to the side of a rusted-out control console, trying not to attract further attention to himself.

At Eye Patch's urging, Garwood led them around the rear of the engines and opened the hatch to the bilge. There was still nowhere for Daniel to run. Except for the hatch, the engine room was another dead end. When it came his turn, he backed through the hole and descended into the sulfurous darkness.

It seemed like a long way down. He stepped off the last rung and into the oily bilge water. The light from the

torches didn't illuminate much. He could barely see the
ceiling overhead, and the bilge walls were lost in the blackness.

Daniel saw his opportunity. While the others stood
around waiting for Eye Patch to join them, he backed up,
slowly moving out of the ring of light cast by the torches.
He retreated very carefully so as not to make splashes, his
right arm stretched out behind him, feeling for obstacles.
The torchlight dimmed with distance. Nobody seemed to
notice his absence. Bilge water filled his boots and it got
deeper. He was up to his knees in it when behind he felt
the warm steel of the bilge wall.

Crouching there, trying not to breathe too loudly, he
could see Eye Patch backing through the bright circle of
light that was the engine room hatch. Gunfire broke out
and the clang of bullets hitting metal resounded in the
darkness. Eye Patch slammed the hatch shut. In flickering torchlight he hurriedly climbed down the ladder.

Daniel watched as the line of torches crossed the bilge.
He could see they were running on a raised walkway,
above the bilge water. The torch in front stopped moving
and there was a loud scraping noise. Suddenly a wedge of
brilliant light cut through the darkness, silhouetting the
escapees. Daniel hunkered down lower in the bilge water,
afraid the light would give him away.

When the engine room hatch reopened, the last person
in the line turned and opened fire. There were more clangs
and much louder gun reports.

Which were answered by a burst of autofire that ricocheted wildly through the enclosed space.

A short string of single shots from the last person put
an end to that.

A tall figure ran into the wedge of light and Daniel saw it was Eye Patch. His pals were disappearing one by one through the hole in the hull.

Movement and light up near the ceiling caught Daniel's attention. He watched as the clutch of CS gas grenades dropped through the opening, and he knew what was coming next. The chilling was going to be nonselective. Anyone stricken by tear gas, staggering around in the bilge was dead meat.

Before his eyes started watering, Daniel made his break. He sloshed around the perimeter, then crawled through the breach in the hull. As he stuck his head out, he saw Eye Patch cresting the top of the dune. Eye Patch didn't look back.

Daniel visualized the terrain leading down behind the ville to the water, specifically the open stretch between ship and shanties, which for a brief interval would leave the deserters visible and vulnerable.

Seizing on the chance to further ingratiate himself in the eyes of his masters, Daniel stepped away from the hull, and without leaving the dish of dune, shouted up at the top deck as loud as he could.

"¡Ay ya, los otros!"

He waved his arms, pointed and kept on shouting the alert.

From the deck high above him came the hollow pops of grenade launchers firing, then from over the top of the dune, he heard muffled whumps as projectile canisters exploded.

"Yes!" he exclaimed in English, pumping his fist in the air.

A gun barked from above and the bullet kicked up sand

behind him, missing his shoulder and neck by no more than a half inch.

As gren blasts continued to rain down on the escapees, Daniel threw back his head and cried, *"¡Soy Daniel! ¡Soy cuentista del fuego!"*

Another guncrack, another bullet whined past his head. Thinking it was his accent, he repeated himself, spreading his arms in supplication and surrender.

In reply, the shooter on the main deck opened up full-auto, forcing Daniel to duck back into the ship.

Chapter Twenty

Harmonica Tom's spirits skyrocketed the second he climbed out of the putrid bilge into full, Texican sunlight. All of a sudden, escape seemed not only possible, but highly likely.

His elation and his hope both faded as he summited the facing dune. Beyond the northeast end of the island, he saw four sets of sails bearing down. The pirates' ships were already through the Aransas Pass and into the Waterway. They had the wind behind them. It was going to be tight getting back to *Tempest,* pulling the hook and making top speed before the pursuit swarmed into the little harbor.

At least it was all downhill from here. The shacks on the outer edge of the ville were still standing. While they'd provide no cover from high-powered rifle fire, they'd block the shooters' view of targets running down to the beach.

Tom lowered his head and really picked up the pace, taking the slope in long, even strides.

The red-haired woman, Krysty, was behind him. She was keeping up, no problem, and she was maintaining a twenty-foot distance, calculated to make accurate sniper fire from the ship more difficult.

When he heard the shouting from the freighter, a chill

rippled up his backbone. He couldn't make out the words, but he knew what their impact would be if the top deck was manned by enemy gunners.

A couple of strides later he heard the shrill whistle of incoming. Whatever it was, it was too damn big to be a rifle shot.

Behind and to the right came a double whump of gas grens bursting in the sand. He didn't look back, but he knew the steady breeze would sweep the cottony clouds over the folks running single-file after him.

In short order, two more whumps.

He heard coughing, but he didn't stop, then heard a gunshot. He hoped the others didn't stop. They had to reach the shacks.

More grens exploded behind him.

There was a brief flurry of autofire, but it wasn't aimed at him. Then he was behind the nearest shack and around the bend. When he looked back he saw he was alone.

"Shit!" Tom said.

He immediately reversed course. Higher up the hill, he saw familiar figures on their knees, shrouded by dense clouds of CS smoke. Some were doubled over and wretching in the sand.

The red-haired woman stood between him and the others, about forty feet away. She was apparently unaffected by the gas, as well. Krysty looked at him expectantly. When he didn't make a move to come back to join her, she abruptly turned away, running toward the smoke and her companions.

Tom just stood there for a moment, his guts twisted in a knot. There wasn't any help he could give her or her friends. He imagined what it would be like trying to guide six blinded, vomiting people to the water, to the dinghy and to *Tempest*. If he did that, no one would get away.

There was something else, too.

He knew the significance of the awnings on the Matachìn tugs. He had seen similar sunshades before. He knew the tugs had been converted into slave galleons. Sharing that fact with Ryan and the others had seemed a pointless infliction of torture. At the time, the odds were better they would end up chilled, anyway. Now he wished he had told them. Bottom line: dead over someone else's oar was definitely not how Harmonica Tom wanted to check out.

Turning back for the ville and the beach, he left Ryan and the others to their fate. He felt bad about it, but he did it just the same. He was man enough not to rationalize the decision. He didn't try to make himself feel better by listing all the other things he didn't owe them.

As he ran past the backs of the shacks, overlooking the flattened ruin of the ville, he heard blaster shots from behind.

Who was shooting, he couldn't tell.

But the redhead had a handblaster, he recalled.

There were six quick shots, then silence. Silence except for the rasp of his boots digging into the sand. Whatever had happened, it was over. He muttered a curse out of reflex, but he knew the additional six shots in his handblaster wouldn't have changed the outcome one bit.

When Tom reached the water, he turned left and raced along the shore, into the acrid smoke blowing off the ville. Nothing but smoke was moving inside the perimeter. Smoke and ash. The rows of huts had been turned into a smoldering rubbish pile.

As he ran past the uncovered burial trench, he realized the whole island had become an open grave.

The dinghy was where he'd left it, and it hadn't been hit by mortar shrapnel. Turning the bow around, he pushed the raft into the water, jumped in the stern and stroked hard for his ship.

Because every second counted, he didn't try to pull the dinghy aboard by himself. He just tied the bow off on a side cleat of *Tempest* and climbed aboard. Jumping into the cockpit, he ducked belowdecks and immediately started the engine. The ship had swung around on its anchor. It was pointed bow into the breeze, 180 degrees in the wrong direction.

This wasn't Captain Tom Wolf's first hasty getaway. It was more like his fiftieth—trouble and close scrapes were part and parcel of the trader lifestyle. He knew exactly what to do and when to do it.

Gunning the motor, he slipped it in forward gear. As the ship moved ahead, it took the strain off the anchor line. He left the ship in gear, left it slowly creeping forward and ran to the bow. He grabbed the crank handle and winched up the anchor as fast as he could.

After he locked it off with the eyebolt, he looked toward the ruined JFK Causeway bridge and his heart did a little flutter. The pirate sails were about a quarter of a mile away and closing rapidly.

Tom raced back to the cockpit and cut the wheel hard over, making *Tempest* pivot to port. It was a painfully slow, tight turn. Before the ship came around 180, he was up on the deck, frantically freeing the lines that allowed him to raise all sails. Wind filled them with a loud snap, and because the rudder was hard over, the ship completed the half turn in a hurry.

A rifle shot whined along the starboard gunwhale.

Then another.

He looked over his shoulder and saw the first pursuit ship coming down on him fast. Two pirates with longblasters kneeled on the bowsprit, shoulder to shoulder.

The water in the channel was calm, perfect for shooting.

The distance between Tom's ship and the pirates had dwindled to about two hundred feet. But *Tempest* was picking up speed, moving faster and faster.

More shots zinged through the lines, punching tiny round holes in the sails.

Tom decided it was time to show them this bee had a sting in its tail. He reached up for the PKM's pistol grip and pinned the trigger. The machine gun thundered, and he swept the muzzle back and forth, sending heavy slugs stitching across the oncoming bow. The full-metal-jacket rounds banged the anchor and skipped off the steel rails of the pulpit. One of the shooters crumpled under the hail, and as he did, he lost his weapon over the side. The other pirate grabbed him by the arm or he would have gone overboard, too.

With the shooters occupied, Tom stood from behind his armored cockpit, took careful aim and gave the bow of the ship another sustained burst for good measure. He streamed autofire down the ship's centerline, blasting holes in the steel masts, skimming the cabin roof and the cockpit.

The second volley made the remaining shooter abandon his post, abandon his comrade and duck for cover, and it forced the captain of the pirate ship to take evasive action, slewing his ship from side to side, trying to make the machine gun miss.

Which meant the ship lost speed.

In the confines of the channel, the slowing lead vessel was like a plug in a bottle. There wasn't room for the ships chasing behind to pass, and if they didn't slow down, as well, they would ram into each other from the rear.

Tom's mind was running triple speed as he turned back for the cockpit. How fast were the pirates really? Could he outrun them? In what kind of seas? Were they carrying RPGs, or something else that could reach out long-distance and sink him? How long would they chase him if he could maintain good separation? Would his fuel hold out longer than theirs if the wind died?

The questions had no answers.

But he knew he had to be prepared for the worst. The worst being that he couldn't get cleanly away, and that the enemy ships would swing in close enough to throw grappling hooks and board him. He thought back to the longest chases he'd ever had. They'd all been eventually broken off by bad weather. That was not something he could count on here.

After taking a bearing on the northwestern tip of the island, he lashed the helm in position with a loop of rope. As he slipped belowdecks the rifle fire from the rear resumed. Bullets slapped into the stern and ricocheted off the cockpit armor.

The pirates weren't giving up.

Tom hurried into the salon and grabbed one of the backpacks of C-4. Then he hauled it up the companionway steps into the cockpit.

He was greeted by slugs plinking into the main boom and chipping divots in the fiberglass deck.

When he looked over the armor, he saw the pirate ships

had broken their single-file formation. The channel had widened. They were coming after him two abreast.

And they were gaining.

He quickly untied the wheel and adjusted course, putting the wind square on his sails. *Tempest*'s hull hissed through the water as it picked up a tad more speed.

"Come on, baby. Come on…" he urged.

Chapter Twenty-One

When Krysty Wroth heard the warning shouts, she didn't turn; she ran faster downhill. The advantage of stealth and surprise was gone. All they had going for them was speed. They had to cover the open ground before the pirates started shooting.

They could make it, she told herself. They could still make it.

She heard the pops of a pair of grenade launchers fired from the top deck of the freighter, the whistle of the canisters as they arced to earth, then the hollow explosions behind her. Not the solid whack of frag grens. More CS gas. Her heart sank. She knew they had landed and burst right in front of the companions. She knew the others had run straight into the caustic clouds.

She stopped and looked back. The dark green cans were hissing, belching plumes of white smoke out of the sand. Ryan, Jak, Mildred, Doc, J.B. and Garwood were enveloped in it.

Even as they tried to run through the smoke pouring toward them, more grens landed upwind and burst, doubling the concentration of CS.

Mildred stopped running and dropped to her knees, clutching her eyes and coughing.

Jak tried to run past the second volley, but he was blinded by tears. He tripped and fell.

Another pair of grens exploded upwind, and it was impossible to see anyone else for the boiling smoke.

Krysty turned to Tom who waited by the edge of the ville. He saw what was happening, he couldn't miss it. He had to know what was coming next, too. The pirates were going to swoop in and clean house. They had to get the companions out of the gas, to cover, if not safety. But the skipper just stood there. She knew then he wasn't going to help. His body language said, it's your problem.

Maybe it was.

Maybe that was the hard truth of it. She had no choice. She had to go back. She couldn't leave the others defenseless. No matter what.

Her eyes streaming, her nose and throat burning, Krysty ran back up the hill. The breeze had blown most of the gas away, but not before it had done its damage.

All the companions were down in the sand. All of them were blinded. Tears and mucous streamed down their faces and dripped from their chins. They couldn't even open their eyes for the pain.

J.B. was on hands and knees, vomiting and moaning.

Somewhere in the back of her mind it registered that the Fire Talker was not among them.

Holding her breath, she ran from one fallen friend to the next, trying to pull them to their feet and head them downhill. "Come on! We can't stay here! We've got to move!" she said.

None of them could get up.

Even if had been able to rise, they couldn't see where to run.

"Ryan, please," Krysty said. "Please, you've got to…"

"You go!!" he said, his voice a tortured rasp. "You can still make it! Go while you can!!"

She couldn't. She wouldn't.

Then it was too late.

As CS gas cleared away downwind, she saw figures popping over the top of the dune. At least a dozen. They were carrying longblasters and heading downhill. She had no doubt who they were.

Krysty held her .38 Smith & Wesson in a solid, two-handed grip and aimed up the hill. She let the murdering bastards get within thirty yards, then she emptied her blaster into them, center body.

Every shot hit its target, but only one of the pirates went down. He fell backward on his butt, but immediately got up again. Like it was nothing.

Armor, she realized. They had body armor.

The Matachìn broke into a trot.

No time for the speedloader. She rolled to her feet and scrambled to reach Ryan's side. She was trying to get his SIG-Sauer clear of its holster when a gruff voice from very close behind her said, "No!"

She looked up. The pirates stood in a half circle around her and her incapacitated companions. They held submachine guns in their grubby hands, and machetes were scabbarded at their hips.

If enemy guns hadn't been aimed at the others, if it had been just her facing them down, she would have gone for the blaster, anyway, taken as many head shots as she could get off before they chilled her. But under the present circumstances, it was something she couldn't bring herself to do.

She didn't want to watch as her friends were murdered.

The Matachìn closed in and started confiscating the companions' weapons. Krysty couldn't tell if Ryan and the others didn't resist the pat-downs because they couldn't see, or whether they realized resistance was futile. Eyes weren't necessary to recognize the pressure of a blaster muzzle against the back of your head.

Krysty stared down a gun barrel and surrendered her empty .38 without a struggle.

Up close the pirates had a style and an aroma all their own. The style was like a uniform, down to the hair. Every one of them wore dreadlocks. Some had piled the lengths of felted hair piled on top of their heads and woven gold chains through them. Their weapons were all of the same design, and it was one she had never seen. The blasters looked like nine millis, but with very short barrels and top-of-action handles-rear sight protectors like M-16s, only scaled down in size. Their armor consisted of overlapping plates of black metal or ceramic, which was sewn into vests of what she knew to be Kevlar cloth. The armor covered their chests, backs, crotches and legs.

The pirate with the highest pile of dreads was ordering the others around. High Pile seemed well pleased. She couldn't understand a word of what he was saying.

Understanding began to dawn on her, as the Matachìn lined up in front of her in order of hairdo height, with leers on their filthy faces. It dawned brighter when they unbuckled their crotch armor, then opened the fronts of their trousers. Some of them were already in a state of extreme readiness.

Daniel Desipio stepped out from behind the last pirate in line. He wasn't tear-gassed, and he wasn't in restraints.

It was pretty obvious to Krysty that he was the one who had given them away.

"You backstabbing little shit," Krysty called to him. "I wish I'd saved my last bullet for you."

The Fire Talker stood well back from her and the other companions, poised to duck behind the pirate's considerable bulk if things suddenly got out of hand.

"We all do what we have to in order to survive," he said with somewhat brittle conviction.

"You didn't have to do this to us," Krysty said. "You wanted to do this to us."

"Hardly," Daniel said. "Seeing you and your friends brought so low gives me no pleasure at all. And I will get no pleasure from watching what comes to you next. But I have to watch because I've been ordered to do so."

"Poor, poor you," Krysty said.

High Pile was at the head of the line. He was the only one who hadn't partially disrobed. He gave up his place in the queue to a much younger, much taller man.

Krysty fought back a start of shock when she realized the guy with the weird eye was wearing a woman's dress pulled down over his body armor. The shoulder and side seams were all split to hell. The dress had bloodstains. It had evil written all over it. The pirate standing in front of her dropped his machete scabbard and belt, then undid his fly.

"What's going on?" Ryan said hoarsely. He still couldn't see for his tears. There was a gun barrel pressed behind his left ear. "What are they doing, Krysty?"

She wasn't about to tell him, although it was pretty clear what was going to happen to her.

If Ryan tried to help, if he went berserk when he found out, he'd get a bullet in his head.

Krysty rose to her feet. Outnumbered, outgunned, she knew she was probably going to die in the next few minutes, and wish she was dead long before she breathed her last. At least the pirates were coming at her one at a time, in some kind of dreadlock pecking order. That gave her some hope for a little bit of payback.

Given the size and strength of the man who was about to attempt to violate her, she wasn't sure she could do the trick unarmed. She had a secret weapon, though, an invisible connection to the power of the earth. Her mother, Sonja, had schooled her in the ways of Gaia, the Earth Mother, passing on the ancient knowledge that had been passed on to her. Krysty rarely tapped into the energy of that potent spirit, and never without good cause. She needed that special help now, and in silent prayer, in the words her mother had taught her, she begged for Gaia's intercession.

The mantra was like flipping a switch, opening a circuit that was always there, always ready.

Gaia came to her as a sensation of warmth, then crackling electric energy. It surged into the soles of her feet, up her legs, filled her chest and arms, illuminated the inside of her skull. She felt a confidence and deep calm.

Time seemed to slow down as the pirate reached for her left shoulder.

He said something in his native garble talk that made the others laugh.

Krysty didn't look down at his protruding manhood. She stared him straight in the weird eye. Her gaze didn't drop to the target until his filthy fingers actually touched her skin. The designated target wasn't his exposed crotch; it was five inches below the point of his dirty chin.

When he touched her, it triggered an automatic explosion of movement.

Precise.

Lethal.

Krysty's right arm shot upward as her legs drove down into the sand. With every ounce of Gaia strength behind it, she thrust her stiffened fingers into the front of his exposed throat. Like a battering ram, her arm didn't flex. Nor did her wrist. Her strike hand was rigid as stone as it plunged into his windpipe. The box of cartillage crunched under her fingertips. She felt it crush to bits against the front of his spine.

One blow.

One stunning blow.

Soundlessly the pirate slipped to his knees, clutching at his throat with both hands. His mouth opened and closed, but no sound emerged. Nothing went in, either. His airway was sealed shut by the massive trauma. Confidence gone, there was panic in eyes shot with blood, bulging as if about to pop from their sockets. The pirate's face turned red under the brown, then purple, then black.

He slumped to his side and died horribly, kicking his legs as he helplessly strangled. He died without emitting so much as a peep.

His fellow pirates rushed over and tried to help, but there was nothing they could do for him. A tracheotomy was beyond their physiological knowledge and medical skill.

At the end, in his last spasm, he fouled himself so badly even his pirate friends had to back away.

The massive expenditure of force left Krysty completely exhausted, as weak as a baby. It was always like that immediately afterward, but this time the strength left her more abruptly than usual. She couldn't repeat the trick without recuperating.

She had hoped a demonstration on one of their kind would make the others rethink their plans for amusement.

It didn't.

They jumped his corpse and gang-rushed her from all sides, easily pulling her down to the sand on her back. She tried to fight them, but was so drained of strength she couldn't push them off. When they had her securely pinned, they began pulling up her shirt and hauling her jeans down around her knees. She felt air and sun and sand on her nether parts.

"*¡Pubis roja!*" one of them howled in delight.

"*¡Jugoso!*" declared another.

"Krysty, what the fuck is going on?" Ryan said, trying to rise to his feet only to be pushed down with the gun muzzle.

How was she supposed to tell her lover that she was about to be raped to death while he knelt helpless not thirty feet away?

Before they could get her boots off and pull her pants off over them to spread her legs, High Pile intervened. He stopped the gang rape with a few well-chosen words.

Enano something, Krysty thought he said. What it meant, she had no clue. That it worked was all that mattered.

The pirates backed away from her, shaking their heads in disappointment as they stuffed themselves back in their flies.

Krysty tugged down her shirt and pulled up her pants. She redid the buttons with difficulty, her fingers were trembling that hard.

She looked to High Pile to convey thanks, but he wasn't paying any attention to her. He barked another order, and his underlings scurried to obey.

A gunny sack was tossed onto the sand. It landed with the clank of metal. Heavy metal. The pirates dumped out the contents: chains and shackles. Before the others could recover, their ankles were cuffed. A short length of chain connected the shackles, making it impossible to run. After similar manacles were clapped on their wrists, chains were connected between wrists and ankles, so the captives couldn't swing a blow.

Krysty was shackled in exactly the same fashion.

And when they were all suitably trussed as individuals, a long length of chain was passed through loops in their ankle cuffs, linking them together.

The pirates jerked and kicked them to their feet. Then they were marched back up the dune, back toward the freighter.

Ryan, Jak, Mildred, Doc, J.B. and Garwood still couldn't see. Tears still streamed down their faces. Their eyelids were almost swollen shut. They were still racked with spasms of coughing.

The new slaves were made to file past High Pile and Daniel Desipio.

As she passed Daniel, Krysty hawked and with a last smidgeon of Gaia power spit square in his face.

The impact made his head snap back.

Chapter Twenty-Two

Harmonica Tom watched as the two fastest pursuit ships continued to close on his stern. He knew he was getting everything there was to get out of *Tempest*. There was no doubt in his mind that in a fair race between the three, he would come in dead last. If he did nothing, the pirates would bracket him in the open water, bring their grappling hooks to bear and swing aboard in droves.

Desperate times called for desperate measures.

Tom cut the helm over to starboard, steering for the mainland shore. He knew the shoals around Padre; he was pretty sure they didn't. Even if they did, it was the only card he had to play.

Holding course with his left hand, he opened the backpack of C-4. He dumped out a couple of bricks onto the cockpit's bench seat, then picked out a remote detonator. Leaning against the wheel, working on the cabin top in front of it, he ran a power check on the remote, making sure it lit up. Setting it aside, he rigged four pounds of high explosive in two chunks.

He wasn't sure yet how he was going to use the plastique. Mebbe he would wait until the pirates got closer and then lob the armed bricks onto the respective decks. Mebbe if things really went downhill, if he got boarded, he'd blow up *Tempest* himself and two pirate ships along with it.

Blasterfire from behind, angling in from both ships, rattled the stays. It forced him to duck momentarily. When he popped back up, he dead-reckoned a line that ran from the northwest tip of Padre with a dip in the bluff along the mainland shore. Then he checked his compass reading in case enemy blasterfire made taking a line of sight a dicey proposition at the last minute.

If he missed the gap in the shoal, if the sandbar had shifted more than ten yards in either direction since the last time he was here, it was going to be all over for him in a big hurry.

If he made it through, he had a fighting chance.

The pursuit continued to gain on him. At the rate they were traveling, they would be side by side with him as he hit the slot.

He had one more trick up his sleeve.

He was still running with engine as well as sails to squeeze the most speed out of his ship. As the shoal came up fast, Tom pulled the motor into neutral.

Tempest slowed sickeningly.

The pursuit seemed to leap forward.

The pirates were so preoccupied with coming alongside, that they didn't see the color change rushing up at them. From emerald green to lime green.

The ship on the starboard side hit the sandbar at what had to be fifteen knots. The keel instantly grounded, the bow pointed up at a sixty-degree angle. The vessel stopped so short that the forward momentum cracked off its main mast at the deck. Undoubtedly it had been weakened by his last burst of machine-gun fire. As the mast and its sheets toppled over into the water, Tom let out a whoop and dropped the motor back in gear.

The other ship cut speed, veered in behind him and followed him through the slot. As they shot through the gap, the distance between them was about twenty feet.

Another hump of sand was coming up fast. As Tom tried to bring *Tempest* to port, the ship slowed a little, and the pursuer, keeping a straight course, sped up and joined. For an instant they were pressed hull to hull. Fiberglass squeaking against fiberglass.

Tom watched in astonishment and fury as the pirates waiting in the bow jumped from their boat to his. No grappling hooks. No lines. They just jumped, landing with loud thuds on his foredeck.

Then the pirate ship stopped dead as it, too, ran aground. Men in the cockpit were thrown up into the sheets, into the booms, thrown overboard. The vessel was stuck good, but it didn't lose its masts.

Tom popped his head up over the cabin roof and saw four men on his foredeck. They were unslinging submachine guns and taking cover in front of the cabin. A glance over his shoulder told him that the two remaining pursuers were following in his wake at a discreet distance. He slipped a loop of line over the wheel to hold course, then drew his handblaster.

Tom rolled out of the portside of the cockpit, and came up against the rail in a shooting crouch. One of the pirates angled around the front corner of the cabin, trying to get a bead on him with his submachine gun. Before he could touch off a round, the big wheelgun barked and bucked.

A hole opened up in the front of the guy's throat, as chunks of flesh and blood blew out the back. The pirate flopped under the rail, his head hanging down loose at an unnatural angle, like a broken doll. Then as the ship hit a line of chop, the body slipped over the side.

Tom caught another movement at the corner of the cabin and fired again. The pirate ducked back, but not quickly enough.

The .45 slug took off half his head, dreads and all.

Sensing that they were losing their advantage, the remaining two pirates rose in unison and sent autofire streaming his way. Then they charged the starboard rail, still firing, trying to pin him down in the stern. As the ship hit the chop of the Gulf, it porpoised and rolled, making it hard for them to keep their balance and stay on target.

Tom jumped back in cockpit and swung the rudder over hard. The main boom swung in the opposite direction, sweeping across the deck and knocking one of the boarders into the water. The sound the boom made against his head was hollow like hammer hitting a coconut. The impact left a smear of blood on the sail.

The last pirate wasn't going to give up. He resumed the attack, rushing down the rail while he fired from the hip.

He ran out of ammo amidships.

Tom popped up from behind the cabin and had him flat-footed, dead in the water.

Grinning maniacally, the pirate dropped the empty blaster and reached behind his back for another clip.

Tom cocked back the Smith's hammer, single action.

The pirate held up the full mag, showing it to Tom, as though he thought the captain wouldn't blast him. Or maybe he didn't care.

Instead of shooting him in the heart, the skipper lowered his aimpoint and put a .45 round through his right knee.

The leg gave way at once and the pirate hit the deck,

no longer smiling. His leg half blown off, he was screaming like a baby. High and shrill.

"There, there now," Tom said as he holstered his
weapon. "Let me fix that for you."

He climbed over the cabin and came around behind the
pirate. Without a word, he looped a line around the man's
neck, cinched a quick knot, then used a pulley to jerk him
up the main mast, hanging him from the yardarm.

The pirate stood on the tiptoe of his good leg, able to
keep from strangling only if he maintained his balance.

Tom tied off the line on a cleat, leaving the man to toe
dance, then checked the other body for signs of life.
Finding none, he dragged the head-shot corpse to the
stern.

As he did, he talked to the toe dancer, not giving a good
goddamn if he was understood. "You dirty bastards chilled
a bunch of friends of mine," he said. "You chilled them in
awful ways."

Looking back toward the stern, he saw that one of the
pursuit ships had stopped to pick up the bodies of the two
pirates overboard, the throat-shot one and the boom-
busted one. Just like off the beach at Padre, the Matachìn
were recovering their dead.

It gave Tom an idea.

The other ship kept coming, and it was gaining fast.

"Know what that gets you?" Tom asked the toe dancer.
"Chilling my friends?"

The pirate had no clue. His neck was stretched to its
limit, the rope creaking under the suspended weight.

"It gets you fucked by Harmonica Tom."

With that, the skipper of *Tempest* flipped up the cockpit
seat cushion and dug out a pair of bright orange lifejack-

ets. Wrestling the corpse with half a head onto its side, he got the limp arms through the lifejacket holes, then rolled the body onto its back. He laid one of the blocks of C-4 on the chest, then folded over the front panels and cinched the binding straps up extra tight.

Tom returned to the mast, uncleated the end of the line connected to the other pirate and hauled on it hard, yanking the guy off his tippy toes. After a minute or so of letting him dangle, when he stopped kicking his good leg and his face went deep purple, Tom lowered him to the deck.

He put the other lifejacket on the unconscious man. This time he stuffed the brick of C-4 into the back of it, where the pirate couldn't get at it, then he really bore down on the binding tapes.

After dragging him to the stern, he threw some water in his face to wake him up. When the pirate blinked at him, Tom tipped him over the side. He did the same with the dead guy.

Tempest sailed on, leaving two men in lifejackets bobbing in its wake.

One of the floaters was conscious enough to wave an arm at the oncoming pursuit ship.

Tom knew the guy wasn't waving to be picked up; he was trying desperately to wave off his pirate kin.

But they didn't know that.

The skipper took out his harmonica, and tapping his foot, started up a lively tune, a kick-up-your-heels-and-dance kind of tune.

Sure enough, the ship closing in on him dropped sail and slowed to pick up the wounded and the dead. The fourth ship was coming up on it from behind, trying to reengage the pursuit.

When the lead ship stopped alongside the floating men, Tom put down his harmonica, armed the detonator and, pointing it over the stern, hit the little red button.

With a tremendous flash and boom, a water spout shot into the sky. Along with it went half the ship's port side. The plume of debris was spectacular.

"Whoo-wee!" Tom exclaimed.

Stuff blown skyward rained down all around the stricken craft, splashing in a wide circle. All of a sudden there were a lot more corpses and parts thereof for the pirates to recover.

As water flooded into the breached side of hull, the ship immediately began to tilt in that direction, the masts angling lower and lower until they touched the water.

The fourth and last ship approached the wreck cautiously, just in case there were more explosives.

The chase had ended.

And ended badly for the Matachìn.

With the pressure off, Tom indulged himself. He laughed and hooted and danced an ungainly jig accompanied by himself on the harmonica.

The moment of triumph passed and the skipper of *Tempest* was left with lingering doubts. Serious doubts. Was what he had just done enough? Did it balance the books? After all, the pirates had murdered a couple hundred people. They had brought down one of the hellscape's living legends, Ryan Cawdor.

On its face it hardly seemed like tit for tat.

Did there have to be more? If so, how much more? Did the payback have to be times ten, times twenty?

He still had a shitload of C-4 that could be put to use. What good was jack when it had the blood of so many good people on it?

It was something he would have to contemplate.

Tom cut his engine and let the wind take his ship southwest, then scooped a bucket of seawater to sluice the residue of brains and skull off his foredeck.

Chapter Twenty-Three

On the beach below the *Yoko Maru,* the new slaves awaited their masters' pleasure. Ryan could see again, as could his companions and the islander boy, Garwood. His eye still burned, still teared a little, but he could see, and he was aware of the totality of their predicament. The situation was beyond desperate.

Disarmed.

Chained.

Held at blasterpoint.

Prisoners all, but to what end? He knew nothing about the pirates, except they were triple brutal, didn't seem to speak English and packed some impressive weaponry. They had slaughtered an entire ville for what? Not for its material wealth. Most of that had burned in the shanty-town or was still burning in the grounded freighter. They had made no attempt to put out the fires or to secure the goods that hadn't been destroyed.

They didn't seem to give a damn about any of it. About any of the things that the people of the hellscape would've gladly chilled for.

It was something that really worried Ryan. As long as their motives were unknown, their future actions couldn't be anticipated.

He was furious at himself for letting Daniel live. He

should have chilled him when they first boarded the freighter. But he'd had no way of knowing he was in league with the Matachìn.

Standing behind the pirate with the tallest pile of dreads, Daniel looked like a pet that was barely tolerated, a creature used to receiving the back of a hand on a whim. Cowed. Cringing. Servile. That's one reason Ryan figured he was harmless. Despicable but harmless.

Wrong.

The nature of the pirate–Daniel Desipio relationship was as unclear as everything else. What had he been doing on the island? Scouting it out for the attack? That didn't seem likely. There was no way for him to pass information he had gathered to the pirates. Not without leaving the place. It was too isolated. And if he had left Padre Island to deliver his scouting report, why had he come back? There would have been no reason to do that.

"We almost made it," Krysty said. "If it hadn't been for that smarmy little bastard, we would have. We were that close."

"At least Tom got away," Ryan said.

"He turned his back on us," the redhead said. "He ran off with his ship and left us for dead."

"He didn't owe us anything," Ryan countered. "There was nothing he could do. And he had the right to save himself."

"Would we have left him like that?"

"If the situation was reversed, I'd say yes. In a heartbeat."

Krysty didn't like that answer, but she knew it to be true.

A quartet of pirates marched down the slope from the

freighter solemnly carrying the body of the man she had killed, evidently some kind of officer. They bore the corpse back to the beach where a funeral pyre had been constructed. The bodies of the Matachìn fallen were laid out in a pyramid on top of stacks of unburned wood scavenged from the ville. With great care they set the corpse among the others.

An explosion rolled over the island, a distant boom from the southwest. The companions couldn't see what it was, but they recognized the sound. There were smiles all around.

"Guess old Tom found some use for that C-4," J.B. said. The Armorer was in a bad way. His face was twisted in pain, and it looked pale and drawn. The CS gas hadn't helped his breathing, and the paroxysms of vomiting hadn't helped his ribs.

"Our intrepid captain," Doc said. "I wish him godspeed."

"Hope he kicked their asses good," Mildred said.

"Mebbe you'd better wait before you light that pyre," Ryan told one of the pirates. "From that sound, it's my guess there's some more of you bastards in need of ceremonial burning."

The man said something back, something fast and singsong. From his expression it was a threat.

"What language are they talking?" Krysty said.

"Spanish, kind of," Mildred said.

"Definitely a variation of the loving tongue," Doc said. "But not Castillian."

"You understand it?" Ryan asked them.

"Some of it," Mildred said.

Doc nodded.

"It would be better not to let them know that," Ryan said. "We might be able to pick up something useful."

"¡Silencio, esclavos!" the pirate snarled.

"Does the last bit mean what I think it means?" Krysty whispered.

"Unpaid labor unto death, I am afraid," Doc said. "We have joined the ranks of the terminally employed."

Along with the handful of other survivors from the freighter, the companions and Garwood were forced to climb into the rafts and then row themselves to the waiting tugs. The Matachìn commander rode in the bow of the companions' dinghy, making notes in pencil in a crumpled little book. Daniel sat at his feet. Two of his underlings guarded the rowers with leveled submachine guns.

The tugs' engines were silent. As they approached the vessels, long oars in a row dipped lightly into the water, holding position. In the skinny shadow of the awnings, gaunt sunburned faces stared back at them.

Hopeless faces.

As Mildred leaned into her oar she said, "I'm getting a premonition of what our job is going to be."

When they came alongside the pirate flagship, after the commander and Daniel had debarked, they were forced to board in a clinking, clanking, clumsy conga line, then they were herded together on the stern deck.

Ryan looked closely at the people sitting under the awning: shirtless men and boys, a few women, also shirtless. Their manacles were chained to the oars so they couldn't let go. There were lash marks on their bare backs and arms.

Some looked to be at death's door, living skeletons with blistered, peeling skin. They were breathing hard though they weren't exerting themselves. Their whip wounds were inflamed and leaking green pus.

It occurred to Ryan that the prisoners from Padre Island were replacements. But for those already chilled or the weak?

When the pirates disconnected the newcomers, pulling the length of chain out of the loops of their ankle cuffs, Garwood sprang away like a tiger. In three great hops he was behind Daniel and had flipped his manacles over his head and down over his neck. Crossing the cuffs behind the startled man's head, the boy twisted his arms, tightening the chain-link garrote.

Daniel's eyes bulged and his tongue protruded. He tried to shift out of the choke hold, but the teenager wouldn't allow it.

Before the boy could break his neck or strangle him, one of the pirates drew his machete and whacked him with the flat of it on top of the head. The stunning blow drove the boy to his knees, taking Daniel down with him. Before he could recover his grip, the Fire Talker disengaged himself and moved well out of range.

The Matachìn raised the heavy blade, winding up to use its long edge to take off Garwood's head at the shoulders. Before he struck the fatal blow, he looked over at his leader.

The commander waved him off impatiently. *"Chico es muy fuerte, necessito no le matar,"* he said.

"I'll get you!" the boy howled at Daniel as he jumped back up. "I'll get you, yet. You wait and see…"

The Fire Talker rubbed his throat. The chain links had left angry welts from ear to ear.

"I'm afraid that's not likely," the commander said.

Daniel looked from the livid boy to a pirate bent over the stern deck. His expression fell as the man opened an inset hatch about four feet by four feet. A pair of pirates swooped in and grabbed hold of Daniel under the arms. They carried him bodily to the opening and threw him in, feet-first. The hatch slammed shut with a thud. One of the pirates twisted shut the latch, locking him inside.

"So the turncoat is a prisoner, too," Doc said.

"That's strange," Mildred said. "It's not like he could swim and get away."

"Don't like the look of that," Ryan said, nodding toward the awnings.

The Matachìn were unchaining some of the slaves from the oars and making them shuffle to the stern.

The weakest ones.

Those who could barely stand were separated from the rest. They were so exhausted they couldn't resist. One by one they were bent over the stern rail and dispatched with single machete blows across the backs of their necks. Their bodies were dumped over the side.

It was a horrible spectacle, barbaric.

Some of the victims shut their eyes tight as the blades whistled down. Others looked off into space. A few looked back to the other slaves. Their expressions said, "Make them pay for this."

Those who had been spared beheading stood huddled in a corner of the stern while the commander took stock of the new arrivals. He felt their muscles, poked their ribs, examined their backs. When he touched J.B., the Armorer grimaced in pain. It was clear he was not in top shape.

At the commander's order, one of the pirates pulled up

the hem of J.B.'s shirt, exposing the multicolored bruising over his ribs.

He waved J.B. to one side.

The side with the other weaklings.

"Are they going to chill J.B.?" Krysty said.

The pirates quickly moved the fresh slaves forward, forcing them to take the newly emptied places behind the oars. The rowers sat three across on crude wooden platforms, all pulling on the same shaft. The seats were unpadded; there were no backrests to lean against. Ryan watched in silent fury as both his manacles were chained to the oar. Mildred sat on his right, closest to the gunwhale.

Ryan laid his hands on the highly polished shaft. Polished by human skin.

The commander climbed the stairs to the pilothouse deck. From that vantage point, he shouted a curt order.

What he wanted them to do was obvious.

Row.

A pirate on the stern deck started pounding a steel drum with rag-wrapped hammers, setting the stroke rhythm. From behind there were the cracks of whips as the overseers urged the slaves to pull harder, pull faster.

It was difficult to get the timing at first. Everyone on the oar had to pull together, and all the oars on the side of the tug had to pull together, as well.

As Ryan was struggling to make it all work, a lash struck him across the shoulders. It felt like a red-hot wire. It made him sit up straight.

He turned and glared up at the man who had just struck him. Dirty face. Dirty hands. Nasty matted hair. He smelled like a bear pit. The pirate grinned as he coiled his short, braided whip for another blow. He clearly enjoyed this part of his work.

Once they had acquired some momentum, the rowing was a little easier. Ryan and Mildred fell into the rhythm of it.

The tugboats headed south, away from the island, to what had to be a prearranged rendezvous point. Three of the pursuit sailboats were waiting for them offshore. Two of the pirate vessels were damaged, one badly. And one of the ships was missing.

"Tom did good," Mildred said.

The commander was not at all pleased. After yelling at the sailboat crews, he gave the order to resume rowing.

Under threat of the lash, the slaves leaned on their oars, once again working up momentum. Facing the rear, Ryan had a view of the still-burning freighter. He also saw some of the pirates lounging at the stern rail. They were laughing. Trinkets were on display. Gold trinkets. It looked like they were making bets.

Then they started dividing the weaklings into pairs and standing them side by side. Short and tall. Skinny and skinnier. Old and young. Male and female. This was the source of more laughter and backslapping among the pirates.

Ryan watched as J.B. was forced to stand next to a much bigger man, older, with a mat of gray hair on his chest. All the body fat had been worked off him. His face was haggard and grim.

From the pilothouse deck, the commander gave another order to his crew.

"What did he say?" Ryan asked Mildred.

"Whoever wins, lives."

Chapter Twenty-Four

Daniel groaned when the pirates hoisted him up by the armpits. He had been hoping for a few more hours, even a day or two of freedom above deck. There was no reason for him to be thrown into the hold so soon. They were offshore and would remain offshore for the entire voyage back home. Casacampo didn't question orders; he followed them, to the letter. By order of the Lords of Death and Atapul X, *enanos* were to be kept in solitary confinement en route to their missions and after their missions were completed. It was supposed to be a safeguard, to keep the plague from spreading to the crew and slaves, and to other unintended targets. The dengue weapon had no antidote. Once it was released in a population, there was no stopping it. It burned through lives like wildfire. If it wasn't used with great caution, it could destroy everything the Lords had built.

Still, and this was what stuck in Daniel's craw, everyone knew that mosquitos didn't fly miles out to sea.

And mosquitos were the only way the plague was spread.

The pirates dumped him through the open hatch, into a chamber just big enough for one person. When the hatch slammed down, he knew to duck his head. He was plunged in darkness. It took a few moments for his eyes to adjust.

The cell had a vent at the back, near the ceiling, about six inches high by a foot long. It was covered with a fine mesh screen to keep mosquitos out. The vent let in a little light and a little fresh air. If he pressed his cheek against the inside of the hatch and twisted his head just right, he could look out at the boat wake.

He didn't feel much like twisting his head at that moment. His neck still ached, and he could almost feel the chain the islander boy had tried to choke him with.

The narrow chamber was furnished with a fiber mat on the floor for sleeping, a plastic water jug, and a covered bucket for excrement and urine.

Cozy was not the word for it.

Daniel shuddered to think how much of his life since his resurrection had been spent in a foul stifling cage just like this.

They only let him out to spread the plague.

And there was no telling when that would happen again.

Daniel slumped to the mat and hung his head in his hands. He knew what the redhead thought of him. What Eye Patch and the others thought of him. But he didn't consider himself evil at heart. The Matachìn, now they were evil. They had a choice in their behavior. They were volunteers in the service of the Lords. They signed on to commit excesses in the name of a greater authority. The Lords, they were even more evil. As in the Mayan myths, they commanded human suffering, sickness and death on a colossal scale. And they reveled in their power, always seeking to expand their territory. If anything, Daniel considered himself a victim of circumstance and his own naïveté.

Was there ever a pat on the head and a "Good job, Daniel?"

Nope.

Was there ever a reward for his diligent service?

Nope again.

His only reward was occasionally being let loose on the world. That was also his punishment. His freedom meant other people's horrible deathes, which he had to watch over and over again.

He couldn't understand why the carriers were always kept apart. They couldn't infect one another. And they could provide each other with companionship, a sense of shared humanity. That might have made the condition more bearable.

In a self-pitying mood, he fell back on a familiar replay: how it had all come down to this. He recalled the day of his arrival on Devil's Island in a kaleidoscope of image and sensation. The heat. The jungle. The screaming of the howler monkeys. Crocs. Wild dogs. Snakes. The overgrown concrete prison. Moldy outside, inside spotless. He flashed back to a spartanly furnished, white-painted cell. To the experiments. All very clinical. Sterile. Injections of serum by little brown nurses in starched white uniforms.

In the preliminary interviews back in the States, no one had said anything about mosquitos.

Or bioweapons.

They hadn't mentioned it was a military research program.

He had gotten sick the first week. All the test subjects had gotten sick. He was one of the few who recovered, and the recovery had taken months. Only then did the scientists of Project Persephone tell him what they'd done to him. After it was too late. They told him they had created a weapon they couldn't control. Morpholinos, anti-sense oligos, the entire genetic engineering bag of tricks, had no effect on the carriers. What had been done to their blood could not be undone. By way of an apology the scientists had offered him an alternative to termination or permanent resident status on Devil's Island.

Daniel shuddered as he remembered the thawing, his waking up in a stainless-steel coffin. He remembered his first agonizing, lung-ripping inhalation.

When he came out of cryostasis, still on the island, he learned that the offspring of the prisoners had renamed that awful place Xibalba.

The Mayan word for hell.

Once again alone in the narrow dark with his recycling thoughts, alone for God knew how long, Daniel Desipio began to softly weep.

Chapter Twenty-Five

Ryan pulled back on the oar, studying the pirates as they argued among themselves on the stern. They were moving the five pairs of combatants around, setting the order of the upcoming fights to the death. When the order was finalized, it appeared that J.B.'s match was scheduled for last.

At the end of the line of fighters, the Armorer leaned against the stern rail, arms folded over his rib cage.

Mildred was beside herself. "J.B. can't fight," she said to Ryan. "Not with those ribs. Look at how big the other guy is."

"Mebbe he can protect them," Cawdor said. He didn't know what else to say. He was plenty worried, too.

"The other guy saw his chest," Mildred "He saw J.B.'s ribs when the dreadmaster lifted up his shirt. He knows where the bull's-eye is."

"J.B. will think of something. He always does." Ryan sounded more confident than he felt. How he felt was pretty goddamn awful. He had been reduced to a spectator. He couldn't help his oldest friend fight for his life and he couldn't slip him a weapon that would tip the odds in his favor. All he could do was watch.

As the coxswain pounded out the tempo for the rowers, the pirates unmanacled the first two fighters and shoved them together in the middle of the stern deck.

The two scrawny men were evenly matched in size and reserves of strength. They both knew exactly what was at stake. They threw themselves at each other like wildcats. The strategy was obvious. They were trying to seize the advantage before their energy gave out. Punches, kicks, claw hands came in frantic flurries as the men stood toe-to-toe. There was no defense, just offense.

The pirates ringing the stern rails whooped and hollered, cheering for whichever man they had bet on.

Blood drops spattered the deck as the two barefoot fighters clenched and grappled. It didn't take long for them to begin to wear down. After two minutes the punch fest became a hug fest as they hung on to each other for support, trying to regather their strength. Their body blows lost power and came in single punches instead of combinations, and at less frequent intervals.

Gasping for breath, neither could gain advantage.

The pirates' cheers turned to boos.

It looked like the stalemate was going to continue, a round-and-round, slow shuffle dance, when one of the men suddenly collapsed to his knees. He was unable to get up, unable to stop the other guy from swinging around behind him, wrapping both hands around his neck and squeezing.

The kneeling man was too weak to fend him off. He couldn't pry the fingers off his throat.

It was just a matter of time.

The squeezer kept up the pressure until his opponent went limp, then he let the body drop to the deck. The other guy wasn't dead, Ryan could see him breathing. He was just choked out and unconscious.

The victor stood over the prostrate loser, hands on hips, breathing hard.

One of the pirates handed him a machete. It had a wicked gut hook at its tip and the main edge looked razor-sharp.

"Good grief!" Mildred moaned.

What happened next wasn't clean and it wasn't pretty. It was a hack job, start to finish. Death, when it came to the fallen man, came as a result of forty shallow chops, instead of one. The rain of blows sprayed blood in a wide fan across the deck and over the stern gunwhale. This drew cheers from the pirates. At least the guy remained unconscious throughout. When the deed was done, the machete was taken away from the man. As he was dragged to an empty place under the awning and chained to an oar, winning and losing bets were paid off.

No one bothered to wash off the deck before the next set of fighters was thrown together: a skinny man and a large woman, both naked to the waist and streaked with sweat and dirt.

"I can't watch this," Mildred said, turning her head away, looking out at the Gulf, as she continued to row in time to the drumbeat.

Ryan wouldn't permit himself to look away from the spectacle. He was hoping to find some kind of strategy that would work for J.B., some plan, some trick he could yell out to him.

There was a lot of punching and kicking between the mixed sex fighters. At one point the man had the upper hand after straight punching his opponent in the face and buckling her knees. But he couldn't close the deal.

The woman, who outweighed him by forty pounds, shot a snapkick to his solar plexus that made her heavy breasts fly almost up to her chin. The heart kick dropped the guy like a sack of rocks, an event that drew cheers from the audience.

The woman did a better job with the machete.

Five strokes instead of forty.

As the pirates dumped the man's corpse over the side, Mildred turned back to Ryan and said, "They're killing each other so they can take a few more breaths of air, so their hearts can beat another thousand times. Look at them. They're all goners."

Based on that assessment, J.B. was a goner, too, but Ryan chose not to point it out. Even if J.B. survived the coming fight, afterward he was going to have to pick up an oar and row, something that his broken ribs would make very difficult. If he couldn't row, he was going to be flogged. A lot. Which would make it even harder to row. There wasn't much wiggle room in the situation.

Two grizzled old men were pushed into the makeshift ring next. Both looked to be on their last legs. They were starved to skeletons. Their skin was peeling off in big white patches, revealing bright pink flesh beneath. Neither one had the eye of the tiger. After some slow circling and a few soft overhand blows, one of the men clutched the center of his chest and dropped to the deck.

"For nuke's sake, look!" Ryan told the doctor.

"Coronary," Mildred said, diagnosing from afar.

The white-haired victor didn't have the strength to swing the machete. He tried several times, but he could only deal out superficial, shallow cuts. At each blow the loser, who was still conscious, let out a shriek of pain.

Finally, a burly pirate seized back the machete. With a single, downward chop he split open the stricken man's skull from crown to the bridge of his nose. He then put his boot on the man's neck and levered the blade back and forth to free it.

The lucky winner barely made it to the port rail without falling himself.

There were boos and catcalls from the pirates. They didn't like the performance. The chilling hadn't been done by the winner. There were disputes over whether bets should be paid off or not.

From the pilothouse deck overlooking the stern came a brusque command.

"What did he say?" Ryan asked Mildred.

"I'm not absolutely sure," she said, "but I think the dreadmaster just changed the rules of the contest."

"Did he give a reason?"

"The winner's too weak to be of use."

In short order the victor received the same treatment as the loser, a machete blade to the skull from behind. Then both of the bodies were pitched overboard. They bobbed together in the tug's wake.

So far, Ryan hadn't picked up anything J.B. could use. Each contest had been defined by the physical limits of the opponents.

The fourth match was only slightly more exciting than the third. The two men were decades younger, with deeper natural reserves of strength and more powerful wills to survive. They had, however, been galley slaves for a while, long enough to be used up and thrown away. They both managed to draw blood from punches to their mouths and noses before their arms hung down limp and useless by their sides.

When the spectators got restless, the Matachìn commander spiced things up by ordering a machete be slid across the deck between them.

The blade stopped at their feet. Both men dropped down on their hands and knees and began struggling for control of the weapon.

This set the pirates to hooting again.

Somehow, in the subsequent pulling back and forth, and the rolling around on the deck, one man ended up flat on his back and the other on top, straddling him. They each had hold of the big knife's handle. The man on top was trying to bring the long edge across the front of his opponent's throat. The man on the bottom was trying to drive the gut hook into his counterpart's neck.

It was another stalemate, but not for long.

Gradually, using the deadweight of his body more than main strength, the man on top wore down the other guy's strength. The blade came closer and closer, and then it bit into his unprotected throat. The man on top pressed down harder, making blood well up around the edge of the blade. Then, with a savage flourish, Top Man whipped the machete crosswise, cutting the man's neck wide open. Blood gushed out onto the deck. The vanquished let out a howl of defeat, his heels drumming. In a few seconds, it was over.

The loser went over the side.

Bets were paid off.

It was J.B.'s turn next.

"You've got to watch this," Ryan told Mildred. "We might be his only chance. We might be able to help him."

"Help him!" Mildred exclaimed. "He can't punch. He can't breathe deeply, so he won't have any stamina, and the other guy is eight inches taller. Ryan, I'll watch, but all we can do for him is *pray*."

The last pair of fighters was shoved together on the stern. J.B. looked extra-small compared to the guy he was pitted against.

"He's left his glasses and hat on," Mildred said. "Maybe he knows something we don't."

Ryan didn't respond. It had also occurred to him that J.B. wanted to die wearing his hat and glasses.

The other guy had much longer arms. J.B. kept moving, circling around and around, avoiding the lunges, looking for a way under the man's guard.

J.B. feinted left, when the man reached out, he booted him in the right kneecap. The impact of bootsole on cartilage made a crunching sound. From the expression on the man's face, it had to have hurt, too. It slowed the guy down, big time.

Sensing he'd lost something important, the next time J.B.'s opponent lunged, he really extended himself. He managed to catch the Armorer by the collar, not the neck as he'd probably intended. Before J.B. could twist out of his grasp, the bigger man body-punched him, laying several quick, hard blows one on top of the other.

For a second all the blood drained out of J.B.'s face.

"Oh, no," Mildred moaned. "No…"

J.B. brought the edge of his boot heel down on the tips of the man's bare toes, which wrung a piercing scream from his mouth. The guy let go and J.B. moved to the right, favoring his injured side.

Then Ryan noticed something about the way the other guy moved. His back was rigid, stiff, like it was locked in place. He didn't twist his torso as he lunged for J.B. He lunged straight ahead. His only plan of attack was to get hold of his adversary and not let go.

A bad back was an occupational hazard for a galley slave. It meant early retirement and a spot in the kill-or-be-killed show.

If the guy couldn't turn at the waist, he couldn't defend himself from a side attack. And if he couldn't do that, he was in deep shit.

"J.B.!" Ryan called. "Flank!"

The Armorer didn't look over to acknowledge that he had heard and understood, he didn't take his eyes off his opponent, but he immediately reversed course, then reversed again.

Ryan smiled for the first time in what seemed like hours.

"Why are you grinning?" Mildred said. "What is there to grin at?"

"J.B.'s checking the guy's range of motion," he told Mildred. "Seeing which side is the least flexible."

"And how is that—"

J.B. showed her how. He faked the big guy into moving toward his stronger side, then before his opponent could pivot back, J.B. stepped forward and heel-kicked him behind the same kneecap he'd kicked before.

With a loud crack, the leg gave way under him, and the man crashed to his back on the deck. He clutched his busted knee and wailed.

Holding his ribs with the insides of his forearms, J.B. didn't waste the advantage. He laid into the guy with a series of snapkicks to the ribs and the side of his head.

J.B. didn't kick in the guy's head with his steel-toed boots, maybe because he didn't want to, maybe because he was winded and didn't have the strength.

As he moved back, his opponent rolled onto his

stomach, then pushed up on his hands and knees. His head hung down. Blood dripped in a steady stream from his face, splattering on the deck in front of him.

It was game over.

But there was one more thing that had to be done.

One more awful thing.

The Matachìn were clamoring for it.

One of the pirates handed J.B. a machete. He accepted the weapon, but the expression that passed over his face was disgust.

If he didn't chop the chop, Ryan knew the chances were good he'd get chopped himself, like the geezer who couldn't make the chill.

J.B. stepped within striking range of his opponent's exposed neck. The man looked up at him with horror and desperation. He didn't want to die like a chicken. He wanted to die like a man.

J.B. gave him a little nod, an almost imperceptible nod toward the stern rail. Ryan caught it, but no one else did. The Armorer raised the machete skyward, then paused as if to summon his strength. The hesitation was on purpose. It gave the doomed man the chance to scramble to his feet and dive headfirst over the side.

The pirates rushed to the stern, hauling out and shouldering their submachine guns, looking for a head to shoot at.

The commander called for the rowers to stop rowing, but the loser never surfaced. Not so much as a trail of bubbles. And the commander didn't order the tug turned around to look for him. They were miles offshore.

Dead was dead, after all.

Evidently, the climax satisfied the Matachìn. Bets were

paid off without complaint. J.B. had clearly won the contest. A pirate snatched the machete from him, then escorted him at blasterpoint to the awning.

J.B. was chained to the same oar as Mildred and Ryan, on the inside empty seat.

"Nice fight," Ryan said. "Never a doubt, huh?"

"That guy messed me up," J.B. said tightly. He was obviously in considerable pain. "I'm not going to be much good pulling on an oar for a while."

"Don't worry about it," Mildred said.

"We'll pick up the slack for you," Ryan said. "You can just coast until you feel better."

From up on the pilothouse deck there was a flurry of back-and-forth Spanish. The commander was talking to someone inside the bridge.

"Did you get any of that?" Ryan asked Mildred.

"We're headed south," she said. "To Veracruz."

"Down in Mex?" Ryan said.

"Uh-huh."

"How far is it?" J.B. asked.

"You don't really want to know," she assured him.

"Yeah, I do. How far?"

"One hell of a long way to row," Mildred said.

Chapter Twenty-Six

Harmonica Tom sat some seventy-five feet above the deck of *Tempest*. He was perched in a bosun's chair he'd hauled up near the top of the main mast. For some, the high, suspended seat under full sail and on choppy seas would have been petrifying, but he was more than used to it. He enjoyed the expanded view and the exaggerated roll of the ship that the vantage point offered.

Though his binocs he was watching the Matachìn fleet at an extreme distance, paralleling their course to keep them in sight. Two of the sailboats were limping along; they hadn't fared so well in the contest of skippers. The third was on the bottom of the Gulf by now.

A smile lifted his handlebar mustache.

He could see the light reflect off the tugs' oar blades. They all flashed at once as the paddles turned and dipped in rhythm. Some of the folks chained to those oars were islanders. It was a safe bet all of them were Deathlanders. He had no way of telling whether Ryan Cawdor or any of his crew were captives. He hoped they weren't dead, but he wouldn't wish the fate of a galley slave on them, either.

Could've been him pulling on one of those oars, he knew, but for dumb luck and a hard, following wind.

Looking through the binocs he had to wonder if he had been saved for some greater purpose, him and all that C-4.

If he could have, he would've attacked the pirate ships then and there, run amok among them with his machine gun and explosives. If he could have, he would've chilled all the Matachìn, freed the slaves and scuttled their evil boats.

A man alone, even a man with a shitload of C-4, a man who was no stranger to excessive violence, had to be cautious when the odds were way-long against him. He had to think hard on his strategy, and pick his time and place to strike.

The skipper of *Tempest,* swaying high over its deck, flying under full sail, addressed the row of little boats bouncing in and out of his binocs' field of view. "You bastards don't know it, yet," he said, "but Harmonica Tom is about to go legendary on your asses."

* * * * *

Don't miss
DARK RESURRECTION
the exciting conclusion of the
EMPIRE OF XIBALBA
duology, available in March

Don Pendleton's Mack Bolan

Colony of Evil

Claiming one hundred square miles inside
Colombia, Colonia Victoria is a sanctuary
for humanity's most dedicated fanatics.
Set up by one of Hitler's minions, this
Nazi Neverland is now a deadly global
threat, and it's spearheading a new wave
of terror. Mack Bolan's hunting party
includes a Mossad agent and a local guide,
and their pursuit of Hans Gunter Dietrich
becomes a violent trek deep into the jungle,
where Bolan intends to dissolve an unholy
alliance in blood.

*Available January
wherever books are sold.*

Don Pendleton
SHADOW WAR

Intelligence has picked up chatter on the launch of an imminent strike of unknown origin and scope against the U.S., code-named Bellicose Dawn. Stony Man must navigate an unknown strike point, fragmented information and a brewing political firestorm. But soon they face the ultimate nightmare—men down, missing, maybe dead, and things going bad so fast that the day every Stony Man member prayed would never happen may have arrived.

STONY MAN®

Available February wherever books are sold.

Look for the 100th Stony Man title in April with a special collector's edition.

POLAR QUEST
by AleX Archer

When archaeologist Annja Creed agrees to help an old colleague on a dig in Antarctica, she wonders what he's gotten her into. Her former associate has found a necklace made of an unknown metal. He claims it's over 40,000 years old—and that it might not have earthly origins. As the pair conduct their research, Annja soon realizes she has more to worry about than being caught in snowslides. With no one to trust and someone out to kill her, Annja has nowhere to turn—and everything to lose.

Antarctica.
The land of snowslides,
alien artifacts and espionage

Available January wherever books are sold.

GOLD
EAGLE

GRA16

ROOM 59

THERE'S A FINE LINE BETWEEN DOING YOUR JOB—AND DOING THE RIGHT THING

After a snatch-and-grab mission on a quiet London street turns sour, new Room 59 operative David Southerland is branded a cowboy. While his quick thinking gained valuable intelligence, breaching procedure is a fatal mistake that can end a career—or a life. With his future on the line, he's tasked with a high-speed chase across London to locate a sexy thief with stolen global-security secrets that have more than one interested—and very dangerous—player in the game....

Look for

THE finish line

by

cliff RYDER

GOLD EAGLE ®

Available January wherever books are sold.

www.readgoldeagle.blogspot.com

GRM595

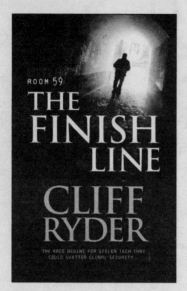